M000014018

G.C. MCKAY

SAUCED UP, SCARRED AND AT SLEAZE

AN ANTHOLOGY OF 8 SHORT STORIES

Published by Gareth Clark McKay 2018

Copyright © G.C. McKay 2018

The amoral right of the author has been asserted.

All characters and events in this publication, other than those clearly in the public domain, are fictitious and any resemblance to real persons, living or dead, is purely coincidental. And inevitable. You are not unique or in any way special. In fact, your whole personality was determined long before you were even born. The author would like to remind you that the idea and very existence of the 'self', at the time of writing this, is being proven to also be fictitious. In an attempt to circumvent any offence taken from the contents of this piece, he would like to insist that you get over yourself, but he's afraid the irony will be misconstrued, if even noticed in the first place.

All rights reserved.

No part of this publication may be reproduced, stored in a retrieval system, or transmitted, in any form or by any means without the prior permission in writing of the publisher, nor be otherwise circulated in any form of binding or cover other than that in which it is published and without a similar condition including this condition being on the subsequent publisher. The author, on the other hand, would like to encourage you to do what you want with this piece, whether as a whole or individually, as long as the credit remains with him. Any knock-off act of plagiarism, in any shape or form, shall be met with the most furious type of Machiavellian retribution and vengeance imaginable. Maybe. All actions are subject to the author's self-aware indifference and nihilistic standpoint.

ISBN: 978-84-09-01654-9

All stories are first published in this piece, with the exception of
Squirm, first published by Abstract Jam, which has since gone into (and at the time of writing this continues to be in) hiatus, which G.C. McKay likes to take personal, though unwarranted credit for and
Bloodhound Lust, first published by Horror Sleaze Trash despite never actually including it in the fiction section of their website, opting instead to mark it as 'uncategorised', which G.C. McKay isn't (he is) particularly bothered by, but certainly doesn't appreciate either. Exposing them in this somewhat passive-aggressive manner makes him feel better though.

abstractjam.com
horrorsleazetrash.com

Cover idea by the author, designed by Graphix Motion from pictures provided by Pixabay.

www.graphixmotion.com
www.pixabay.com

gcmckay.com

CONTENTS

*This book is dedicated to the
debauchery it was inspired by*

SAUCED UP, SCARRED AND AT SLEAZE

SOMETHING BORROWED, SOMETHING BLUE

I was drunk in a club, blacked-out but still standing upright. Of course, I didn't know that at the time, but when the woman who'd been twirling her tongue around my mouth comes back from the bar, she'll inform me of the fact. Going by the sultry glaze in her eyes and the touchy-feely nature of her disposition, my place of kip for the night seemed already booked.

I'd been living like that for about a year, losing myself inside any woman who'd let me; preferably one who didn't know me at all. Whatever meaning I might've once possessed had vamoosed, leaving my sorry arse behind as it disappeared into the dust along with my skin particles. I don't know how it'd happened, but I felt like a total stranger to myself, and so, only a fellow and complete unknown seemed appropriate, especially when it came to my sexual proclivities.

"Are you awake?" the woman shouted, over the monotonous song played the week before and the one before that. Somehow, it always seemed to provoke the same ecstatic arousal from the crowd. My eyes snapped open in a panic, blinded by the glaring light of her phone, filming me in my pathetic, unconscious state.

"Urm, yeah," I replied, holding my hand up to block the light, sipping my saviour with the other. A true drunk never drops his drink, conscious or unconscious.

"I've never seen anybody fall asleep inside a club before!" she shouted, cutting the light and slipping her phone away. "I've got something back at home that'll wake you up. What d'you say? Think you've got it in you for an older woman?" asked the nameless stranger. The promise of class-A drugs allowed me to forgive the lack of fresh drinks in her hands. I nodded in my feigned, carefree, showmanship manner. Maybe she knew it, but I hadn't been with a woman twice my age before. She seemed more turned on by the idea than I was though. My target market was anywhere between eighteen and fifty. Fourteen if I could get away with it. Sixty if she was a lush looking to splurge the wealth she'd accumulated during her better-looking days.

A cab ride and a gram or so later, we were in her bed. I don't know whether she told me she was married, now that I think about it, but the videotape resting on the bedside table, with its label Our Wedding Day glaring at me during our sloppy romp soon made it apparent. She assumed my whisky-dick was down to the coke, but I think it was due to that videotape. I didn't have a problem with banging another man's woman but having him watch (in a sense) didn't make it easy. It must've been a while for her, as she sucked me off for near-on an hour to get my coked-up cock into a rideable state. I wanted to keep her a stranger, but within hours I'd been made aware that she was married, into cocaine and seemed to be nuts. You don't leave videotapes lying around for strangers to see without a good reason. By morning, I learnt that reason was an upcoming divorce.

She was showering when I sprung up in the early hours, humming the same song as in the club to herself, but never singing any of the words. I was on the sofa, my dick sore from the aggressiveness required to get it hard. She told me she was clean and that I could come inside her. If she thought that comment was sexy, it wasn't, but I did it anyway. The woman, still nameless to me at the time, was very vigorous. She came out of the shower with her hair still dripping, stepped into the open-plan kitchen and started making breakfast without saying a word. I lit a cigarette and snorted-up some of the leftover coke. As the drop slithered down the back of my smoke-tarred throat, she plonked a couple of bowls of muesli on the table, along with a carton of almond milk. Unsweetened almond milk to be specific. I'd rather suckle on an udder than drink that shit again. I asked for a coffee, black. She told me she didn't have any sugar. I never asked for any. After handing me a mug the size of a tit, she sat down opposite me to my left on the other side of the L-shaped couch. Despite already sleeping with her, this was the first time I looked at her properly. She looked great. Clearly older, but still great. Droplets of water fell from the tips of her long, brown locks, whilst her nipples threw me little glimpsing kisses between the loosely-tied folds of the lilac silk dressing gown she had on. "I'm old enough to be your mother," she said, just before sucking on a straw dunked into what looked like a cup of urine. "Oh, this. It's apple cider vinegar, diluted with boiled water and a spoonful of honey." Good for arthritic problems, apparently. She really was old enough to be my mother.

"So, Richard. How old are you?" she asked.

"Nineteen," I said, slightly perplexed at being called Richard. I was in the habit of making up names for myself with many a stranger, but I couldn't remember if I opted for that one. Ricardo would've been more my style. It always amused me to see if I could make the unbelievable believed.

She stirred the honey at the bottom of her glass with the straw until it blended, then lifted her feet onto the edge of the couch and spread her legs wide. I had a panoramic view of her pussy, glistening with its own helping of honey. My real breakfast looked a lot sweeter.

"I'm forty-two," she said, clapping her knees back and forth, acting young but coming off old. "I teach yoga."

"I realised that last night," I said, lying. I took out my phone to check if any of my friends from the club had got in contact. They hadn't. After a year or so of disappearing from clubs, they got the hint—never interrupt a man in the middle of a mission. I started filming her instead. She knew it from the off, even seeming somewhat delighted by it.

"You wanna see me squirt?" she asked, staring into the lens. Then the phone dropped to the floor along with my knees. I began crawling over to her, but she clicked her fingers and pointed at the phone. I picked it up with my mouth and continued with my crawl. A jaw-ache later and she filmed herself squirting over the youthful face of her stand-in son.

I showered afterwards and shaved my balls with what I presumed to be the same razor she went to work on her pussy with, then brushed my teeth with her toothbrush. When I came back, she was gone. On the coffee table sat a freshly cut line and a folded note. I went into the kitchen first and raided the larders and fridge, looking for some much-needed protein. There wasn't shit. Not even an egg. I figured she must've been a vegan or on a strict diet. The only protein that was in the flat had been emptied into her mouth, so I was left wanting. I made another coffee instead and kicked my hunger to the curb with a cigarette and the white line. Then I picked up the note and unfolded it, when a tenner dropped out onto the carpet:

A growing young man such as yourself needs a good, hearty breakfast. Go and treat yourself. I've got your number. I'll be in touch. Sorry if your jaw aches. Raquel. X

I thought her name was Rachel. Raquel suited her better though. I sat there for a while, thinking

5

that I could make a decent living by eating vagina. If Raquel's was the average per hour, I could earn about £60 for three hours of pussy munching. Then I noticed some hand cream on the coffee table. A second, better smelling squirt soon followed and I masturbated away the morning build-up. I went into the bedroom afterwards to get my jacket. When I got there, the same videotape that had compromised my boner during the night was sitting on top of my threads. I picked it up. The back just read: Our Wedding Day—Richard and Raquel. Then I remembered why she called me Richard. I told her to in order to get me hard. It worked. I took the tape with me as I left, hoping that the latter end of it was a more pornographic declaration of vows.

I ducked into a McDonald's to get the cheapest breakfast possible, wolfed it down after flirting with some dorky-looking Asian girl who probably didn't have a clue what I was saying, then took the £8 I had remaining and invested it down my local off-license. The guy who ran it knew I was a drunk alright, so he treated me accordingly. Fuck the customer. The drunk is always right. I got twenty-four cans of out-of-date Stella for my modest investment, and a bag of salted peanuts to boot. The only catch was lugging them up the four flights of stairs to get to my dump of a bedsit.

I realised why I took the videotape when I collapsed into my flat with the cans. I actually had a video player, left behind by the previous tenant. It was a few years since the DVD killed the videotape. I'd never used it, nor had any reason to up until then. I stuck it in the player, hoping it wasn't just some boring bog-standard wedding. Admittedly, this wasn't exactly sticking with my plan to keep Raquel anonymous, but to me, it didn't matter. I doubted I'd see her again. I hit play. That's when things turned bizarre. It was her at about thirty, getting married to a dude that could've very well been my own doppelganger. They were fully in love, from what I could see. It reminded me of the high-school sweetheart I'd spent three years with, as she used to look at me in the same way. We'd broken up about a year and a half, maybe two years before.

Long story short: Guy meets girl. They fall in love. Guy gets bored of fucking Girl. Guy breaks Girl's heart. Guy realises Girl will whore herself out for love. Rinse and repeat. Girl realises Guy is a piece of shit. Girl gets her revenge by fucking one of Guy's ex-(shitty)band members. Girl finally sees that most men want to fuck her, just like Guy once said. Girl gets free expensive cocktails, candlelit dinners and class-A drugs until she forgets about Guy. Guy pines for the pussy he once had but lost. Girl tells Guy her new man has a *bigger cock than you*, specifically. Guy and Girl part in mutual, silent animosity. The end.

By the time Raquel and Richard were repeating empty promises to one another, my boredom had forced me to hit fast-forward. Through the static confetti was thrown, the cake was cut and the first dance, with all eyes watching, was performed. I hit play again. I wasn't sure why, as it was about as interesting as any wedding to a stranger. All the family members wished them well and all that crap, then the party began. A lot of the women were desperate or jealous, making most of them mildly doable. Then Raquel plucked a boy out from the crowd for a dance. I was dumbfounded. That boy, I watched on in amazement, was me. I couldn't believe it. The shock even made me drop my can of beer. As it frothed over the already-stained and hopeless carpet, I crawled over to the television, double-taking in disbelief. Then I remembered, when I was eight-years-old, being dragged to that wedding.

I rang my old man.

"Dad? You there? How drunk are you?"

"Yep. I'm here. Not drunk enough, but I'm working on it. What d'you want?" he said, cracking open a can in the background.

"Alright, this'll sound weird but fuck it. D'you remember us going to a wedding when I was about eight or nine?"

"Fucking hell. You're not getting married, are you? Don't be an idiot. Just look at how I turned—"

"No, Dad. I'm not. Just answer the question."

"How am I supposed to fucking know? Maybe. You're talking about something that happened fifteen years ago."

"Eleven years ago, Dad. I think their names were Raquel and Richard."

"Raquel... that name rings a bell. Think she used to work with your Mum. She's cooking right now. You want me to ask her?"

"I'm only asking you, Dad. If you know what I mean."

"Gotcha."

"Where did they work together?"

"Well, you probably don't remember but your Mum tried her hand at teaching for a little while. She only lasted six months, tops. She left after one of the kids accused her of giving him a clout. Whether she did or not I couldn't tell you."

"So, Raquel was a teacher?"

"Yeah. She was the only one your Mum liked. Said the rest were a bunch of cunts. I think I tried it on with that Raquel once. Great arse."

"You tried it on with her at the wedding?"

"No, no. I ain't that fucking daft. Your Mum sent me down the school after storming out to collect her stuff. Raquel was in the office, putting all her shit away. She had a tight, pinstripe skirt on. Lovely it was. I had to give it a shot. I got a slap for my trouble, but she took it well enough. A no harm, no foul kind of girl. She wished me and your old dear all the best, and you come to think of it, and then I left."

"Okay. Thanks, Dad—"

"What the fuck you asking me all this for?"

"No reason really. I just had a nightmare. Speak soon, Dad."

"Yeah, yeah. I won't wait up for that. Bye."

By the time I'd hung up the phone, the wedding had finished. If dancing with a woman I'd fuck in the future wasn't weird enough, there was a dirty movie at the end of it and it was an exact replica of the sex I'd had with Raquel. Every position, each chronological order, even the way she came; all were exactly the same. Freaked out by this, I stopped the tape and went out again that evening, hoping to find another stranger. But as I went to leave the bedsit, my phone beeped:

Raquel: Hey.
Fancy another
white night?
I'm with a friend.

A female friend...

So back to hers I went.

"Richard, this is Veronica. Veronica, Richard," said Raquel, after kissing me at the front door. Veronica was sitting on the same part of the sofa where I got my face sprayed. She seemed to be hiding behind her purple-dyed hair. The layers of white dust on the coffee table told me they were both high as fuck.

"Drink?" Raquel asked me. "I've got some rum or whisky. Which would you like?"

"Whisky," I replied. Raquel darted off to the kitchen whilst Veronica cut up three lines. I whipped off my jacket and flung it over the sofa. I was still a little freaked out about the tape, but the night's promise soon helped me forget all about it.

"You go first," Veronica said suddenly, "you're playing catch up, after all."

"Thanks," I said, taking hold of a luminous pink tube that was once a straw. Veronica patted the sofa and I sat down. I guessed she was about the same age as Raquel, possibly older. She had a slightly haggard look, but it suited her. Upon sitting I noticed the smashing set of tits she had, hiding behind her weird shawl-like clothing. I snorted the line and went to pass the straw back, but Raquel intervened. "Here's your drink," she said. I switched the straw for the drink and had a sip. Raquel moved around the sofa. "Now kiss Veronica," she said, placing both her hands on our heads, guiding us. Veronica seemed reluctant but got into it. She broke away, took the last line, then kissed me again and moved on to my neck. Raquel planted her lips on mine whilst Veronica's mouth moved further south.

"Don't worry," Raquel said between kisses, "if you're wondering why Veronica is so... forward, shall we say, it isn't because she's a whore. She's got cancer." "So, why not be a whore, right Raquel?" Veronica replied, laughing.

"For real?" I asked them both.

"Yep," Raquel replied, "and she's up for anything. Pain or no pain. She's dying. Stage three already." She turned, dropped to her knees and began to cut-up more lines. Veronica unbuckled my belt.

Within minutes of being there, my cock was inside a dying woman's mouth and for some reason, I had no problem at all with getting a boner that time around. There's some theory I think, that says we fuck to spite the inevitability of our demise. What I learned that night was a person who gets down with death looking over their shoulder, does it like their existence meant absolute shit-all. It was amazing, precisely because of how little I needed to do. Raquel and Veronica went at one another like they wanted each other dead. There was an array of hair-pulling, faces being shoved into crotches and lines snorted off arse-cracks, nipples and clits. Raquel seemed determined to make me come in her mouth, which I welcomed far more than her 'come inside my clean pussy' demand. When she kissed and donated it to Veronica's mouth in return, making her swallow by clamping her nose shut, I nearly fainted. They didn't stop fucking each other the entire night, I just joined in whenever I wanted to. It was perfect. The reluctant, yet willing animosity never failed to stiffen me. I could've died a happy man that night.

When I woke up Raquel hit the shower again. I was hoping we'd get all soapy together, but her and

Veronica seemed to be adhering to a morning-after agreement of non-speaking terms. I guessed the drugs had worn off and there they were, fuelled-up by pointless inhibitions and respectable boundaries again. So, whilst Raquel soaped herself down, I exchanged numbers with Veronica, thinking I could easily commit to a soon-to-be-dead woman. Then I got the hell out of there, fearing a repeat of the breakfast and the possibility of Raquel noticing the missing videotape, which was still back at my place.

The glory of my debauched night of tantalising hedonism, of course, wore off by the time I got home and had a proper snooze. I was still buzzing, but that buzzing was starting to itch. I wanted more. More cocaine. More crazy pussy. More fucked-up threesomes. *My cock is your chemo, Veronica, now come and take your medicine.* I wanted to bed her again, purely because she was decaying more rapidly than I was. I'd texted her in the hope that further penetration would make her hair fall out, but she didn't reply. Then, like she instantly forwarded it to Raquel, my phone beeped again:

Raquel: Hey big
boy. Have you
watched my
wedding video
yet?

Me: What the fuck?!

I didn't send that but came close. I'd been so distracted during the past twenty-four hours that

I completely forgot about my weird, eight-year-old self, dancing with a bride I'd one day share a sordid threesome with. All I could fathom was that she did know who I was somehow, and she wanted me to take the tape. But for what purpose, I had no idea.

Raquel: I know
you took it.
Fancy a drink?
I can pick you up.
X

So, for the third night in a row, I was to see Raquel again. As much as I would've loved another ménage, in truth I was exhausted. A quiet drink sounded good, but the unknown potential of the tape was alarming. Whilst I waited for her, I rewound it and stuck it in the case, then handed it back as soon as I entered her brand new (second-hand) emerald-green sports car. She was wearing a leather jacket, like myself, and a pair of ultra-light blue jeans. They were old and tight and torn aplenty for an effortless, future finger-slide. Irresistible.

"Where we going?" I asked.

"You'll see," she said and planted one on me. Cocaine bells rang behind her eyes. "Did you like the video?"

"Who says I watched it?"

"Your face did when you saw me last night."

"Fair enough. Yeah, I gave it a watch. Me, dancing with you. Then you, fucking your husband the same way you did me. Bit weird, I must say. Is there a name for that particular kink?"

"There's more than that. Watch the rest."

"What's on it?" I asked.

"Watch it and find out," she said, sticking the just scooped car-key under my nose. After a sniff and off we went.

She took me to the edge of some cliff. Beachy Head or something. She paid her respects to the latter part of its namesake as soon as the handbrake was yanked up. I wanted to finish in her mouth again, but she placed my hand on her arse, indicating her desire for a top of the cliff fucking. I was in that half-drunk, half-asleep state of tranquillity, which helped me fuck without thinking. She came twice, I think, but realised that I hadn't. After keying-up some more coke, she handed it to me and put her mouth to work again. I followed suit, then lit a cigarette and leaned back. I imagined she was Veronica and listened to the waves below as they crashed against the cliff, to the stretching of leather and to Veronica's slurping saliva, desperate for the little life elixir swirling around my balls. I came inside non-existence.

Raquel wiped her mouth with the back of her hand with the crazed conquest of triumph radiating from her pores. It was the first time that I realised how beautiful she was. There was a glow to her. It wasn't the naïve, hopeful attractiveness which sometimes made me sick. Raquel's was an experienced, trampled and trodden-on beauty, riddled with anguish, sadness and disappointment. It was no wonder why she fucked so well.

After a couple more keys, she whipped out a bottle of vodka and took one of my cigarettes for the first time. We both lit up, then she popped the roof of the car open. The stench of sex disintegrated into the ether almost instantly, like it never happened. The chalky-cold air was a welcome change though. We sat there for a while in silence, looking out at nothing in particular.

"So," Raquel said, shifting her legs around to my lap and resting her back against the car door. "Did you masturbate to the tape?"

I shook my head but immediately regretted it. Lying would've been the better play. "I was going to but seeing myself in it put me off."

"What do you mean?" she asked, gesturing for the vodka.

"I'm on the tape. That's what I mean."

"Are you?"

"Yeah. Don't make out like you didn't know that."

"Of course I don't know that! How old were you?"

"About eight, I think. We danced. You danced with an eight-year-old boy that you went on to fuck. You're a degraded paedophile with the worst kind of patience. Fucking you has been an honour," I said.

"Are you really in it? Or are you just messing with me?"

"Oh, I'm in it alright. You used to work with my mother."

"Who's that?"

"Susan Archer."

"Susan Archer is your mother!? Wow! What a fucking small world after all. I remember that bitch! Oh, sorry."

"Nah, don't be. She's a bitch alright."

"How is she doing these days?"

"Dead," I said, lying. Didn't like the chance of Raquel somehow getting in touch with my mother.

"Oh. I'm sorry—"

"Don't be. I see death as the reward for being forced to live through this shit. Don't worry about it."

"Wait. Your old man—"

"Yep. He's the one who tried to bone you when my mum walked out of the job. He shares my appreciation of your physical frame. Especially that tush of yours," I said.

"Wow. I honestly had no idea you were in the video. Well, not consciously... do you believe in fate?"

"No," I replied, "but I do lean towards determinism. Fate's just its bullshit sister, full of misplaced romanticism and sugar-laced with hope."

"Are you a nihilist or something?"

"I dunno. Maybe. I just think that reality is too tough for most. Hence Gods, systems of belief and the poppycock notion of karma."

"Well, I do happen to believe in fate, Richard Archer. We were destined to meet. I'm sure of that now," she said, looking out at the stars.

"What makes you say that then?" I asked.

She turned the key in the ignition, winked and said she'd tell me in the pub as the roof closed in on us.

I resisted the urge to keep asking her just what in the fuck she was talking about on the way and cut up some lines on the video-cassette case. Raquel stopped outside a burger joint. She made me wait in the car to cut up more lines whilst she went in and ordered. The spots posing as a teenager gawped at her like she was there to bust his cherry. I imagined that he could smell me on her breath. She paid for the whole meal without even thinking of asking me for some cash. Another jaw-ache that night seemed inevitable.

When she got back in the car, she kissed me like I was her man, hawked-up the line waiting for her and poured the rest of the vodka into our drinks. Whilst munching away on my chilli-burger, I glazed over the videotape again, back to front.

"That's yours to keep, by the way," said Raquel, delicately eating some vegetarian nut-burger or something. It looked disgusting.

"Well, I love weddings just as much as the next man, so thanks. Yours was especially beautiful. I like seeing how in love you once were before I come along and ravage you. But why are you giving it to—"

Here I turned and saw that Raquel was crying. Not the bullshit, melodramatic, give-me-attention tears so many women learn by the age of three, but silent, downtrodden, can't-be-fought-back tears of genuine pain. I felt like a cunt.

"Hey, I'm sorry. I didn't mean that. I was just playing around," I said.

"No, it's fine. I know that," she said. I handed her a napkin from the bag. She delicately dabbed her eyes. I put my hand on her shoulder and after a minute or so, she regained her composure. She picked up her soggy burger and threw it out of the window. I offered her the rest of mine. She hesitated at first but then wolfed it down with aplomb. I kissed her afterwards and waved to the ball of puss flipping burgers as Raquel drove off.

She said she was fine inside the pub, but something had changed. Once you make a woman cry, for whatever reason, something always changes. I kept myself entertained with thoughts involving the only other female in the place. She was behind the jump and looked pissed every time she had to pull a pump, an easy eight, nine or ten pints before you would kind of broad. Resting bitch-faced women always look great giving head mind you.

Raquel and I played pool for a couple of hours and drank the most ridiculous, luminous cocktails you can imagine. I was surprised the place even served drinks like that, as it was a proper dive bar if I ever saw one. Loads of old biker types leered at Raquel's fine arse, which prompted me to give it a few territorial taps now and again. They gave me rotten looks all night, but I didn't give a fuck. Raquel didn't seem to mind but also didn't seem to care. She wasn't there in the pub with me, she was somewhere else, somewhere she didn't want me to know about. She slipped in and out of the bathroom at least twice as much as I did. That didn't bother me, it was her coke after all, but the regularity did alarm me a bit. It was awful; I was starting to care about her.

Everyone watched as we left. I planted my hand firmly on her arse and kept it there until we reached the car. "I'm going away for a bit after tonight," she said whilst driving, "for about a week or so. You can fuck whoever you like, but I'd still like to see you a few more times afterwards. How does that sound?"

"Fine," I replied. I wondered why she said 'a few more times', but as the evening had taken such a strange, unknown turn, I didn't push the subject.

We went straight to bed once we got back. She told me that I could do whatever I wanted, but the manner in which she said it didn't bring about any sordid thoughts. So, in the dark, I went classical and made love to her missionary style. I felt her tears caress my cheeks as I kissed her, but neither of us said a word. She held onto me tight as I climaxed and seconds later I fell asleep still inside of her.

By morning, she was already gone. I lay there, stretching out my arms, wondering what the fuck I was doing with this woman. Like most chicks, or people for that matter, the social mask she wore for strangers had withered away and the real, troubled and anxiety-ridden train-wreck she tried to hide had kicked the poser off the stage and stolen every other role. Her underwear was still on the bed. Sniffing them gave me a boner, so I wrapped them around my face and whacked off. After showering, I found a little bag of coke on the coffee table, along with another note:

This'll help you get laid. Sorry about last night. I'll explain everything soon, I promise. Raquel. X

I got the fuck out of there soon after reading it. There was a picture of Raquel and her husband sitting on the entertainment centre that seemed to be staring at me, instilling me with paranoia. I kept wondering why this husband wasn't around and feared he might just pop over whilst I was there, to get some coke or talk or whatever.

After resting for a few days in my humble abode of depression, I decided to hit the club where I first met Raquel. Back in those days, I was a machine. The itch that must be scratched would only give me about a week's worth of rest before it made me go nuts and send me diving into some skank. There was also part of me which liked seeing how many women I could fuck in a week. Three seemed to be my limit.

It was a bust. My cock craved to score with someone who had a bit of colour. I was sick to death of white chicks and their fucking weddings and their yoga. I wanted some tight-pussied, tit-less Asian girl who'd gasp in horror and delight as my monster flopped out in front of her subservient mouth, or a self-loathing black chick with a huge arse, who would scream in disgust that I was nothing but a dirty nigger-fucker whilst I brought her to orgasm. But like most fantasies and potential outcomes of pleasure, I was left with my tail between my legs and bailed a good hour or so before the club closed.

Things picked up after that though. After getting a box of spicy-fried chicken from the greasiest, rat-infested, knock-off KFC in town, I checked my phone:

Veronica: Hey.
You awake?

Me: I am now.

I rang her immediately. She gave me her address. I hopped in a cab and told him where to go. He looked disapprovingly at my meal. I offered him a drumstick. He waved in refusal. So, I stripped off all the chicken skins, wrapped them around a handful of chips and tucked it down my throat whilst chucking the box out of the window. "Drive fast," I said, munching away, "there's a dying woman at the end of this route, craving cock like a porn-star late on rent."

He didn't drive as fast as I would've liked, but I gave him a decent enough tip all the same. The prospect of fucking rapidly decaying matter had put a spring in my step. The cabbie with a grudge against chicken drove off as Veronica answered the door, looking far fresher than she did when I first met her. She'd done her makeup close to perfection, with straightened hair to boot. Her clothes, on the other hand, left a lot to be desired. She wore a bubbly-cottoned, faded-colour dressing gown with a missing tie, a baggy old t-shirt with only the outline of the logo it once had and a pair of red football shorts. But as her nipples hardened, so did I.

We started exactly where we left off. Kiss, squeeze, sip. Sip, squeeze, kiss. Under the light, Veronica looked like a different woman almost. Her skin didn't look as hollow and dead as before. There was even a radiance about her. She said it was a one night only deal and that she was going to delete my number afterwards. So, I gave her my best in the hope of making her come crawling back for more, just so I could refuse her. I wasn't having some forty-odd-year-old woman dictating things, even if she was dying.

After unloading on her tits, Veronica popped into the bathroom to clean up. I had a little snoop around her room and to be more precise, her closet. I wanted to see if she had any skimpy outfits for the following morning. When I opened the door, however, I was taken back by the sight of a wedding dress, waiting inside its plastic wrapping. I didn't know what to think but must've stood there staring at it, as Veronica gave me a jump when she returned.

"Don't worry about that," she said. "I'm getting

married in a couple of weeks. Take it as a compliment. You're my last taste of freedom," she said, laughing it off.

"You're getting married?" I must've asked with a judging tone, as Veronica looked at me for a second with a straight face until it dawned on her that she was dying.

"Oh, that. Right, you know what? Fuck it, I might as well just tell you. I'm not dying. Raquel is."

"You're joking right?" I asked. Veronica chose not to respond, but casually opted for a seat on the edge of the bed.

"No, I'm not. I've been having an affair with her husband since they got married. Now we're getting married, finally. Raquel doesn't know. She lied to you about getting a divorce. She's been divorced for over a year and dying for close to two."

"Shit," I replied. "You people are fucked up."

Veronica shrugged. "I don't know about that. Best friends always betray each other at some point. It's a shame I won't get to see if we'd get over it together, but that's life."

"Why did you have the threesome then?" I asked.

"Cheating with your best friend's man doesn't make you feel so great. You weren't the first. We did it when Raquel first got married. Literally, I should add."

"With Richard?"

"You guessed it."

"Right. Well. Shit, I'm speechless."

"Raquel told me about you. Said you were young, eager and a bit of a dish. When she suggested another threesome, I thought, why not? I'm not getting any younger and she's gonna be dead soon.

The only person who could fuck up my life because of it is you."

That must've been the reason she asked me over, to make sure I kept my mouth shut. I turned towards her for confirmation. Her hand was gripped over the hem of the towel wrapped around her firm chest. She slowly peeled it off, then caressed her breasts with outstretched fingers, with one gesturing for me to come closer. "I'll assume discretion is an essential part of your vocation. How much do I owe you so far?" she asked.

"I'm sorry, what?"

"For tonight. You got £200 for the other night, right? How's another hundred, plus a bonus?" she said. Shit. She thought I was a prostitute and for a second, I nearly ruined it.

"£150."

She looked me up and down, saw I was ready and nodded. "Okay," she said, "but you must leave afterwards. No sleeping here."

"Deal."

I walked straight over, seeing a completely different person in front of me. I thought she was a sweet, caring and loyal friend. Instead, she was a cunt. But a cunt who was willing to bribe me with blowjobs.

***

Raquel was living rent-free inside my head for the next couple of days. I couldn't get the cancerous bitch out of my mind. In some sense, it was ironic. My original aim was to keep her a stranger. But what little I thought I knew about her, turned out to be bollocks, which made her an even bigger stranger. I didn't hate her for that or anything, but the stupid narrator in my head had woken up and wanted some answers. The fact she was dying did explain a lot, but there seemed to be something missing. I couldn't figure out what though. Then, whilst drinking and open new-tabbing my way towards a wank, I remembered the videotape. Raquel seemed obsessed with the idea that I watched it all. So, once I found it amongst my crumpled clothes and trinkets, into the player it went. I skipped all the crap I'd already seen but stopped anytime somebody wished the lovebirds well with a series of benign, colloquial phrases bereft of any significant meaning until I found Veronica. I didn't even recognise her at first. I think she must've been going through some hippie/goth phase or something, like one of those annoying as fuck women who spout shit about how the universe will fulfil your dreams for you if you just ask it nicely. I tried to watch the tape without thinking about my recently updated perception of Veronica, but it was difficult. She genuinely seemed quite happy, but there was, I was sure of it, an underlying sadness in her words. Every time she said Richard or looked at him, there was a sense of yearning in her. Confirmation bias? Perhaps. Anyway, I fast-forwarded onto the fornicating with two motivating factors: One: Rubbing one out, and Two: Watching it till the end.

The first couple of minutes helped me achieve my first aim. It starts off well. Raquel gets the party started by lifting her dress up and tossing it away, revealing a white, lacey, silk-set of underwear and suspenders, then drops to her knees, nice and close to the camera. A cock flops into the frame. She teases it to perfection, with a hesitant yet hungry mouth. From there, things soon go tumbling down towards the dull. Whilst the outcome of factor one coagulated around my stomach, the happy couple started fucking like I'd already seen and done. After that, I had to sit and watch the we're-so-in-love-with-each-other fucking. Twenty-five minutes of teary-eyed, missionary misery. It depressed me severely and was even worse after that. They started talking (for another twenty-five minutes no less) but their voices were too low to be heard. I decided to skip it all until the end, but just as I went to hit fast-forward again, the screen moved, zooming in on them both. Somebody else was in the room. Richard notices, smiles, looks at his wife, then at the person holding the camera, then back at his wife. Raquel had that pang of remorse, mixed with a reluctant need or want expression on her face that you see on many a woman before and after their first pornographic performance. Richard must've been trying to convince Raquel during the ball-achingly dull interval to have a threesome, on his fucking wedding day no less. I will have to buy him a drink for that if I ever get the chance. All things aside, that took some balls. Then Raquel gave the tiniest nod. The next shot was just a frantic blur, which was quite a fitting metaphor for the blind rush of impending hedonism, till the tripod was moved to a better angle, not just the shitty straight shot of their profiles, but a diagonal one at the corner of the bed. When the picture re-achieved clarity, Veronica was there, already working away on Raquel. Factor one came back for another round. Pretty soon Richard reappears and dives straight into Veronica, with notably more enthusiasm. I guess he was trying to seal the old dutiful, respectful wife coupled-up with the slut-enriched mistress deal. Can't blame him for that.

So, yeah. That was it really. He ended in Veronica's mouth, which I found fucking funny for some reason. She swallowed whilst Raquel stared, then the screen soon cut off. Whilst it did enable a couple of semi-satisfying tugs, I still felt clueless as to why Raquel had wanted me to see it. Let alone own it. Was the tape a joke of hers? Did she want me to do something with it? Was she trying to move on from her pointless marriage? I didn't have a fucking clue. But I knew I needed some answers and waited out the last couple of days, eager to see her again. The tape even forced an amateur move out of me; I contacted her the day she got back.

She told me to meet her in the same dive-bar she dragged me to before she disappeared. Despite my reluctance to go back there, off I went. As soon as I walked through the door, there she was, with some guy about the same age as me.

"Oh, hey you," she said, casual as fuck, kissed me and introduced her friend. Darren was his name. Or Warren. I don't know. He looked pissed I was there. Sensing something was up, I whispered to Raquel that I wanted a word. She shrugged me off and bought me a drink instead, which pissed me off as well.

"I watched the whole tape," I said. It caught her attention. She looked at me, searching for answers. Then she turned towards her date.

"I'm going to go now. Would you like to have a threesome with us?" she asked the dude. I wanted to interject, but the guy just looked Raquel up and down, then gave me a quick once-over and shook his head.

"No bother. Nice meeting you then," said Raquel

The guy just smiled and turned on his stool.

"Let's go," she said, taking my hand as we walked towards the door.

Without another word, we got inside her car. We did a couple of lines in silence, till my patience thinned beyond tolerability. "So, what's the deal with you Raquel? Why did you give me that videotape?"

"What made you watch it?" she asked.

"What?"

"You didn't seem bothered by it before. What's changed?"

"You're the one with cancer. That's what."

Raquel looked at me, then ran something over her mind.

"I take it you fucked Veronica again."

"Yeah. I did. She told me—"

"Everything. That woman is determined to take everything I have, I swear," she said, not really to me but herself.

"You said I could sleep—"

"No, no, no. It's not that. That's fine. She thinks you're a gigolo after all. I take it you got paid?"

"Yep. £150."

"Okay, good. That makes me feel better. So, what did you think of the tape?" she asked, dismissing the subject.

"What d'you mean?" I asked.

"What did you think of the tape?"

"Urm. I thought it was alright. Got a few tugs out of it. It's a wedding. Not really my forte."

"And the threesome? What about that? Did you think I wanted to do it?" she asked, weirdly reminding me of a child.

"Why are you asking me this?"

"Because I want to know. I've never really spoken about it with anyone. It was the last thing I had left of my marriage and in a way, the very thing that ended it. That's why I gave it to you, as a warning. Veronica and Richard both think I don't know about their affair, or that they're about to get married."

"How do you know that?"

"After my wedding night, Richard told me the threesome was a one-off. I only did it because I loved him so much. He fucked her, my supposed best friend, behind my back during the entire eleven years of our marriage. Probably before that as well. They both think they got away with it too, but I have something planned. And I'd like you to execute it."

"And what's that? Does it involve me being a prostitute again?" I asked with hope.

Raquel turned the ignition key. "No. More of an actor."

"Same difference," I said, smiling.

"I'll tell you back at mine. Let's fuck first."

"Oh yeah. What was that in the bar? Who said I was up for a threesome with a dude?" I asked, flirting.

"You don't like the idea of fucking me in the arse whilst I suck on another guy's dick?"

I opened my mouth to speak but came up short. She had a point. Off we went.

Everything felt different once we got back. It was almost like during Raquel's absence, death had finally crept into the flat. It was cold, lifeless and isolated somehow. It even smelt dead. Maybe the fact I knew she had cancer affected her confidence or something. We drank without laughter and snorted without relief. We started fucking, which was fine, but something was missing, and I got bored.

"What are you doing?" she asked as I pulled on her hair. We were in the spooning position.

"I want to see you," I said.

"No way. I look hideous... like I'm dying. I am dying... I'm dying. I'm dead. You're fucking a dead woman," she said, beginning to cry. I went to pull out, thinking she was having a breakdown, but she insisted I carry on. So, I did. I told her she was beautiful and all that crap, but it felt meaningless. Then she said, "You know what's weird? I'm not on any protection at all. There's part of me that wants to die with something living inside me. Is that sick?"

That's when I came.

Things picked up after we fornicated. We managed to get back to a good place. Or an even better place, really. Raquel was smiling, ruffling my hair and walking around with a sway in her hips. She was the sexiest soon-to-be corpse of all time. We'd warmed the place up with our bodies and lay on her rug, naked, drinking wine and smoking cigarettes.

"Life really is a cunt," she said, "I spent most of my time trying to look after my health, believe it or not. I was a vegetarian and even went vegan for a bit, only to be rewarded with arthritis and cancer. And here you are, a burger-scoffing, alcoholic chain-smoker in full health. I know you're young and all that, but still. There really is no correct way of living. I wish I became a drug-addicted porn-star or something instead. What does any of it matter once you're gone?"

"It doesn't. You're right. At least you got the drug-addicted part down," I said as she flipped away from the rug to cut up another round of lines.

She laughed and looked at me saucily, with a delight that can only be provoked by evil-doings. There was a camera lying nearby. She picked it up and said, "I've still got time for the latter," and handed it to me. I began filming her.

Pretty soon the rug was soaked.

Afterwards, as we lay there laughing like disobedient children that just got away with doing something destructive, I asked, "But how did you find out? About the affair and the upcoming marriage?"

"Well," she said, caressing my body with her fingernails, "after I found out I was dying, I went straight to Richard and told him. He disappeared for nearly a month and told me a load of crap about being devastated. Then he filed for divorce. I was shattered, but mostly confused. I couldn't understand why. All he could answer me with was that it was too hard for him and blah blah blah, which made me very upset. Meaning, I had a mental breakdown. I know people can be dicks during times of grief, but I was his wife and I wanted answers. Eventually, he told me he was having an affair, but wouldn't tell me who it was. He even went for the cliched, 'she's twenty-five, blonde and full of life,' which inadvertently gave him away. He thought he threw me off the scent with that younger woman shit. Then, I just knew. Everything kind of fell into place. Our entire marriage. All the times he got home late, took a shower immediately, how often he disappeared whenever Veronica was about to come over. All of it. Maybe I always knew in some ways. It even irks me to think that that's what brought on the cancer, but I guess I'm just trying to connect dots that aren't there. Just to find out for sure, I bugged Veronica's bedroom. You can take it if you like. It's behind the headrest of her bed."

"I love you," I said and meant it. I really had fallen for her; the evil, cancer-ridden, bitter and twisted beauty.

"That's sweet of you. But you're just in love with the idea of me. I'm not really this bad normally. I just figure if I'm going to be a ghost soon, I might as well start haunting them now."

"Till death do they part, Raquel," I said, going for a toast. She lifted her glass.

"I certainly hope so Rich—no wait. What is your real name?" she asked.

"I didn't call myself Richard?"

"No. I called you that for laughs when you fucked me. You just went along with it. Or maybe your cock did. That's another reason why I thought you were special in some way. You seemed to understand, somehow."

"Well, maybe when this is all over, I'll tell you my name."

We chinked our glasses, yawned simultaneously, smiled at each other with serenity and eventually fell asleep with our limbs entwined.

*****

"Alright, here we are," said Raquel, parking the car a

short distance away from the reception area.

It suddenly dawned on me. "Ahh, that's why you got a new car. Nobody knows it's you inside."

"Quite the bright lad, aren't you?" she said.

"I just thought you were having a midlife crisis," I said.

"Well, a bit of both. If I wasn't going to be dead soon, I'd say you were right."

We shared a laugh.

"Alright," she said, "here's the play. With this camera strapped around your neck, you go inside and start taking pictures of everyone."

"Wait. Don't all these people know that you and the groom were once married? Don't they care that he abandoned you for your fucking best friend?"

"Of course they know. That's another reason I went away for a bit. Everyone in there thinks I'm travelling around India. Feigned sympathy can't travel across continents I suppose. I'm sure Richard charmed them all with a load of shit about pining for Veronica over all these years. I don't know. It doesn't matter."

"I guess not. Sorry. Right. What's the play? I go in there and start taking pictures."

"Yep. Nobody will suspect anything. People always pretend to be happy at weddings and cameramen are expected. You can hide your face behind the lens too. It's perfect."

"It is. And so are you." In truth, she probably looked rough and haggard as fuck, but I'd fallen hard for the bitch. At that moment, in my eyes, she was perfect.

"Once you're inside, drop these into the wedding bags," she said, handing over a load of special souvenirs.

"What the hell is a wedding bag?" I asked.

"They'll be at every table. It's basically just a bag of jokey stuff. Condoms, lubricant, maybe some poppers for the gays, that sort of thing. Kind of fitting to chuck a porno into the mix, don't you think?"

I just nodded, laughing like a little girl. Then I kissed her without even thinking about it. She pushed me back, laughing as well, even blushing. "That comes later. Please, focus."

"Aye-aye captain."

"Right. After you plant the DVDs, you need to locate where the projector screen is. It shouldn't be hard to find. I heard Veronica say that her ditsy, dumb as a dodo friend called Leeanne is in charge of that. Just look for a woman who dresses twenty-years too young, with her fake tits on full display. Give her a flirt, your number. Whatever. She loves young guys. Tell her Richard hired you to make a small montage video of him and Veronica, of their annual little trips to some cabin in the middle of nowhere."

"That's true, as well, isn't it?"

"Yes. It is."

Suddenly a load of cars began to drop people off around us, all clearly from a wedding. Raquel looked at me. It was show-time baby. Maybe I was doing too much coke at the time, but I didn't care that a bunch of strangers were unknowingly about to watch me fuck the groom's dead ex-wife.

I got out of the car on the driver's side and locked it, on Raquel's insistence, and put the keys in my pocket. Before even entering the building, I began to take pictures of people loitering outside, all except for the bride and groom of course, who weren't around anyway. The one person who couldn't see me was Veronica. She may not have done anything if she saw me, but the risk of it was too high. After a few flashes, I slipped through the door into the foyer.

"You must be Ed," some fat woman said upon seeing me.

"Urm yeah, that's me. I just need to check the lighting in the hall, so I know what filters to use."

"You're doing that now? Why so late? You could've prepared a little sooner, don't you think?" she asked. I knew her type. Everyone knows bitches like that. One of those busybody know-it-all critics, who love nothing more than to stick their noses into other people's affairs because they have no lives of their own.

"Yeah, it was done this morning. But one of the lights went out. I need to check if it compromises my plans. You don't want to be responsible for ruining the pictures, by refusing me access to the lights, do you?" I asked. Throw in a snarl and an authoritative, cunty undertone and they usually back down. Seeing my point, she just waved her hand and carried on boring some poor couple like before. I walked on without looking back.

Once inside the main hall, there were a few people scurrying around trying to get the last-minute stuff done. Planting the DVDs was a piece of piss. Raquel calculated exactly the right amount; forty-two, plus one extra for the projector. Then I had to wait it out until Leeanne turned up. I went back outside, took a bung load of fake pictures and helped myself to all the free booze I could get on the sly. The happy couple were there then. I always kept them at about a twenty-foot radius from me, but they were too busy lost in their over-elaborate excuse for attention and had their own photographer anyway, so I was safe. Veronica was beaming, but the groom didn't exactly look all that happy. Maybe he'd just made the same mistake twice. In some ways, he had. Christ, it was dull as fuck. They cut the cake. Yay. Everybody pretended to care. Woo. They had a dance. Aww. Women cried. Guys drank. Terrible music was played. I'll never understand why people still choose to get married.

Finally, the grub was served. I had a few sausage rolls and chips and started searching for the dumb blonde. Raquel must've known these people very well; her description of Leeanne was right on the money. She was mildly doable, but I think I only thought that because I'd never got my hands on a set of plastic tits before.

"Leeanne," I said whilst approaching her.

"Alright young man," she said, placing her hand on my shoulder immediately.

"Veronica asked me to give you this. She wants it to be the last video. Don't worry, it's pretty short."

"What is it?" she asked, looking at the case which read: Our Wedding Day. I put my hand on her shoulder, near the neckline, switching her focus.

"It's a montage of their intimate moments, out in a private cabin they rent every year. Sadly, it isn't as saucy as I'd hoped, if you know what I mean, Leeanne." I gave her a wink and a shoulder squeeze. She laughed and gazed at me all drunk and dreamy.

"I can trust you to manage this, right?"

"Sure thing, young man. Just make sure you

dance with me later," she said, with her fingertips caressing silicon. Lonely, dumb and older women are fucking great.

"You have my word," I said, thinking the exchange was over.

"I want more than that," she said.

"Well," I said, stalling, "I'm going to take your picture, whilst you write your number down on... this napkin. How's that for more?" I asked, patting around my pockets, pretending to look for a pen. Classy Leeanne soon helped me out by producing lipstick from her handbag.

"What's your name?" she asked.

"Glen," I said. Not sure why. Never met any Glen's.

Leeanne wrote her number down whilst I watched on through the lens. She seemed to like it when I focused on her arse. She finished by signing it with a kiss. Elegant bird.

"Here you go. Bring the camera with you next time as well, if you like," she said, with the lust of an STI shining through at its potential prey.

"Oh, I always do," I said, pinching the napkin from her hand and slipping it into my pocket. "Find you later."

"You better," she said, running a fingertip over her lip, as I walked away backwards, taking more pictures.

I probably should've left at this point, but I didn't. I wanted to see Raquel and I's masterwork on the big screen, in front of its oblivious test audience. After going out back for a smoke and a cheeky key, I grabbed a few more bottles of beer and drank them, wondering whether a pair of plastic tits was worth a virtually guaranteed trip to the STI clinic. Whilst

I did all that, the bride and groom bored everyone senseless with their empty speeches as the guests ate their food. I went for a piss. After I came back, the first film began to roll.

I was momentarily stunned. It was a carbon copy of the beginning of Raquel and Richard's wedding video. Not the actual wedding, but the separately recorded congratulations that showed before. All the same people were in it, only older and more downtrodden. A lot of them had switched partners too. They had filmed themselves wishing the happy couple well with all the same meaningless words. This wedding was more like an incestual celebration of all things middle-class and mundane. It was truly horrifying. Like a glimpse into the future if you fall for the wrong value system. I couldn't believe it. Then, after it all finished, a picture of Raquel came up, with the words: In Loving Memory Of, followed by an audience 'aww'. They were all congratulating themselves for doing what in the traditional sense was the right thing, but conveniently ignored the fact that A. Raquel wasn't even dead yet and B. Her fucking husband was marrying her fucking best friend.

But the threat of vomit passed as soon as the next DVD went into the player. I whipped out my phone to begin filming all the reactions. The silence was deafening. People looked at each other at first, but then couldn't take their eyes off the screen. I was especially looking forward to the part when Raquel said to the camera, that she'd been sleeping with me since I was fourteen. To hell with the truth, just planting the seed into the heads of the crowd was enough. But then, I couldn't avert my eyes from the screen either. It wasn't the porno Raquel and I had recorded. It was the threesome. Not the wedding night threesome either, but the one we had with what I thought was the dying Veronica. Raquel had filmed it. From numerous places all around the flat. Each camera hidden to perfection.

Veronica was sat on the couch where I'd first meet her. Raquel came onto the screen. They kissed. All the guys in the audience perked up. Some of the women too.

'We have a guest on the way,' Screen-Raquel said.

'Who?' asked Veronica.

'A young man with a penchant for older women. He's a gigolo. Pre-paid as well,' she said and snorted a line.

'He's all yours, thanks.'

A flash-cut of me undressing Veronica spliced onto the screen, then back. The test audience liked the opening sequence.

Inside the hall, Veronica dropped her cutlery. Richard, in a beautiful moment of misremembering, held his hands up in the air like a guilty party, until he realised his balls had been tarnished by the laws of gravity far more than the ones that just flashed on the screen. They both sat there, as stunned as their guests.

'Veronica, I'm a dying woman,' Screen-Raquel said, 'with only one wish. Do you remember our first threesome? I don't think I've ever been that turned on before in my life.'

'But you didn't even seem to like it?' Veronica questioned in disbelief.

'That's because I was too petrified of my feelings,'

Raquel replied, really laying it on thick. 'But now, I just want to do it again. One more time. Please. I promise it'll be worth it.'

Flash-cut: Veronica's eyes rolling around the back of her head.

'Oh, I don't know, Raquel,' said Veronica, clearly warming to the idea. Raquel was leaning over her, moving in. Slowly, they kissed. 'Come on,' said Raquel between smooches. 'We've done it before. And now, we can do it again, but with a young stud this time. What's stopping us? I'm single. You're single. I don't see why you wouldn't want to?'

Flash-cut: Veronica on her knees with Raquel over her shoulder, holding her arms back.

In the hall, Just-Married Veronica said, "No! Please," only to be interjected by another flash-cut of her slut-screen self, screaming 'Oh, yes, that's it! Don't s—'

"Stop the video!"

Flash-cut: My hand pushing Veronica's head between Raquel's legs.

'Please?' Raquel said, back on the couch, toying with Veronica's hair. 'It'll be more than worth your while...'

'Oh, okay. Let's just see what happens, I guess,' said Veronica, the reluctant and oblivious porn-star. 'I'm sure one last time couldn't hurt.'

Flash-cut: The money-shot; Raquel spitting me into Veronica's mouth.

"ARRRRRRRGGGGHHHHH!!!!!!" Gate-Crashed Veronica screamed across the entire hall, but the audience was still too transfixed to even notice. She made to run, but, after struggling passed some chairs, she tripped up under the fabric of her own wedding dress! Whilst crying she continued begging for the video to be stopped, but it kept right on rolling. In fact, nobody else moved at all, not even Richard.

Ding-dong.

'Oh, and I want you to pretend to be the one with cancer,' Raquel said. Before Veronica could reply, the front door was opened and into the frame I walked. Veronica starts chopping up some lines. I go to take my seat next to her. During which, more freeze-frames began slicing into the story, of me, doing all the degrading shit I was just about to do to them. It had the exact desired effect, as those shots kept everyone watching, frozen and gobsmacked.

I thought the DVD was going to be cut-off, but as Veronica made her way out of there screaming, with Richard walking behind, I turned my frame towards Leeanne, who also seemed to be loving the show. She couldn't keep her eyes off it. Who knew the dumb mule had a dark horse in her? Then something clicked. She recognised me. She looked over, then back at the screen. Three times. As the guests of honour had already departed I decided to follow suit and leave the crowd behind, who were now all acting appalled despite not being able to avert their eyes. Leeanne began pointing at me as I bolted for the backdoor, so I waved the STI goodbye and blew her a kiss as I exited and ran without looking back.

When I got back to the car, Raquel seemed to be asleep. The satnav had the location of the cliff punched into it. So, despite not having a license, I'd driven an automatic before, and as I seemed to be untouchable that day, I drove my very first sports car with the devil sleeping by my side.

Raquel was still unconscious when I arrived, so I decided to join her and have a nap. Must've needed it a lot, as I didn't wake up until dark. When I woke up it became apparent that Raquel hadn't really been sleeping at all, unless smoking heroin counts. "Hey," I said, sleepily.

"Hey you," she said in a daze herself, "you want some?"

I hesitated. The only reason I'd never done heroin was that I'd never been offered any. I always thought I'd leave it until I was dying myself. It felt rude to refuse her offer though. So, I had a few goes. Then I threw up the free food I ate at the wedding. I didn't feel like doing more after that.

"I threw up the first time as well, don't worry about it, it's normal," said Raquel.

"Fair enough. I feel good now anyway."

"So, how did it go?" she asked. "Did you watch it too?"

"Oh, I watched it alright. I was as stunned as everyone else. For a while anyway."

Raquel started laughing. I joined in.

"I'm sorry I did that to you. Well, actually I'm not really, but still. I'm aware it wasn't very nice. Are you annoyed?" she asked, knowing I wasn't.

"I thought I would be, but no. Not at all. It was one of the best things I ever saw in my life. I should've known you filmed the threesome. I dunno why, but it feels like I should've done," I said, taking out my phone. "Have a look at this."

"No, no. It's okay. I don't want to watch it."

"Really? You sure? There's some real gold on here."

"Yeah, I'm sure. Just tell me about it," she said,

sitting back.

I gave her all the details. She didn't laugh, cry or really betray any emotion at all. At first, I put it down to the heroin, but there was something in her that prompted me to ask if she was okay.

"Oh, yeah. I'm fine. I didn't really want to ruin their marriage, per se. I just wanted to make them suffer for it. If they really care about each other, they'll get over all their friends and relatives watching a DVD of the bride, with her dying best friend she betrayed for years, both fucking the shit out of some teenager. The vows he gave to me only lasted for a few hours. Now the vows he gave to her are the same. They got everything they deserved. I can die at peace now."

We made love for a long time after that. It was a sloppy daze, dreamy sort of fuck. She let me take her wig off half-way through. Even though she did look like a cadaver, the pain and suffering still present in her eyes made her look perfect to me. Once we finished, I stayed inside her for ages, with both of us clinging to each other by the sweat of our skin and the endless tears that streamed from her eyes. Before we got changed again, I told her my name. Then I got out of the car for a piss.

"Eric," Raquel said through the window as I let rip, "promise me you'll never get married."

"I never planned to anyway."

"Good. Don't forget that. I'm sorry, but you're going to need to walk home tonight. The nearest town is a couple of miles back. You can get a cab there."

"What?" I asked, zipping myself back up. I headed towards the car again, when Raquel tossed a rucksack out and drew-up the window she'd been leaning out of.

"I didn't tell you the whole plan. I'm dying tonight," she said through the remaining gap.

By instinct, I went to open the door, but it was already locked. "Raquel, don't fuck about—"

"I'm not. My disease is only going to get worse. I don't want to be confined to a hospital bed. All the people I used to know would find out, I'm sure of it. I don't want them to see me like that, or hear about what an evil bitch I am. I'd been planning my revenge for a long time, but I never planned on meeting you. I couldn't have ever pulled this off without you. You were sent to me like some sordid angel. Falling in love with somebody new was a beautiful way to go. I can't have you watching me rot. This is the perfect time."

I went to speak but couldn't. Instead, I started to cry because I knew she was right. There wasn't anywhere left for her to go, nor for us. "What are you going to do?" I asked.

"Smoke a shitload of heroin, then let this car roll off the edge. If the fall doesn't kill me, the water certainly will."

"Yeah. Can't argue with that."

"I've always loved this place. Just look out at the landscape and the stars. It's the only time I've been able to feel my own insignificance and not fear it. It's the perfect place to die. I left you some money and the rest of my coke, among other things. Now kiss me and leave."

I obliged her request. "Wait," I said, as I pulled back. I took out my phone. "Not that I'm ever going to forget you, but I want a picture of us."

"Go right ahead."

I took one single photo. She looked like the cancer patient that she was. I looked like the alcoholic teenage drug addict that I was. It was perfect.

"So, what are you going to do with your life?" she asked.

"I'm thinking of training to be an actor. Pretending to be someone else is pretty fun. Helps me see inside humanity a bit."

"You'll be superb at that."

Here, she pulled me towards her again. We kissed with an empirical understanding of one another. Afterwards, we looked into each other's eyes with the hope that we'd meet again, but with the resignation that we knew we never would. I couldn't tell you how long it lasted for.

We kissed again for the last time. I turned, slung the rucksack over my shoulder and began to walk away. Once I reached the road, I looked back. The car was still sitting there, but tiny. Nothing but rock and chalk. Then, like she knew I was watching somehow, it began to roll. Time seemed to stop as it coasted towards the edge. I turned as it was tipping and walked on. There wasn't any Hollywood explosion. There wasn't a series of house lights suddenly flickering on. There wasn't even a crashing sound. She was just gone.

I walked all the way home. When I got there, exhausted, I flopped on my bed and had a look in the rucksack. Raquel left me two grand with a note that said she'd maxed-out her credit card for me. There was the camera I'd used at the wedding, a couple of grams worth of coke and my own copy of the DVD. The next day, I edited it so that my face was never on screen and uploaded it to some porn sites. I liked the thought of Richard, just getting over the trauma of his wedding, stumbling upon the video of his two wives whoring themselves out with a stranger. Then I signed up for an acting workshop and decided to leave women alone for a while, hoping that one day I'd find a Raquel my own age, despite knowing that I never would.

THE IMPORTANCE
OF SAFE SEX

If you happen to be eating whilst reading this, I suggest that you swallow whatever you're chewing and push the plate aside before continuing.

I'm a married man nearing the middle of my thirties, who recently quit his job as grocery manager in one of your favourite supermarkets. I won't mention which, for fear of judgment. I live a quiet life on the outskirts of a small city, surrounded by fields of green and the such. It's my wife's parents' place but thankfully they're both dead, so now the house is ours. We moved here around a year ago to start a family. With that in mind, we may as well have moved here yesterday, as the circumstances since have remained unchanged. I don't know whether my boys are slow swimmers or if my wife's womb is a barren wasteland. We start the tests soon though, so time will tell. Considering our pasts... well, let's just say that all bets are off. As of yesterday, we dismissed our concerns by becoming first-time pet-owners of a female Great Dane. Perhaps this purchase is the reason I'm telling you this tale, or maybe it's because of the banana I've just eaten. Either way, by the end, I think you'll agree that my intention is to simply raise some awareness over the importance of safe sex.

It was my solitary summer of the early twenty-first century, or the 'noughties' as they were sometimes referred to as. My older brother of three years had just turned eighteen and vanished from the family home to travel, whilst my workaholic parents decided that even more overtime would fill the hole left behind by his absence. The short preferred over the long, my parents were disappointed by my brother's decision and so, dealt with it in the best way they knew how. What they neglected to consider was that I was a fifteen-year-old male, alone in an empty house, with nothing but time and an internet connection. Hence the word solitary in regard to the summer I'm speaking of.

I remember I was on my knees, hunched over in a sea-horse posture, picking polyester pellets out of my foreskin. Staring up at me from the floor below were the blackened eyes of my favourite childhood toy, Ashley; who on this day was re-christened and baptised, Ashleigh. Please spell the two if reading out loud. Stood upright, Ashleigh was a teddy bear of around two to three foot tall. Beneath her now female arse and about the ground was a large array of even more pellets, strewn across the carpeted floor. I recall it being carpeted because my knees were fairly-well grazed after the act I'd just subjected her to. There must've been hundreds if not thousands of the squidgy little things. The toy looked identical to what it did during my childhood, with one notable exception: the desperate, crass slit slashed across its groin. Yes, there's no other way of saying this, I had just fucked my favourite childhood toy. You see, I was on the verge of fucking a real, breathing, animated girl the very next day, and in my adolescent logic, I thought I'd better get some practice in first. So, I dug-up and pornified the bear. Little did I know that it would prove to be more animated than some of the girls in the years to come, but that's a whole different story.

As the last pellet fell from my slightly raw, flaccid member, down into the collected pile of semen-soaked ones, the forever lingering scent of smegma was in the air. I remember being slightly traumatised by that stench, as a few months prior I'd only just peeled my foreskin back. I don't know whether I was a late bloomer or not, but as the excess skin finally broke away from the head I was confronted by a bright, thick and pungent halo-shaped ring of smegma. It was spread as if by a connoisseur of a crumbly French cheese; who'd omitted the addition of herbs as they would've been cancelled out going by the taste suggested by the pong. Upon the reinforcement of such a memory (which I was still struggling to pacify) the computer to my side suddenly sprang into life, informing me of a new message from the girl whose charm had sealed Ashleigh's unfortunate fate.

Hannah: Hey. You there?! It read. This was at a time where if a program stated that you were online, you actually were. It was also a period where people would feel a pang of guilt for not replying, instead of contentedly ignoring one another like they do now.

In a swift haste, I booted the bear under the bed, pulled up my boxer shorts, but left my torso bare. I was in that puberty-plagued, hormonal-gangbang age when I thought my bordering-on-the-anorexic frame could easily be confused for a muscular, toned body. After taking my seat, there was a new message.

Hannah: Did you try the banana thing?

I started typing.

Me: Hey. Yeah, just now. Gives a whole new meaning to the words 'banana split'.

After apparently laughing out loud, she began typing again.

Hannah: So, did it feel like the real thing?

Me: Urm, maybe. It was slippery. I wouldn't know. But you knew that already...

Hannah: Well, you'll find out tomorrow...

Me: We're meeting at the station, right?

Hannah: Vid?

Here I span around to check whether the bear could be detected through the lens. Jacking off with a banana was one thing, but wrapping one over your cock, then duct-taping it closed through frustration, to finally slitting a hole in a comforting childhood plaything and fucking it was another. My dirty little secret was safe though, as the brutalised bear was back in the dark again, fucked, and I suppose literally (for the lack of a more charming phrase) torn a new one.

The hypnotically spinning loading sign retracted itself from the screen and Hannah appeared, still dressed in the uniform of a school the next town over. She'd made all the customary adjustments to her clothes in a bid to come off as sexy. It'd be a good few years until she realised she resembled something just short of a gullible prostitute with naïve notions regarding male sexuality. Ah, to be young again. Hannah had fallen into the habit of playing with her dog during the opening ceremony of our conversations. At first, I found it rather adorable. By this time, it was aggravating and somewhat strange.

"Hey. So, yeah... about tomorrow. We're meeting at the station, right?" I asked, slipping my hand underneath the desk to caress my testicles whilst she played around with her mutt. Looking back at it, I'm sure it was intentional on her part. I'd often say nothing in the first few minutes of our video chats, as she always seemed to wear something that kept my interest instead. Knee-high socks killed me. Ripped tights with muddied short skirts killed me harder. And the curious way her buxom cleavage shook together never failed to leave my mouth hanging agape. This could've been dismissed as a hindsight bias had I not come to into knowing what I now know, but I was sure Hannah loved being leered at whilst goofing around with her pet.

Truth be told, Hannah's body, though appealing to my innocent eyes was not without a layer of puppy fat. I think that fact benefited me overall though, as many a man would've been attracted to her had she not possessed such a glaring threat of imprisonment by the obviousness of her adolescence. It was that very fact that attracted me to her. She carried herself off as a sassy, carefree type, with a cute, albeit incessant need to be found desirable. She often held her hair up in clumps, with items she seemed to be forever sucking upon in between: pens, pencils, paintbrushes and the like. Her clothes were often creased and sometimes even stained. She wanted to be seen as a new age hippie type, full of liberal ideals and meat-free preferences. All she came across as to me was dirty. And that excited me. I should mention that this was a Friday night. Friday night had recently evolved from Let's Talk About Our Feelings Night to I'll Show You Mine If You'll Show Me Yours Night, hence my decision to go into the conversation already half-naked. The week prior she had shown me her breasts. That night I imagined she'd be keen to see my penis, but I was hopeful for an equal, simultaneous exchange.

"Hannah," I cried, just as the dog's butt began to creep into the frame, blocking my peeping tom view.

"Urrmmm. The station, tomorrow at six. I'll bring Boomerang with me. Won't I boy, won't I?" said Hannah, continuing to play with her dog, who was apparently named after the strange shape of his tail. It always confused me at the time, as his tail never appeared to be anything other than straight as a rod. A far cry from a boomerang.

"Is that the banana, then?" she asked after shooing Boomerang out of the door. I was too busy perving over her to notice any looks she might've stolen from the lens whilst she played around. I'd forgotten where I put the banana post-coitus. It was lying on the corner of my desk on the right side, limp, used and layered with ejaculate. My fingers were poised over the prickles of my ball-sack. Reluctantly I pulled them away and pointed at the sorry-looking piece of fruit.

"That is what I just destroyed," I said, making a joke but also trying to sound masculine. I still don't know why we males associate that with destruction and violence so much.

"Oh yeah?" said Hannah, "did you fill that bitch up?"

"Sure did. Only peeled one flap back beforehand. Look at her now. Broken in from every angle."

Hannah slapped her knee, let out a laugh and raised her foot to the edge of her chair. Whenever she playfully flopped her legs from side to side or tapped her knees together like that of a pendulum, my tongue would stick out of my mouth through its own accord. She certainly enjoyed provoking that action.

"Show me it," she said. "I wanna see that big, creamy fat load of spunk," she uttered in an actor-esque, sonorous whisper, but ruined it with the guffaw that followed. Hannah then nodded for me to pick the banana up. Between my index finger and thumb, I dangled it in front of the lens. Thinning droplets of semen fell onto the keyboard (not for the first time, mind you). She leaned forward with her head at an angle, examining the banana with investigative eyes.

"D'you see it?" I asked.

"Urm. Sort of," she said with a scrunched face, "looks a bit see-through."

"It gets like that the longer you leave it. Or it

coagulates," I said.

"Coagulates? What's that?"

"Urm. You know how bits of dough become loose sometimes, so you have to rub them together to form a shape?"

"Yeah?"

"Well, semen does the same. The clumpy bits seem to anyway," I said.

"Gross."

I nodded. "It is a bit."

"Would you like to coagulate over these?" she said, stunning me into silence. Without warning, she removed her blouse and sat back in her chair. Sadly, she was wearing a sports bra, but at the time I wasn't going to complain. Hannah's eyes crossed over and a cheeky, mischievous smile arose from her lips. "Hey. Will you do something for me, if I do something for you?" she asked.

"Maybe. Like what?" I asked back, placing the banana in the same place.

"I want you to lick the banana."

"No way. That's disgusting—"

"Oh, come on! Just a little bit. For me. It'll be hot. If you lick it..." she said, teasing me by popping a finger into her mouth.

"If I lick it..."

She broke the finger away from her lips. "I'll go get one from downstairs and..." she trailed off and flushed. Her hand slowly moved in front of her crotch and she began to mock penetrate herself. "I'll let you watch me. You can masturbate too, if you want."

"Deal," I said, grabbing the banana like a starving monkey.

"Wait. Hold it the other way around, so the skin

hangs like when you eat one," she said. I twisted my hand around. There was still a pool of spunk in the centre, with a few stringy pieces of banana swimming inside.

"Mmm, this is making me wet already," said Hannah.

"Really?" I asked in a different octave.

"Uh-huh," she said. All I saw were her shuffling, opening and closing legs, teasing, taunting, titillating. "Give it a good, long sniff first," she said, laughingly, covering her face with her hand.

Obeying my orders, I gave it a good, long sniff. It didn't have a particular smell. Just your standard banana flavoured semen. I'd tasted my own semen before anyway. The week summer began I tried my hand at self-fellatio at the cost of reshuffling my organs into foreign regions and nearly snapping my spine in half. I did manage to get the tip into my mouth though. I didn't swallow, for at the time it seemed to be too homosexual. Ah, was I really ever that blissfully naïve? I could've admitted it to Hannah without judgment, but I was trying to make an impression I guess.

"Don't make me wait, Max. Just stick your tongue in it and swirl it around. It'll be more good practice for tomorrow as well," she said. "Just follow my lead."

"Okay," I replied, a tad turned on by her instructive manner.

"Stick your tongue out. That's it. Now, from the bottom of one flap, run the tip of your tongue along the whole thing. Slowly."

I did as Hannah directed, but kept a small distance between my tongue and the banana.

"Hey! I can see you're not touching it, Max. Come on, do you want to see me play with my pussy or not? she asked, biting her bottom lip. "I shaved it today."

I pressed my tongue down immediately.

"That's it. Good boy. Now run it along slowly, swirl your tongue around when you reach the top and let's get down to business."

"Like this?" I asked. With a deep breath, I slithered my tongue over the semen-laced skin all the way to the top (or bottom, if you prefer) and dipped it into the tiny paddling pool of ejaculation product. It tasted like... well, of semen, hinted with banana. When I looked back at the screen, the lip under Hannah's teeth was quivering and for the first time in our relationship, her finger was gently stroking the vaginal lips underneath her panties.

"Go and get that banana," I said, reaching my hand under the desk again. "I'm more than ready."

"I can't wait to taste you," she said, horny as hell. The pale skin around her cheeks always pinkened when that was the case. She removed her finger from her underwear, then revealed her breasts. I started beating off immediately, but in a sudden movement, she re-covered them, sprung off the circular-spinning computer chair and merrily skipped out of the room. In the meantime, I focused on a picture-frame sat on the bedside table, of her mother, and masturbated over her instead.

I couldn't help feeling astonished that I was going to be the first one out of my friends to get laid. I knew they'd never believe me, as Hannah went to a school none of us had ever heard of before and committing to a long-distant relationship before you're even legally able to have sex didn't seem so viable. But all of that didn't matter. From what I'd learnt, Hannah was keener on experimenting with someone she didn't know so well, so that she'd be more than adequate when sleeping with someone she actually liked. At first, this admission hurt my feelings a bit, but then she showed me her tits, and all was right again. Of course, her real reason was that she wanted to fuck men twice her age. But I was more than willing to be her kinky little Guinea pig.

Hannah returned with a black bottle of deodorant in one hand, but nothing in the other. "No bananas here I'm afraid. My stupid brother must've taken the last one when he went out. God, it's steamy in here. I think I better... take some more clothes off."

"Great idea," I replied like a gimp.

The bra came off first. I gulped. Then her short skirt.

"Leave the socks on," I said as she attempted to roll them off. The rainbow-coloured stripes were rather alluring. She popped the cap off the deodorant can and sprayed under her armpits.

"I swear, even though I haven't technically had sex yet, that I really stink of it. Sweating always makes me think of sex. And I'm flustered all the time."

A rivulet of my own sweat streamed down the side of my ribs. Hannah sat down on the chair again, placing both feet on the edge. "You've heard the song 'Smells Like Teen Spirit' right?" she asked, clicking the cap back on, her hand firmly gripped around the can.

"Nirvana? Sure. Who hasn't heard it?"

"Here's a fun fact. Did you know that Teen Spirit

was a deodorant?"

"Was it?" I asked, a little miffed at where the conversation was going. I could fuck a soulless teddy bear with a makeshift vagina, but the thought of a dead guy blasting his brains out didn't do my erection any favours.

"Yeah. That's where Cobain got the idea from. Get it? Smells like teen spirit?"

"Oh right. Yes, sure. Clever."

"I believe so. What do you think? Shall I make this bottle smell like my teen spirit?" she asked, but I wasn't paying attention, as she was busy pulling down her underwear with her delicious rainbow foot. Unfortunately, Teen Spirit was cock-blocking my view of her vagina. "Don't gawp at me, Max. Pay attention. What do you say? Shall I turn this can of cheap crap into a brand-new teen spirit or what?"

"I'm not sure I know what you mean," I replied.

Hannah took the can from the desk and showed herself to me. There it was, the first vagina I'd seen without the help of a porn site, with a far smaller slit than the one I made in the teddy bear.

"This is what I mean, Max," she said and plunged the can of deodorant straight into her vagina. In terms of circumference, it was a fair match for my manhood, but when it came to the length, the big black bottle was a tad intimidating. Honestly, though, I didn't care. I was watching a fifteen-year-old girl dildoing herself with a can of bubble-gum-scented deodorant. God bless you, Kurt Cobain.

"I wanna be ready for you tomorrow, Max," she said, in between her most likely feigned orgasmic moans, pumping the can in and out of her pussy. Another pool of cum was present in the room at that moment, pre-cum to be exact, around my urethra. "Show me your cock," said Hannah, reading my mind.

I stood up so fast that the room spun around all before me. The sunlight glaring behind the closed curtains seemed to invade the room, blinding me towards fainting, but all I could hear was Hannah's gasps and cries of pleasure. So, I vowed to myself not to fall unconscious.

"Oh yeah, that's it. Tease me," she said, watching my cock swing from side to side. "You want me to touch my breasts?"

"Yes," was all I replied, as I waited for my sight to return back to normal.

"Are you ready to fuck me tomorrow?"

"Yes," I said again.

"Talk to me, Max. Say something dirty."

"I'm going to... I'm gonna... stick my dick in your head," I said. More weird than dirty now that I mention it.

"Oh yeah? Are you gonna stick that filthy banana dick into my mouth? Oh god, I can't wait," she said.

Indulge me once more, but thinking back, I'm sure Hannah is the reason that I prematurely ejaculate to dirty talk of any kind.

"I'm gonna bring a banana tomorrow and... and... put it in your arse whilst I fuck you from behind," I blurted out.

"Oh, you are a dirty boy, aren't you, Max? Oh, look at you jerk off. You're so fast. Let's do it in the same rhythm," she said.

I didn't have a clue what she was talking about, but my vision had returned. On the screen before me Hannah was busy, circling the deodorant can around her pussy, whilst fondling one breast, pinching it at the nipple. "Oh fuck, Max. I'm nearly there. Tell me you're going to come. I want to hear you say it."

"I'm going to come," I said.

"Oh yeah?! Are you going to come all over my tits? Or in my mouth?" she asked.

Like a spaceship in full throttle, my cock was convulsing and throbbing inside of my hand. "Both. In your mouth, over your face, in your arse, over your tits. I'm gonna fuck you till... till my balls are shrivelled up like raisins."

"Oh yeah? In my arse? You wanna see my arse?"

"Yes, I want to see it. Bend over the edge of your bed."

"Oh fuck. Yes, sir," she said. Continuing to thrust herself with the bottle, she kicked her chair to the side and grabbed the laptop. For a few seconds, all I could see were her tits. I pumped myself harder. The screen scrambled, but as it came back into focus, all I could see was Hannah's shapely behind. She'd positioned herself at an angle where the arse was the main point of focus but upwards you could still see half of her face. She was biting her lip again, pinching the other nipple and fucking the can of deodorant so hard that I thought it might explode. On my own side, things were much the same. I was masturbating so intensely that a squidgy sound from the head of my cock repeatedly rang around my ears, I assumed because of the moisture left behind by the banana.

"Oh fuck, Max. I can't take anymore," said Hannah, easing into a slower movement. All I could see was the bottom of the bottle, being engulfed by her spewing vagina. It was too much for me to take. The twinge of imminent ejaculation shot through my shaft.

"I'm coming," I said.

"Oh, please. Go on, Max. Come all over my arseeeeeee..."

I wanted to watch her as I came, but the bright light from before invaded my senses again, forcing me to close my eyes. Under the glow of supreme rays of golden glory, I blew the biggest load of my life. It seemed to last for much longer than any orgasm up until that point. All I could hear were panted breaths of arousal, satisfaction and an eagerness to play. Naturally, it passed too quickly. I opened my eyes, eager to see how much I had unloaded. Nothing was there. Not even a drop. I checked the floor. My feet. My legs. Even my arse, for some reason. My load had seemingly disappeared.

"Hey boy," said Hannah.

I looked at the screen. Hannah's face was flushed all over.

"Did you come?" I asked.

She nodded her head, exhausted but still raring to go again. "That was much hotter than watching you fuck a teddy bear," she said and began laughing, still toying with the can.

I sunk, literally, sunk down into my chair. Through shame, I couldn't even look at the screen.

"You should take more care of your privacy, Max."

"You were watching me?"

"Watching? I was masturbating to it. You know, I've done some pretty weird shit like that too."

"Oh yeah? Like what?" I asked, now pretending to look around for the spunk to avoid looking at the monitor.

"Jump up boy," said Hannah. I could hear Boomerang breathing. The weird shit she was referring to, was apparently going to be saved for another day.

When I used to smoke, I used to go mad looking for a lighter when I couldn't find one. And I mean nuts. That's what I was doing whilst looking for my load. I wasn't pretending anymore. I guess, in my anger at having been caught out, the disappearing spunk became a convenient distraction. This was before I realised how handy a sock could be when it came to ejaculation. But no matter where I looked, not a trace was to be found.

"Well," said Hannah. "I watched you in secret. Now you can watch me," she remarked, but there was something in the way she said it that caught me off guard. I hesitated, then lifted my chin up towards the screen. Then I saw it. Covered over the screen. Running down Boomerang's legs from the centre of his arsehole, was the heavy load of Hannah-provoked spunk, egg-like under the glaring light. It stared at me like a cataract eye, already blind but seemingly all-knowing. Hannah was staring into the lens, smiling at me. Boomerang's true boomerang was protruding from his hairy covering. It was thin. It was long. It was pink and bent, like a curved, Peperami hot stick. I don't know how I reacted. Hannah leaned towards the lens... as her dog began to mount! I couldn't move. I couldn't speak. Nor could I stop myself looking at the screen!

"We all have our secrets, Max. I'll keep yours if you keep mine. See you tomorrow at the station. Six o'clock. Don't worry. It'll just be you and me tomorrow. I'll leave you alone now, with Winnie the Pooh." She blew me a kiss, gave me a wink and clicked the exit conversation button. But before the video closed, Hannah bent down on all fours, swung her hand around, grabbed Boomerang's boomerang and slid it into her vagina! He began to ravage her like a... well, like a dog. The last thing I saw was his quaking arsehole; the staring cataract eye, crying the singular, milky-white tear that was my semen. Then everything cut to black and at that moment, my own teen spirit died.

I think I must've sat there for an hour, maybe two, not only stunned at what I'd just seen but also horrified that she'd witnessed me fucking Ashleigh as well, my favourite childhood toy. I dug out the bear again that night and hugged it like a child of trauma whilst I slept. Or more, tried to sleep. I guess I felt guilty about what I'd done to it, but I also felt terrified of what might happen if I didn't show up at the station the following day. Hannah could've filmed the whole thing; from me cutting a hole in the crotch, to wrapping a banana skin around my cock, penetrating the bear whilst the pellets somehow slipped through the slits of the banana flaps and worked their way inside the lingering smegma folds of my foreskin. My mind was nothing but an eight-hour nightmarish montage of my five-minute romp that day.

By the morning, I had come to a decision. What Hannah had seen me do could not possibly be compared with what she was doing with her dog. I packed my rucksack with some spare clothes, resolving to meet her at the station to explain that no funny business was going to take place during my visit and that any sign of the dog would prompt my swift exit. This I swore to myself, as the front door of my house swung behind me. A couple of minutes later though, I let myself back in. I went to the bathroom, had a second word with myself, then slipped some condoms into my bag. On my way back, I stopped at the front door and pondered for another moment. Then I turned back and headed for the kitchen. I had forgotten the banana.

Speaking of front doors, I just heard mine right now. My wife has returned with our new Great Dane, back from their first walk alone together. She's going to the doctor's tomorrow for a few tests, so for my first time, the dog will be left alone with me. Her name is Ashleigh.

A LESSON
WORTH UNLEARNING

When I look back on my youth, I'm sure I'll often wonder which out of the following is worse:

One. What Dad could've said and done, but never did.

Or *Two.* What Dad did say and do, but never should have.

This story concerns both.

Instead of procrastinating, I'll just come out with it. Dad had just caught me masturbating. Like a true amateur, I'd got down to business without checking if I was alone, as he was supposed to be at work. Then again, I was meant to be at school. I'd decided to do a bunk (not out of pleasure, funnily enough) to finish a homework assignment already a day overdue. It was for my English class. Normally I get the work done straight away, but Dad's been a bit of a wreck recently. He drinks and talks at me until his eyes begin to droop. As the Sandman begins to sprinkle, I then take his place and do the same, except I'm only ever talking to myself. But I guess that's all he's doing as well. We've been doing this for a few weeks now, which I think must've made me forget about the homework. I feel bad about that. In truth, I like the teacher (yes, *like* like) a lot. Not just in the way all the other boys do as well though. I don't know what it is, but there's something very comforting about her. Reassuring, you know? She makes me feel safe; at ease. At around this time her heart didn't seem to be in the job. The other kids came across as a relentless disappointment to her and she seemed stressed with their collective indifference. I just didn't want to be yet another contribution to that. Anyway, I'm now left wondering whether part of myself was undone due to my absence from school, almost like an immediate consequence. The unfortunate cause and effect concerning my task at hand (ahem) soon led me to think about Miss English (that's actually her name too) which transpired into the swift removal of my trousers and the opening of a fresh and private browser. The double-association created by her namesake surely doesn't help with the matter either, but I'm probably just making excuses. In secret, I've fancied Miss English since day one of secondary school, long before any orifice was gazed upon in the pleasurable sense.

Anyway, whilst I was in the middle of things,

shall we say, Dad decided to barge into my room without warning and caught me in the act. We both froze whilst my substitute teacher on the screen began her countdown, intended for my impending climax. During the 'Not yet, six, keep going, five, oh yeah, that's it, show me how much you want that A-plus, now faster,' Dad seemed to shift three-sixty and vacate the room without actually moving his feet, whilst the pulse in my hand pinballed around my stomach before it began its descent down the bottomless pit that is now my chest. As my hands concealed my uncertain erection, Dad told me, in the simplest manner possible, to go and wait in the hallway whilst he went for a shit. Normally, I would've ignored this and left the house without saying anything, but like I said, things at home have been tough of late, especially for him. I guess that made me feel obliged to stay and obey his orders.

So, there I stood, re-imagining the horrific moment when Dad double-took between me and the woman on screen, dressed in a casual-smart fashion, with large-rimmed spectacles and an authoritative aura, demanding that I touched myself exactly how she commanded. After an unknown quantity of minutes, the toilet flushed. Following that, as usual, was a guttural hack of phlegm, the running of the sink, then a sneezing fit. Dad had taken to using the tweezers Mum left behind to pluck the hairs out of his nose, which always seemed to provoke him into a relentless, five-to-ten-minute frenzy of sneezes. As the ringing after-flush hiss faded from the house along with the *'ahh-chooes!'* the bathroom door opened.

"Son, grab your coat. We're going on a little trip,"

said Dad from the landing, still sniffing. "Grab mine 'n all and go start the car while you're at it."

"*Argh, what?*" I said. "What d'you mean? Where are we going?"

"Never you mind where… *you naughty little boy,*" he said, scoffing himself into the silent moment that comes just before a sneeze. I'm sure he was thinking about that joke whilst shitting.

"*Ahh-choo!*"

I made no further protest, hoping the lack of a response would stall the litany of jokes that promised to follow behind us during our mysterious outing. I recall thinking as I opened the car-door that I only watched that particular video because I'd become somewhat bored with pornography. Sometimes I just want a woman to talk to, even if she's doing all the talking, demanding that I jack off as she does so, even (or especially) when she's just telling me how filthy and wretched I am. Part of me enjoys thinking of myself as disgusting. I don't know where this psychology comes from though.

Dad never did any of that father/son crap when Mum was around, so I had no idea what he was planning. Since she left he's been hitting the sauce hard. When he's not here chewing my ear off, he's down the pub boozing instead. This week he's taken it to a new low by waking up on the sofa with a half-eaten kebab under his head for a pillow; an array of the saddest chips I've ever seen scattered about his person, the couch and the floor, like tears of potassium and grease. And, as you already know, bunking off work. I guess he misses her, somehow. If anyone asked me (nobody ever has) I'd say we were better off without her, or would be, if Dad just got his shit together. I didn't even know if I missed her. Still don't in fact. You see, she's something of a cunt. I'd like to tell you why this is the case, but I can't. She's been playing the disappearing act ever since my need for nappies expired, eloquently spouting off about her 'artistic, creative mind and its unquestionable need for solitude in order to prosper and bloom'. She's the reason I can actually speak English properly though, which I'm secretly grateful for. Fuck knows how she ever ended up with Dad. I did read her poetry once as well. It sucked.

Perhaps this is the best place to mention that Dad doesn't really talk to me as a son (though he's fond of using the word), but more like a mate sat next to him on a barstool down his local haunt. You'll soon see what I mean.

Whilst sitting in the car, staring at the overcast clouds all around me, I had the feeling that this day was going to be like so many others: forgotten in no time at all. Almost like he read my mind to contradict that thought, Dad opened the car door and gestured for his coat. I passed it over. Once inside, he said, "Got the hots for one of your school teachers have you then? Been there, son."

I said nothing but felt myself flush.

He winked and said, "Thought so," just before stabbing the key in the ignition.

"Can't we just forget about what happened Dad?" I asked in a last-ditch attempt to abort ship.

"I'm afraid not, son. Usually I'd let your mother deal with this, you know that. But she can't right now, for obvious reasons. Don't worry about it though. I'm not pissed or nothing. If anything, I'm actually quite proud of ya. It's good to see you've got a bit of your old man's blood in your veins. Normally you've got your head stuck in a book. Look at you now. Bunking off school so you can say hello to your monster. Next thing ya know and you'll be drinking beer. This'll be a nice, father-son moment. Trust me. Have a bit of faith in your old man."

"You've got chilli sauce on your face, Dad."

"Have I?" he asked, checking the rear-view mirror. "Oh yeah, so I have." He swiped the mark, licked his finger and then patted me on the back and laughed it off.

"Wait," I said. "You were just in the bathroom. You didn't just eat that kebab from the other night did you?"

"Waste not, want not, son," he replied.

"You stubbed a cigarette out in it."

"Well I didn't eat that, did I?"

"It was on the floor for three days! Think of all the bacteria that grew during that time. Just looking at it made me feel sick."

"You've gotta give the immune system something to work on. If you leave it bone-idle too long it goes soft on ya, and everything's liable to make you ill then."

"But Dad those things are bad enough as they are. I don't think you should be contributing to its already non-nutritional state."

"Ark at you with the big words. I'll tell you what. When your fancy talk brings home the bacon, you can buy the most gourmet, organic, well-to-do, lar-dee-da free-range whatever, whenever you like. How's that sound?"

"Dad. You always do this. There's nothing wrong with using the words of the language you speak.

And yes, I know I don't have any money. I'm still at fucking school in case you forgot. I shouldn't have to advise you that eating a kebab, especially one that's spent the majority of its life on an un-vacuumed carpeted floor is bad for you!"

"All right. Calm down. What's up with you? Teacher not like the apple you brought her?"

"Just drive."

I asked him where we were going again but he ignored me, checking to see if the road was clear instead. As soon as he pulled out, he said, "I've got a little story to tell you, son. Now listen up and listen true."

With that, I knew the drive was going to be a long one.

As we coasted downhill towards the first traffic light, he began. It was a little difficult to concentrate, as for some reason when I saw the amber switch to red, it dawned on me that Dad was the first person to see me with an erection.

"You kids these days have no idea how good you've got it, I swear. You've got everything at the end of your fingertips on a twenty-fucking-four-hour basis, but when I was a kid, things were different. For one thing, we had to work for our wanks. Most of the time we were stuck using our imaginations, which was bad enough at the best of times, but every once in a while, somebody'd find a porno lying about in the woods somewhere. Seemed to be the same in every school that, a porno in the woods. No idea why. Anyway. D'you remember your grandmother's place, at all?"

The traffic light still shone red.

"Yeah, I remember. It was boring," I said.

"That's because you don't know how to occupy your mind without a phone in your hand. D'you remember what it looked like? Or d'ya need to google that 'n all?"

"I remember what it smelt like."

"No - *you cheeky bastard* - not inside the house. Around the neighbourhood," he said, driving on despite the traffic lights speedy blink back to scarlet.

"Urm. Sort of. Lots of small houses all rowed together. Long driveways and gardens. Urm, huge fields near enough everywhere, a small forest—"

"A small forest indeed. That's exactly where I had my first porn wank, son. Beautiful place," he said.

"Really?"

"Really," he repeated whilst turning right, where, out of habit, I thought he'd turn left. I still knew the area, but only in a vague sense. "That's right, my boy. Now listen up. I was about your... wait, how old are you son?"

"I turned fifteen last month, Dad."

"Did ya? Right well. Yeah, I was your age if I remember correctly. Maybe fourteen. I dunno. Anyway. There were these bunch of rumours going around about one of my teachers at the time. Mrs Darwin her name was. Apparently, she'd done the dirty on her husband with a younger man or something. That's what everybody was saying anyway. All the lads fancied her, but she came across as far too uptight for any of the rumours to really ring true, if you know what I mean. Most of us thought she was a dyke, as she was always screaming at the lads but never the girls. We all figured her husband had been the one playing away, as her wedding ring had suddenly disappeared during the time of these rumours."

"All right. What's this got to do with masturbating in the woods though?" I asked.

"I'm getting to that. Just laying the foundations here. Anyway, me and the boys were all disappointed because she hadn't bothered to turn up that day. *Ha,* I only just remembered that. The crafty old mare. Oh well," he said, talking to himself rather than me.

I gave him a quizzical look, to which he returned an oblivious smile. Then he made another right, towards a motorway I'd never seen before.

"Anyway, yeah," he continued. "It was just before second period; the class Darwin was supposed to be teaching. Whilst we were banging on about her, one of my mates, Johnny, said he saw a porno mag in the woods. He said it wasn't old and tattered with all the pages stuck together like most of what we'd found before though. He said it was brand new."

Weirdly enough, it occurred to me that despite all the pornography I'd watched, I'd never seen a magazine either. Still haven't, in fact. "Okay. What was it then? Penthouse? Playboy?" I asked.

"Ah, nothing as upmarket as that. Urm... can't remember now... nope, nothing's coming to me. It doesn't matter. Anyway. Obviously, I asked my mate where the mag was, thinking he must've taken it home with him, but he said he left it there. I didn't believe him at first, but back in those times if your old dear found a porno mag in your room you'd be in for a clout. When you lot get caught doing something naughty, you get a back rub and a few hours' worth of free therapy. It's *nuts.* Anyway, even though I was suspicious of my mate, I still wanted to see me some porn. I'd looked all over my house for something and always came up short, except for some old lingerie catalogues. I'm still not sure if they were your grandpa's or your grandma's, come to think of it."

"*Argh,* Dad—"

"But! As you can very well imagine, they got boring fast. I was fifteen. Or fourteen. Tits were blooming about all over the place. Arses were forming shape and claiming all my attention. I needed to see the real thing, even if it was just in a shitty old magazine. I guess part of me was jealous that my mate had seen it and the only tits I'd ever seen were your grandmother's."

"*Argh, Dad!* That's gross."

"You're telling me. Gravity didn't go easy on the poor lass, let me tell you. Those things hung down to her knees, like a pair of veiny, flesh-stretched wrecking balls. Kind of like the way my own balls are going now."

"Dad! You always do this. Stop commenting on your story and just tell it, will you?!"

"Right, right. Sorry. Just trying to give you a bit of advice over the reality of things, for what it's worth. Anyway. After the bell rang for class, I thought, fuck it, did a bunk and headed straight for the woods. Even though my mate could've been lying, I still thought it was worth the gamble. I was the only other kid who lived around that area as well, so if it was still there, I figured it'd be all mine. And more importantly, all mine alone."

"And was it?" I asked.

"Oh, you can bet your blue balls it was there. The whole thing was like a dream. How's this for a description: A bed of endless autumn leaves covered the whole place, crackling and crunching under each step I took. Winter sunlight broke through the gaps between the branches in golden waves. Birds sang and fluttered, as if melodically guiding me towards my first porno wank. That's when I saw it, lying smack in the centre of a tree stump, opened at the centre-fold. Mint condition 'n all. Somebody'd had the fucking thing laminated. Which, come to think of it, was a pretty damn clever idea. You didn't have to worry about the pages sticking together then."

"Dad. Jesus Christ. Why the hell are you telling me this? I can feel a fresh psychological scar slicing across my frontal cortex."

"Frontal cortex? You mean your loaf?"

"Loaf?"

"Of bread."

"Oh. *Head.* Yeah, that's what I meant. Sort of anyway."

"Then why didn't you say that? I mean, I know you're into all that psychology lark 'n all that but it's all gobbledegook to me."

"I'm just failing to see the reason you're telling me this charming tale, Dad. That's all."

"You've got the attention span of a drunk without a drink, that's why. Have you forgotten what happened this morning already, or do you need a little reminder?"

"No, thanks. I will always remember it."

"All right then. This'll make sense in a minute, just stop interrupting me. Anyway. I don't know what took over me, but as soon as I saw all those lovely tits and huge, untrimmed bushes—that's right—hairy muffs! Sure, back in my day, women didn't have as many rights, but at least they could choose to have a big old bushy vagina if they wanted. Nowadays you can't even find a well-trimmed one. This obsession with youth has made you all crave baby pussies, which is just fucking weird if you ask me."

"Nobody did Dad—"

"Anyway. It was a good couple of hours before school finished, which also meant a few hours before our folks stopped working. So, I thought I had more than enough time."

"Enough time for what?"

"To jack off, of course. What d'you think I'm banging on about 'ere?" he said, lighting a cigarette. I truly had no idea where we were at this point. My main fear was that Dad was taking me to the very place he was talking about.

"You started masturbating in the middle of the woods, on a school day?" I asked, lightening up a bit. It was quite funny.

"Yup! The sun was just the right temperature. The air was hot yet cool. My dick was strong and confident. You'll know what I mean by that once you get to my age. And the porno was just about the best thing I'd ever seen. Everything was exactly how any kid would want their first porno wank to be. However, what I should've realised is, if it's too good to be true, it fucking ain't."

He paused, so I paused as well. He started looking around as if to remember where he was going. Meanwhile, my own anxiety had transferred into a mild sort of car sickness. "So? What happened?" I asked, mainly for the distraction.

"Just as I was... well, nearing completion, shall we say. I got the funniest feeling I wasn't entirely alone."

"Why?"

"I don't know. Maybe there's something to do with it in those psychology books of yours. I just *felt* like I was being watched or something. I stopped without even realising it, after hearing something like the scattering of leaves. That's when she spoke."

"She? What she? There was a woman watching you?"

"There was a woman watching me. I thought you'd get excited about that," said Dad, rubbing it in with a wink. In exchange, my statue-esque expression served as a cue for his swift continual. "There I was, blinded by a shift in the sun, half-dazed with my dick in my hand, when I heard *'you naughty little boy!'*"

"*Bullshit—*"

"Bull-*true*, son," Dad said, holding his hands in the air, "I have no reason to lie to you about this."

"Keep your hands on the wheel, Dad," I said, pushing one of his arms down. I thought about it. He was right, so I told him that I couldn't see why he'd lie about it either.

"Good. Now, guess who it was."

"You knew who it was?" I asked.

"Of course I did. I lived in a village. Everybody knew everybody. Not like now where nobody knows nobody."

"Well, I have a suspicion, but considering this morning's events there's a big part of me that hopes it was Grandma."

"Well, sorry to disappoint ya son but it wasn't."

"Thought not. I can only presume it was Mrs Darwin."

"You're bang on the money, son! There she was, the hot, uptight teacherly piece of arse every lad at school had jacked-off over at some point. She was staring at me, arms akimbo, doing her angry teacher pose. She didn't say anything else, just stared, with her glasses resting on the tip of her nose. That's what I remember best. The light shimmered across them so intensely that I couldn't really see her eyes. Thinking about it, that's probably what attracted me to your mother. She used to wear those type of glasses all the time."

"Dad, I don't want to know how I came about, please. Just tell me what happened next. This is the best masturbation story I've ever heard."

"Is it? You really mean that, son?"

"For sure, Dad. I mean, it's not like I've heard or read every masturbation story that's out there, but I'm sure this one would be in my top ten. So what happened next?"

"Well, nothing."

"Nothing?"

"*At that moment,* nothing. I shit myself and ran home, leaving my fucking rucksack behind 'n all."

"You shit yourself?"

"Yeah, you'd love that, wouldn't ya? Not literally, you cheeky git. I was scared. Teacher's had power to give you smack back then. And Mrs Darwin had caught me not only doing a bunk, but also with my pants down, out in public to boot."

"Go on," I said, genuinely on the verge of soiling my own pants.

"I'm glad you're getting a kick out of this. Anyway, yeah. I ran home and managed to sneak inside without my old dear noticing that I was short a rucksack, not that she'd have noticed anyway. I never knew whether she was coming or going at that time. After dinner I just moped about in my room, wondering about what was going to happen. I didn't sleep a wink. The next day I went to school and tried to keep my head down. I went to the woods beforehand but my bag and more disappointingly, the porno, were both gone. At first, I thought Mrs Darwin had thought it best for us both to just forget about what'd happened. Or more, that's what I was hoping. But then, about half-way through the class, she suddenly accused me of doing something improper and told me to stay behind after school. None of the lads could believe it, as I'd done fuck-all wrong, but obviously, I knew it had something to do with the day before."

"Dad, sorry to interrupt, but where the fuck are we? I feel like I've been here before, but I can't remember when."

"You'll see soon enough, son. Let me finish first. Things are about to get even juicier. Believe me."

"All right. So, she kept you behind. Did you start jacking off again or something?"

"Very funny. So, yeah. I knew Mrs Darwin was up to something. I had no idea what, mind you. A few of my mates said they'd wait behind for me after school but I told 'em not to bother, as everyone knew she was a strict one and usually kept kids behind for an hour, minimum. I was honestly bricking it. I'd got it into my head that she was going to use the day before as some sort of leverage against me. It was always going to be my word against hers and back in those days nobody gave a shit what the kids had to say."

"That's rough."

"Yeah, it was. I mean, most kids are full of shit, but at least you lot get listened to nowadays. The problem comes from it all being too one-sided. Treating kids like angels only leads them to act like cunts, just like with adults. It's as if all that human psychology you bang on about has been tossed aside for the unquestionable word of a fucking teenager. Talk about bonkers. Anyway, there I was, alone in the classroom with Mrs Darwin. Guess what happened next."

"Urm... did she get her tits out?"

Dad laughed. "No, no, no. Nothing like that at all. She stayed silent for at least an hour, just watching me. Once it got to about four thirty or something, she gathered her things and from under her desk, she picked up and threw me my rucksack."

"Oh. So she took it with her?"

"Yep. Then she said, 'Time's up. Gather your things and follow me. I'll give you a lift home.'"

Dad stopped speaking here, then looked at me. "Don't you wanna say something to that?" he asked.

"Not really, no. I want to hear what happened."

"You sure?"

"Yep."

"You sure you're sure?"

"Yes, Dad. I'm sure. Carry on."

"Okay. So, I went outside with her and we got into the car. It was the only one left in the parking lot. Then I started thinking that she planned the whole thing to be that way, but I still didn't know what the hell for. I was fucking shaking as I got in the car, but once again, she stayed silent and just drove. I thought she somehow knew where I lived along the way, until she pulled down some side road and hooked around the same forest we caught each other in the day previous. I honestly had no idea where she was taking me though. She parked around the back in some secluded spot. After she cut the exhaust, she looked at me and said, 'Open your bag, young man' and started tying her hair up. So, I unzipped it and there it was..."

"What was there?" I asked, but I could see his attention was already drawn elsewhere. Through years of experience, I could always sense the exact moment he ceased bothering to listen to me.

As I turned to see what he was looking at, he said "Oh, Christ, I'm starving. Let's continue this by making a little pit-stop in here, shall we?"

"Argh, what? No, carry on with the story, Dad. What are you doing? Don't pull in here!"

"You used to love this place when you were a kid. Come on, even naughty little boys like you have gotta eat!" he said, chuckling away at his own joke, before and after he exited the car. By the time I got out he was already walking inside. He wasn't being rude, as I always ordered the same thing anyway. It was just so typical of Dad to get to the meat of a story and then stop due to a sudden pang of hunger.

After entering the place, I ignored him and started looking for a booth, but instead of allowing me that small piece of freedom, he started waving at me to come over.

"What now?" I asked on approach.

"Hey, don't get lippy with me boy. You forget who's paying for this meal you're about to have."

"I didn't ask for a meal. I asked where we're going."

His neck stayed turned towards the fryer. "Never

mind that now, son," he said. "Tell me what you think of this one."

"Huh?" I said, but then I saw who he meant.

A teenage goth girl brought our order over. Instead of trousers she wore jeans. She had the right shirt on underneath her apron, but the buttons were all loose. Her black hair had light-pink streaks at the front and her bottom lip was pierced on the side. I think she wore a touch of black lipstick too. Pretty. Sexy. Angsty. And way out of my league. As she turned back from handing over the tray, Dad asked for ketchup. After she nodded and turned again, he actually hooked his thumb towards her behind and scrunch-pouted his lips into his 'take a gander at that' expression. "That's the kind of arse you should be seeking out son," he whispered, "not a bunch of internet hussies' already way-passed their sell-by-date. Mmm," he said, shamelessly eyeing her up. "Corrrrr. Juicy. I'm hungry. Let's eat."

I took the tray away before the ketchup arrived. Despite Dad's crudeness, he was right. The girl had one of those taught, upright arses, perfectly proportioned inside those ripped-up black jeans. I found a booth and sat down whilst Dad flirted for free ketchup and the reputation of a pervert.

Normally I would've waited until he returned before I started to eat, but he began yakking on his phone instead, waving over at me to tuck-in if I wanted to. I was halfway through my burger by the time he reached our booth, and was still on the phone.

"Right yeah, I know. You said I'd be back before I knew it. I know, I remember. I'm not coming for me though, so don't get your hopes up. Well, maybe my arm could be twisted. Alright. See you soon. Bye."

"Who was that?" I asked.

"Ah, nobody. Just some clown from work. Right, where was I? Urm—"

"You were in your teacher's car, near the woods from the day before," I said, stuffing some fries into my mouth, "she just told you to open your rucksack."

"Right! Yeah. Good to know you were paying attention," said Dad. "Just a second." He flipped off the plastic lid of his coke, looked over his shoulder as he whipped out a small bottle of rum from the inside pocket of his jacket, uncapped it and poured the whole lot in. He didn't notice that the sexy goth was staring at us the entire time. When she saw the booze she just smirked, then shrugged and started looking at her phone. She kept scratching one of her breasts as she scrolled. I imagined somehow finding her online when I got home and filling the screen she was staring at, possibly with my cock.

"You should ask her out," Dad said. He must've noticed me gawping at her. "Those goth types are usually just as dark in the sack. She could sure teach you a few things."

"You think so?"

"I know so. Be a doer son. Nobody likes a spectator."

"She wouldn't go for somebody like me."

"You don't know that. Anyway, if she says no, who gives a shit? Nobody's going to find out."

"You will."

"And? I'm your old man. Come on, get on your haunches and ask her out."

"Finish the story first," I said.

"Oh, so now you're suddenly interested?"

"I was interested, Dad," I said. "It's called listening."

"Fair enough. But you're not leaving here till you've asked her out," he said in his 'serious' voice.

"Fine. But I don't understand why you care so much."

"I care because that's exactly the type of girl you should be taking out. You can't sit in your room all day with your dick in your hand. I know you like to do all that arty shit as well, and that's great, but you must realise that the only reason any bloke ever picked up a paintbrush or plucked a guitar, was so he could get himself inside some lady's panties. Or many ladies' panties for that matter."

The goth girl laughed. Dad looked over. I wanted to as well, but I just couldn't. "She keeps looking at you," he said, "I reckon you're a shoo-in there."

"Just open the rucksack already, Dad," I said, trying hard to stop myself from blushing, if that's even possible. "What was inside?"

"This isn't over," he said, returning his gaze to me. "Anyway, yeah. I unzipped the bag. For a long while, I couldn't believe what was inside. You want to take a little guess what was in there first?"

"No idea... a dildo?"

"A *dildo?* Fucking hell you have been watching too much of that online shit. How long have you known about dildos? Actually, don't answer that. No, it wasn't a dildo. Or any sex toy for that matter. Now guess again."

"Dad, I have no idea."

"Only the very same porno."

"Really?"

"Yep. I didn't know what to do when I saw it. Seemed weird to take it out and have a look. So, I thanked her, expecting to be taken home. But then she took it out for me."

"Right. This is getting weirder by the minute. What did she do with it?" I asked.

"Well, after taking it out she skimmed through it for a little while, half-looking at the pics and whatnot. Then she suddenly said, 'There have been some rumours going around about me recently, hasn't there?' I just sort of nodded. 'Would you believe my husband had this laminated?' she then said. 'Really?' I asked, 'why?' 'Because he's trying to get me sacked from the school, that's why,' she said. I didn't understand what the hell she was talking about. Before I knew it, she was crying. Or more, sobbing uncontrollably. You'll learn all about that as well in the next couple of years, for sure. Anyway, I didn't know what to do really, so I hugged her. She held onto me tightly, almost desperately. We parted, and she seemed to settle down again. After a minute or so, she passed me the magazine and told me to turn to page fifteen. At first, I didn't see it. I felt too embarrassed to look at the magazine properly, especially with the teacher there and all. But she quickly got wise to that and asked me what I thought, so I had to give it a proper look. Page fifteen had this brunette woman, naked except for some tiny overalls, all oiled-up and dirty, posing inside some garage. In the main picture, she was holding a dripping petrol pump and pointing it at herself. Streaks of oil were all over her tits and falling from her chin. It took me a while to see it, as she didn't have her glasses on."

"What the fuck!? It was your teacher?"

"Yep. It was her. I didn't know where to look, let alone what to think. She saw my embarrassment.

I think she enjoyed it 'n all. Her whole personality seemed to change. She kept telling me that it was okay for me to look at it, that it was perfectly natural and all that. She knew what she was doing. After my initial shock, all I could hear, or thought I could hear, was the greased-up woman in the photographs, telling me how normal it was for me to find her arousing. So, naturally, I became aroused before I even had time to realise it. But that didn't stop Mrs Darwin noticing. She pushed the magazine closer to my face with one hand, and planted the other... you know where," said Dad, smirking like the teenager he once was.

"Wait a minute. I just need to get a few things straight here. Your teacher started giving you a hand job whilst you were looking at the very porno magazine she was featured in?"

"Well, it started off as a hand job. Pretty soon she had it in her mouth, but she insisted that I kept looking at the magazine until, well, the end, let's say. It was weird. It was confusing. It was fucking mind-blowing."

"I don't believe you."

"I don't care if you believe me or not. It happened. Don't be jealous, son. You'll have your day yet. I promise."

"Jealous? Some paedophile teacher—"

"Paedophile? God, you lot really are snowflakes these days. That woman weren't no paedophile, son. She was a saint sent down from heaven to bust my cherry—"

"You had sex with her?"

"Sex? Son, that woman taught me everything— *and I mean everything*—I needed to know regarding women. I mean, yeah sure, she was a pervert. But she was my own personal pervert. For a while at least, anyway."

"Right," I said, scoffing involuntarily. My jealousy disguised itself as disbelief. It was hard not to be a little envious. I mean, what teenage lad wouldn't be? I knew the story couldn't have ended well, so I wanted to hear how hard reality came gate-crashing into this indecent arrangement. "So, what happened after that?" I asked.

"Well, after she gave me a blowy, she shoved me into the backseat and sat on my face—"

"No, Dad. I mean, what happened during this affair? I don't need all the sordid, graphic details thanks."

"You sure? She did some pretty messed up shit with me. I thought you'd be interested in that."

"If I didn't come from the very same penis you're describing, I might agree. But I did, so I don't really want to hear it."

"What's wrong with you lot these days? You think your parents never got off themselves or something? Seriously, you've all got a very warped perception of sex."

"Oh, do we now? That sounds a bit rich, Dad."

"Maybe."

"So? Go on. I'm still interested here."

"Are you? Okay, then. Well, after she ravaged me in the back seat of her car, she drove me home. Any time she wanted more she'd just keep me behind after school like before. Sometimes we just did it in the classroom. Everything was hunky-dory for the first month or so. Maybe two. The best part was being in the sex education class. She'd talk about all these things we'd already done with each other, occasionally looking at me in that 'remember when we did that' way, if you know what I'm saying."

"Just tell me about when it all went wrong."

"Well, it was hardly going to end well now, was it? Let me see. She told me her husband had done a runner, so sometimes we did it at her place. Everything was sweet as you like during that time. I couldn't believe my luck. The only annoying thing was not being able to tell anyone about it. I'd have been a legend at school if I could've done, but I knew I had to keep my mouth shut. It would've ruined everything. Of course, time did that anyway, just like it always does."

"Go on."

"Right yeah, well," he said, finishing off his large rum and coke. Neither of us had any food remaining. "As you've already guessed, it wasn't going to end well. After a month or two we agreed to stop doing anything until the weekends, as it was too risky doing stuff out in public, let alone inside the school. So, the weekend that followed this arrangement, I made my way over to her house. Things just weren't the same. Without the whole teacher/student vibe we'd lost our magic. After an hour or so of awkward sex, she started looking through her husband's wardrobe, searching for a white shirt and a black pair of trousers."

"Why?"

"She wanted me to dress up like a schoolboy again, that's why. She found what she wanted, laid it over the bed and popped off herself to get into her own teacher gear. That's when it hit me, I guess. She was just using me because she had a thing for schoolboys. It was just dumb luck that I'd found the magazine. I'm sure if anyone else found it, they'd have been in the same position. That's the problem with kinks son. They're usually very one-sided. When she came back from changing, I pretended that I felt sick and wanted to go home. I could tell she was pissed, but she seemed to understand at the same time. To support my claim, I took the next week off school, just to avoid her. I don't know why it bothered me so much really. I guess I just didn't like feeling like somebody else's tool."

"Okay. Something must've happened when you went back though, surely?"

"Oh, it did. I can assure you of that," he said, standing up. "But first things first. I need another shit—"

"Again?! How could you possibly need another dump?"

"I think I've been boozing too much recently, that's why, son. Turned my guts to sludge. I won't be long though. In the meantime, you can ask out the goth."

"Dad, I dunno. She's only going to say no."

"You don't know that until you try, son. Think about it, a good-looking girl like that must have a pretty damn fine mother 'n all. If you like 'em older, just take the daughter as your in."

I looked over at the girl, trying to picture the mother. I must admit, Dad had a point. I knew I was too young to get any older women, but if I did date a girl my own age for a while, there was a slim chance, admittedly a very slim chance that I could land a Mrs Darwin of my own.

I turned back towards Dad, but all I saw was the swinging toilet door a few booths beyond. Instead of sitting there like a chump, I plucked up my courage, stood up with the tray and walked swiftly over to the bin. After dumping it inside, I turned towards the girl, who smiled pleasantly at my consideration. Then I went up to the counter.

"Hey," I said, stuffing my hands into my pockets so I wouldn't be able to fiddle with them.

"Hey, can I get you anything else?" she asked.

"No, I'm pretty full thanks. The food was really good."

"Okay," she said. "I'm glad. The food here is shit though."

I laughed and nodded. "Yeah, it is quite."

"But you just said it was really good."

"Oh, yeah. I know. I was being polite. In honesty, I thought it was total fucking garbage. My Dad likes it though. I feel sorry for his taste buds."

"Right," she said. It wasn't going well. "So that's your Dad, is it?"

I nodded.

"He looks familiar. Have you been here with him before?"

"No, first time."

"Must be someone else then. So, where are you headed?"

"Honestly? I have no idea. He won't tell me."

"Really? Why? Have you been a naughty boy or something?"

I let out a single, puffed laugh. Strange she would choose to use such a specific set of words. I heard the toilet flush behind the wall. The girl was still standing there, unmoving, waiting for my reply.

"Maybe. I don't know. He doesn't usually even pay attention to me, so this is all pretty weird. Hey, can

I ask you something?"

"Urm. Yeah, sure."

"D'you want to go to a movie with me sometime?"

Her eyebrows creased. A slight, pitiful smile arose. "How old are you?" she asked.

"Seventeen," I lied.

"Sure you are," she replied, not buying it for a second. "You look about fifteen to me."

"Would that bother you?"

"Well, yeah. Course it would. I'm not a paedophile. Maybe you should stick to girls your own age for now."

"Yeah, maybe. They don't seem to like me much either though."

"Aww. You're sweet.

I felt a hand on my shoulder. "You bet your life he's sweet," said Dad. "Right, we done 'ere or what?"

"Yeah, I guess so. Let's go," I said, unable to look at the girl again.

"Cheers," Dad said behind me as I headed towards the door. I knew that girl wouldn't agree to go out with me, but I let my Dad convince me otherwise. I still don't know why I fell for his bullshit.

"Dad, can we just go home now?" I asked as we got into the car.

"Not yet, son. We just have one more stop to make."

He started the car without another word and pretty soon we were back on the endless motorway, going to who-knows-where. After a while, I asked, "Don't you want to know what she said, Dad?"

"Not really. She must've said no. That much is obvious. That girl's too old for the likes of you anyway, son."

"Why did you make me ask her out then?"

"Why not, that's why. So, she said no. Big whoop. The world didn't end, did it? You can't see it now, but I'm doing you a favour here. Trust me. The whole dating game is just a law of averages. Get your knock-backs in early and it's only a matter of time before one of these broads says yes. That's just the way things go."

"But I knew she'd say no all along. What good is confirming what I already know?"

"Because you don't fucking know, that's why. Yeah sure, you'll probably be correct ninety-odd percent of the time, but until you put your thoughts into action, you'll never really know who might be interested in you. Don't be a pussy, son."

"Whatever, Dad."

"Do you really feel that bad about getting knocked back?"

"No. It doesn't feel as bad as I thought it would."

"There you go then. This shit builds character. Or so I've been told. I know I go a bit hard on you sometimes, son. But I do it all for the right reasons. I hate the fact that you see yourself as some kind of wimp. You should be going for girls your own age, or even younger, just like the goth said."

"Christ. How long were you standing there for?"

"Not long. If you were her age and she was yours, she would've said yes for sure. Guaranteed. Believe me, there's nothing wrong with what you're into. It just concerns me that you're a bit young for those dominatrix types. Most men usually only get into them after they've had a few women chew 'em up. You're still young and fresh. The world doesn't look like the rubble of shit it really is yet. It breaks my heart to see you already so keen to get pussy-whipped."

"Alright, Dad. Thanks for the splendid advice. So, what happened with you and your teacher, after she broke your little pussy heart?"

Dad chuckled. He always liked it when I gave back as good as he'd given. The whole thing with the goth girl already felt far behind me somehow. My anger had faded.

"Right, well. Let's see. The night before I was due back at school, I thought to myself that I'd simply lay low and hope Mrs Darwin was going to do the same. I figured we'd had our bit of fun and all that and thought it best if we just left it where it was."

"And was it?"

"I wish. Now, the next part of the tale doesn't exactly reflect well on me, son. I just want you to know that. I was young and stupid. I was gullible and naïve—"

"What did you do?"

"Well, I went to school with my mind set. Everything seemed to be fine, but of course, Mrs Darwin's class was coming up. I was nervous as hell walking in, but all seemed well in there too. However, what I quickly realised was that Mrs Darwin was giving me the complete cold shoulder. She wouldn't even look at me. Then, whilst she was handing out papers or something, one of the girls in my class hissed at me for a word. After asking if I felt better and all that crap, she started telling me that Mrs Darwin had started picking on Johnny boy instead of me whilst I was away. Apparently, she'd started busting his balls instead of mine, keeping him behind after school for reasons nobody else could grasp, except for me, of course. Now, I don't know why I felt the way I did back then, but it's just the way it was. I was pissed off. I was jealous. Not only did that bitch use me for her own perverted games, but she'd had me replaced quicker than we came to be. I was furious."

"But you said you didn't want her after that weekend?"

"Yeah, I know. I was a teenager. Nothing they do makes any sense. She was the first woman to play with me, and she was already playing with somebody else after a week, a week in which, according to her and everyone else, I was sick. I couldn't believe it. After the class ended and Johnny was kept behind as expected, I headed back to the woods like before. I had the magazine in my rucksack still. I'd planned on giving it back to Mrs Darwin as a gesture of no hard feelings, you know. But after finding out that I meant fucking nothing to her, I wanted me some fucking revenge."

"So, what did you do?"

"I went back to the woods, lay the magazine on the stump like before and jacked-off all over the younger, hotter version of Mrs Darwin. Then I had a cigarette—"

"You smoked at this age too?"

"Yeah. Everybody did. Nobody cared back then. I was smoking it for a different reason though. When the cherry reached the filter, I stubbed it out over the picture in the mag, all over her boat race, burning the bitch good. Once that was done, I left the cigarette inside, slammed the magazine shut and headed back to Mrs Darwin's to give her a surprise through her letterbox. I know how it sounds now.

Pretty sordid, right?"

"I can understand it. You were angry."

"Thank you, son. Yes, I was. Anyway, after biking it over there, it was already starting to get dark. I walked across the porch and went to deliver the magazine, but I saw that her garden gnome was lying down."

"Garden gnome? She liked those?"

"I dunno whether she liked 'em or not. They weren't your typical ugly Snow White dwarves though. Hers were more like those religious paintings. You know, the ones with angelic-looking kids but in statue form."

"Male or female?"

"Oh, all hers were male."

"A faunlet then."

"Right. Well, whatever they were, I didn't like 'em. Anyway, Darwin told me that if I ever popped over unannounced and the gnome faunlet thing was lying down, it meant that she had someone in the gaff. Most likely romping now I fucking know better. If it was standing up, however—"

"It meant that she was open for a romp."

"Exactly. I thought she only told me that as a hint to get me to do it whenever I came 'round. Which I did, but I used to just kick the fucking thing over. So, when I saw the creepy midget thing at the door, I figured that One: She was in there with Johnny boy, riding away on some more young meat and Two: By posting the mag I was actually giving her a chance to see it first and get shot of it before anything bad happened. It seemed about fifty-fifty of that happening and I didn't like those odds."

Dad turned down some side road here, which

looked like it'd been abandoned long ago. All I could see in the distance was a large, low-ceilinged building. Rectangular, with only a single door on the left-hand side. We drove steadily towards it.

"So, I thought I'd hide and wait for Johnny to come out. I was going to tell him what Mrs Darwin had done with me and how she was doing the same with him. I didn't know if he'd buy it or not, but at that point I had the magazine to prove it, in some sense at least. He was the one who mentioned it in the first place, but I didn't have a clue if he knew Darwin was in it. He never mentioned nothing, so I reckoned he knew nothing. So, I dumped it on the first step of the porch and hid behind the nearest bush I could find, after chaining my bike to a post across the other side of the road. I think I was there for at least an hour. The only light on in the house was the one I was already familiar with, round at the back, but you could only see the outline of the closed curtains in front of the window. I kept wondering if Mrs Darwin was doing all the shit she did with me with Johnny, you know, buttering him up with some porno mag and shit. After an hour, I was pretty fucking cold. Just as I was about to give up, a car came charging down the road, swaying from left to right, screeching and struggling and all sorts. I thought whoever was driving was gonna crash straight into my bike, but luckily, it stopped right outside Mrs Darwin's house. After a minute or maybe two, the car door swung open, quickly followed by a pasty leg, with a black shoe and a pulled-up black sock. As the bloke got out, I soon realised that he was dressed up as a schoolboy. It was only fucking Mr Darwin himself!"

I wanted to listen fully and enjoy the story as much as Dad was telling it, but we'd parked just outside the singular red door of the desolate looking building we had just been heading towards. Dad ignored any misgivings I may have betrayed about the place and simply shut off the engine before continuing with his story.

"He got up out the car, fell over dead drunk, then got back up again. He had the shoes, the socks, the fucking shorts, a white shirt with the typical school-tie and even had an apple in his hand."

"An apple?"

"Yeah, like a teacher's pet! I couldn't believe what I was seeing. I wanted to die with laughter, but I was way too near him to make a sound. Now, at this point, I really feared for Johnny. I thought the forty-odd-year-old schoolboy could probably take him, even if he was drunker than sense. You should've seen him stumbling about the place! He walked straight over the porno mag lying on the path without even noticing it, managed to get himself up the steps, took out his keys, but stopped himself just before sticking one in the door and stared down at the gnome under his foot. I assumed he was privy to the code 'n all after he booted it."

"Oh shit," I said.

"Exactly! That's what I thought. But wait. He turned around, nearly fell down the steps, then started walking towards the window, the same window with the only light on in the house. Something in his manner even seemed to sober up. He crept up to it and peaked his head between the tiny gap. Then he unbuckled his belt!"

"He unbuckled his belt?!"

"Yep. Before I knew it, he was standing there with his pants around his ankles, tugging away under the moonlight. I couldn't believe what I was seeing. I was laughing my bollocks off—*as quietly as I could*—until it struck me. Mrs Darwin was always pissing about with the curtains in that room, especially when we were about to get physical. Then an avalanche of memories came crashing down on my mind, of all the times I'd been in there, how many times Mrs Darwin made me stand in the exact same spot, how she even positioned me when we were going at it."

"No fucking way!"

"Yes, but still, yeah, *no fucking way!* Her husband had been jacking off the entire time I was there. It was their own little indecent arrangement. Everything made sense. Mr and Mrs Darwin were just kinky perverts. She didn't give a fuck about teaching, except to fuck the ones she was supposed to be educating. She was the one who had had the magazine laminated! It was all her idea in the first place! She'd planted it there, knowing one of the lads would find it! I reckon her husband, or her, must've seen Johnny boy stumble across it, but something spooked him, probably her husband's crusty cock, so he left it there in the woods. Mrs Darwin even had the cunning to know that he wouldn't keep his mouth shut about it, so she did a bunk and I was the chump who went back there to find it! I went into some weird space. Everything turned black. I thought I was going to throw up, or faint, or even die! Until I heard the most high-pitched scream I've ever heard. I shifted my neck to see Mr Darwin, running towards the front door whilst trying to pull his pants up. All the lights in the house snapped on. The front door swung open, crashing against the wall. Out came Johnny, so stressed out that he was screaming like a bitch, whilst desperately trying to get his clogs back on. Darwin saw him and tried to rugby tackle him to the ground, but because he hadn't done up his trousers, he tripped himself up and landed face first on the magazine, smashing his nose up rotten. Blood spurted out everywhere! Johnny boy hurdled over him and started bolting it. Then Mrs Darwin joined in on the scene, with nothing less but a fucking whip in her hand! I thought she was going to chase after Johnny, but the sight of the gnome stopped her in her tracks. I hadn't noticed it, but when her hubby gave it a good kicking, he only knocked his little pecker off. She scooped it up and tossed it at her husband's loaf, then started cracking the whip across his arse, screaming about what a pathetic little wimp he was. I nearly screamed myself. She was terrifying! Whilst she was giving her hubby what for, I scarpered out of the bush, ran across the road, unlocked my bike chain and got the fuck out of there just as all the nosy neighbours began to come out of their houses for a gander."

"Wow. So, what happened after that?"

"Well, nothing really. The next day Mrs Darwin didn't turn up. I went up to Johnny to try and speak to him about it, but he seemed a bit fucked up over the whole ordeal, you know? I could tell that he'd rather not talk about it. The next day Darwin didn't turn up again. The day after that the headmaster announced that she'd decided to move on to a different school. Nobody heard anything about her ever again."

"Amazing," I said. "That's quite a story, Dad."

"You're telling me. I still can't believe some of it when I look back. Catching you with your pants down this morning brought it all back to me. Life's a funny old game. Anyway, we're here now. If your Mother ever asks, don't tell her I told you that story. And don't ever mention this place either. Let's go," he said, opening the car door.

"Where the hell are we?" I asked after vacating it too. To the right of the building there was a forest that birds were flocking to. Decaying leaves were scattered everywhere, scrunching under Dad's footsteps. "Dad?" I asked.

"You see, son. Even though Mrs Darwin was clearly shit-bat crazy, she sure knew how to please a man. It was only when I discovered one of these places that I truly appreciated the beauty of that skill. You might not agree with me right away, but after a few years, I'm sure you will. Happy belated birthday, son."

The red door in front of us suddenly buzzed and opened, swinging like it knew we were coming. Beyond the frame there was nothing but darkness, with the occasional puff of smoke sweeping across. Dad just walked in like he owned the place, leaving me standing there. He turned at the frame and told me to come in when I was ready, then he disappeared into the black.

Everything fell silent, except for the occasional muffled voice beyond the walls. The small forest behind the building appeared to me as very sinister, for some reason. In all honesty, I got a bit scared. Pretty soon, I headed straight for the door, not wanting to be alone. Once inside, the door shut behind me. Everything was so dark I could barely make anything out. All I could see was the outline of a rug, a few beaten-up old sofas and a reception desk, which I thought was empty, until a head popped up from below. It was a woman, smartly dressed, about ten or so years older than my Dad, just like my Mum. She smiled at me and told me to walk down to the end of the hallway and stop at the door with the buzzing lightbulb above it. Number fifteen. Then she slipped through some curtain and was gone. I walked down the corridor, calling out for Dad, as I guessed he was playing a prank on me or something. But nothing I did or said provoked any response. When I reached the door, I went to knock, but something stopped me. Then the light above it turned off, and the door swung open. I walked in, calling Dad's name again. It was a hotel room. At least, that's what I thought at first. Everything was coloured red. The air was dank and hot. It was like nothing I'd ever seen before. Then a toilet flushed and out-stepped this woman from the only other door in the room, who was at least double my age, if not triple. "You're the only Daddy I see around here," she said, walking up to me. "I hear you've been a naughty little boy," she continued, and pushed me onto the bed. "Well, it's time teacher taught you a good, hard lesson."

She climbed on top of me and started touching me all over. I felt paralysed but unable to stop myself becoming aroused, almost against my own will. She said all the right things, like she'd had access to my internet searches before we arrived. Part of me was horrified, but the other half was even more terrified by how desperately turned on I eventually got. As soon as that happened, she took me for a ride and taught me a lesson.

A lesson I'll never be able to unlearn.

When it was all over, I didn't really know what to think. The woman who'd made quite a teacher of herself turned out to be a pretty terrible human being. At least, that's what I felt when she told me that my time was up and to get my fucking scrawny arse out of there. It made me wonder whether all the woman I'd watched on the internet were the same as soon as the camera was cut. The thought hadn't crossed my mind before that. Since the drive home and even up until this day, Dad hasn't said anything about it. Not one word. I'm unsure whether to be appreciative of that. His overall mood is better though. I think he believes he done me a great service or something and prepared me for the world outside.

I'm more or less happy for him to believe that.

We still haven't heard anything from Mum.

What really shocked me was when I went back to school. I still find it hard to believe, even now. After we got home from the brothel, I wrote this piece. I planned on handing it in as my homework assignment. I'm not sure why. If Miss English asked, I would've assured her it was a work of fiction; not some cry for help. I went to class earlier that day as well, hoping to speak to her before the lesson but really just looking forward to spending some time close to her. But she never turned up. And she won't. Ever again. Some mishap (according to the rumours anyway) with the school she transferred to needed her to begin right away. A private all-girls boarding school, no less. When it was announced in class I burst into tears. Why, I don't know. I guess I just felt... alone. Maybe Mum's absence finally hit home. Perhaps the irony of Dad's story creeping into my reality did it. I just don't know. All I do know is that I wish I didn't cry. I must be the only kid in history to be one of the first boys in school to get laid, only to then become its biggest laughing stock. It doesn't really rattle me too much though. Unless I stop to think about it.

The good news is I've stopped watching porn altogether. Now I think about Miss English every night as a stroke myself to sleep. Sometimes I get lucky and she travels with me into my dreams. We never have sex though. She simply reads my homework. This piece in particular. We speak about love and whether it can be unconditional, discuss our thoughts on life and my hopes for the future. All the while she laughs at my story, occasionally blushing and looking pleased. Her outfits change but they're always the same style. Tight-fitted blouses with medium-length skirts. She sits on her desk with her legs wide open, heels resting and toying on the edge of mine. I know her vagina is there, but due to the lighting it's always pitch black. Mysterious and unknowable. I want to touch her, run my fingers through her hair, thrust myself into her and listen to her moan for eternity... but I never do. I'm just happy that she lets me masturbate in front of her without her ever acknowledging it.

THE
PERFECT CLIENT

With a sallow hand poised for knocking, a man stood in front of a shaded door. Seconds ticked by, but no knock was made. The light above him flickered but failed to take hold, as if mirroring his own doubt, causing him to drop his arm and pivot. He looked around the hallway like he expected someone else to be there, but the surrounding yet distant identical doors suggested no change. Whether he could see much at all remained as sombre and concealed as the shaded clothes that covered him. He pulled the sleeve of his shoulder-stretched trench-coat up and checked the time. As he peered over the watch, the lightbulb above his head finally blinked into life. A red rose tint soon outlined his frame, but the rest of the narrow corridor stayed in the shadows. The only sounds that could be heard were the distant drones coming from a handful of floors below and the rain which rattled above his head; near yet somehow distant. The other rooms about his person betrayed nothing. He straightened himself up central to the door again with his feet slightly apart, took a quick, uncertain breath and then re-raised his hand. More ticking ensued, louder this time as the face of the watch lay adjacent to his ear. Instead of knocking, he pulled the sleeve back over the time-telling device and turned around once more, murmuring to himself. The dust-covered trilby on his head was pulled down hard, silhouetting the face due to his slouched posture. All that could be seen of him was the protruding pot-belly around the midriff. Unbeknownst to the man, a cockroach had appeared under the gap of the door he was having so much trouble making contact with. The man scrunched and then squeezed his face with his palms—when the cockroach darted under his crotch. Seeing, or perhaps hearing the insect caused him to shudder and thrust backwards, thumping the top of his head against the burgundy-shaded door behind him, but the hat remained as if untouched. Not realising he'd finally managed to make the sound of his arrival, he chased after the roach, stamping his foot down along the zigzag trail of scatter-brained movements. He missed. Then missed again. And again. Refusing to be outwitted by a non-sentient bug, he scurried after it whilst stamping, spinning around on the spot from left to right, but the insect somehow managed to evade all attempts of its murder. As the last failed stomp landed, it disappeared under the fire escape a few doors down. The man, overspent from this ridiculous ordeal, bent over exhausted and tried to catch his breath.

"Hello?" said a young woman's voice from beyond the door. "Was that meant for me?"

Whether the man registered it or not wasn't clear. He creased his brow as if he had heard something, but it could've just been from the strained breaths which continued to struggle forth from his mouth. Returning upright and after a moment, the man hushed himself down. During his confrontation with the insect, he hadn't noticed the strengthened illuminance of the bulb above his head, which, in an ironic sense, had risen in accordance with his impotent rage. His attention, however, was drawn to the walls on both sides of the door. From the top to the middle there were streaks of scarlet that had been painted by large brushes, only for the lower half of the wall to be left unchanged and seemingly abandoned. Through consequence what remained in the centre were bumpy rivulets of vermillion, forever falling yet frozen in time. The man stood, stunned by the sight until a sudden crackle of frequency forced the bulb back into a weakened state and once again made the man's presence nothing more than a walking shadow. Though no distinguishable features were betrayed by the lacklustre light of this desolate place, the glimmer of duress behind the man's eyes could not be denied. It appeared that he was carrying the shame of a decision before he'd even put it into action. This was only suggested further by his startled jump as the faucet fuelling the shower somewhere behind the door he was so desperately in want of knocking upon came to a screeching stop. What seemed to keep him standing there, exchanging stares between the door and his watch, was the haunting yet calming, familiar yet distant hum of the female in the room, which had replaced the running water he previously mistook for the rain outside.

Inside the room, a girl still shy of eighteen was wrapping a towel around her head. She glanced at the clock above the door (behind which glowed the bulb interrogating the man) as she always did on countless occasions during one of her shifts, and tsk-and-tucked her disappointment of its passing more quickly than she had imagined. Shuffling the towel around her head faster than usual, she soon threw it to the floor and began to straighten her hair, ignoring the singeing sounds its dampness provoked. Once satisfied, she began to put on her clothes, or more, the undergarments she wore beneath her normal clothes before and after a shift: black stockings with matching suspenders, along with a satin-made piece of lingerie, also black, except for the large embroidered X around the crotch, stitched with a thread of blood-red. She picked up a corset lying limply over the bed, shrugged, tossed it across the room and then hooked on the bra that was underneath it instead. My tits look better in this anyway, she thought with a passing shrug. After changing she slipped on a black silk dressing gown and walked over to the mirror. Just one more month. One more month and I can get the fuck out of here for good. She re-checked the time. The penultimate client was already ten minutes late. Considering it rude to keep her waiting and exercising the tiny snippets of power she had in this place of ill-repute, she slowed down in her preparation for the man. The late ones are normally the easiest to please anyway. Some of them don't even seem to enjoy it. It's like they come here on a bet or just for the thrill. Half of these men can't even look at me. She was standing in front of a body-sized mirror that was slowly revealing her appearance due to the steam that'd fogged over it. All she could see were the blotches across her chest. Seven scorching showers in one night seems like overkill to me. Better the quiet ones than the talkers though. All they do is drone on and on about their unhappy marriages, how disappointing their children are to them, or how they yearn to do something different with their lives if only they got the chance. Then they take their cocks out. She laughed, remembering one of her first clients, who'd shown her a picture of his missing dog instead of his new-born son. Though she preferred the quieter types, it didn't mean she liked the silent ones. Those men freaked her out, as they gazed upon her like prey to a predator, making all their actions, or lack of them, put her on an edge she couldn't quite understand.

The girl swiped the mirror and her face appeared inside the streaks. Avoiding eye contact with herself, she applied a touch of lipstick to her already reddened lips and some extra eye-shadow in the hope of maintaining anonymity outside the walls. Once satisfied, she flicked a look at the clock again and moved towards the bed. After throwing herself on it, she positioned herself into her 'come-over-here-big-boy' pose she'd had the most, and quickest success with. With her already ample cleavage further exposed, the chance of premature ejaculation was always enhanced. Seeing that the man was now nearly twenty minutes late, she reached out to the bedside table and took a smoke out of its pack. The lighting of a cigarette would sometimes threaten her hopes to get rid of the client as quickly as possible, but most of the time the image of her lying sprawled across the bed outweighed any of their health concerns. It is a brothel after all, she thought, perplexed by some of the concerns raised by previous punters, especially the ones who'd agreed to pay more just so they wouldn't be obliged to wear any protection.

The man now stood with his ear against the door, listening to the creaks of the bed springs and the scratching of a stubborn flint. The halt of falling rain had made her movements easier to hear and, by appearances he looked to be more at ease with his surroundings. Still, no attempt to make his presence known was made. It seemed like he was content to simply listen to the girl and imagine her beauty and physique within the walls of his mind. Then an unexpected, sensually-fuelled sigh of smoke left the lungs of the girl, which caused his knee to jerk and strike the door. Once more, instead of making his presence known by his own design, he'd made it by mistake.

The girl went to say something upon hearing it but stopped herself when she realised that it was the real her who wanted to speak. After tossing her hair back and cupping her breasts up for better exposure, she composed herself to speak in her 'sex' voice. "Hello?" she purred, throatily emphasising the final vowel into a salacious slur and even dug her fingernails into the bed like a cat does with its paws. A moment passed. Silence encased the scene until the light threat of more rain brushed over the only window in the room. She shrugged, recalling it was only his own money that he was losing. Whoever her next client was, he was now running close to thirty minutes late. In roughly twenty minutes she'd only have another hour to endure. She flicked the ash of her cigarette into the already over-filled ashtray and took another drag. As it dispersed from her lungs she watched the smoke drift away from the cherry with a distant, albeit palpable wonder.

Smoke had been wafting from side to side due to the shaking hand of her mother. She was sitting in the kitchen, carefully peeling the label away from an empty bottle of wine. The prolific amount of stubbed out cigarettes told a colossal amount of truths, but the slamming of the front door told the one that hit the girl the hardest. The piled-up letters mostly marked with red held the secret of her mother's next move. At the time, the girl had believed that money was the sole cause of their problems. Never in the manner of which it was to be later obtained.

The girl leapt off the bed, put out her cigarette and grabbed the half-emptied bottle of champagne brought in by her previous client. He'd celebrated the birth of his firstborn by receiving oral sex inside a bubbling mouth full of sparkling wine. She spat the first gulp out in dismissal of the memory, then began to chug away on the bottle as if to overwhelm and drown the lingering threat of an embedded association.

As the mouthful of wine splattered across the

carpet beyond the door, the man, before consciously registering it, had grabbed at his groin. A woman who sultrily disperses smoke from her reddened lips was one thing, but one who openly spits out in anger was apparently another. He stared at the door and slowly rubbed his crotch against it, seemingly in a different world to the one he was actually occupying. Going by the noise the woman had re-screwed the cap of the bottle and was now peeling something away from wherever it was glued. The recommencement of rain prevented him from hearing anything further though, until the sudden sound of scribbling could be heard on the other side of the door. The man looked at the top of the doorframe and light above it as if expecting to see some sort of insect scurrying around. Before too long the scratching stopped but the man continued looking as if transfixed. His attention was held so strongly that he didn't even notice when a note soon slipped under the door, in the very same place the cockroach had poked its tiny head.

Instead of lying sprawled on the bed the girl was now sat upright, tying the last tassel of a pair of strappy high-heels. Before standing she lifted her legs up and admired how they and her feet looked in them whilst wiggling her toes. As she rose she stumbled, grabbing the end of the bedpost to keep herself upright. After a deep breath, she began to pace about the room, wobbling on occasion. I mastered this before, she pondered with frustration. Why is it so difficult now?

"Stop looking at your feet," her mother had said. They were alone together in the living room, both wearing heels. "Now stand up straight. Make the heels work for you—not the other way 'round."

The girl looked at her feet, then rolled up her spine and expanded her chest.

"Now walk," her mother said.

The girl did as she was told, walking in slow paces but smoothly all the same. She could manage the steps well enough, going by her expression, but the command over her body was lacking. Standing firm and upright seemed an impossible task, as each stride shot an ever-increasing pain through her spine.

"That's better," her mother said. "Nice and straight. You must own these things. Look," she said, waving her arm for the girl to move aside. "Like this, you see? I'm controlling the heel, the heel isn't controlling me." She walked casually around the room, sometimes even appearing to spin around as she turned—in the girl's mind at least. "It's not easy, but once you get the hang of it you won't ever forget." The girl went to continue walking, but her mother protested after seeing the clock on the wall. "Why don't you go practice in your room instead? I bet in two or three hours you'll be a pro." Instead of replying the girl simply nodded and made for the stairs. As she turned on the landing she saw her mother still looking at the clock, but paid it no further notice, as she was too eager to practice and show her mother that one day she'll be just as good as her.

Two hours later the girl walked out, excited to show her mother how good she had gotten in so little time. But as she stepped on the landing, hearing what she thought to be her own heels, she saw her mother striding down the hall. She was wearing the same strappy red high-heels as the girl was in the brothel, with a black PVC short skirt and a tank top with straps around the shoulders as thin and slinky as the ones wrapped around her ankles and calves. The girl had frozen upon the sight. Her mother hadn't noticed her presence, but just as she reached for a trench-coat the girl had never seen her wear in all the time it'd hung inside the closet, their eyes had met. Inside that tiniest of exchanges a truth was exposed. A truth to a thousand questions which were thought of, but never asked. A glimpse of instant interpretation. An admittance spoken through a palpable silence. What the girl couldn't know then was just how much that look would pave the way to where she found herself now...

The man stood with the torn wine label note in his hand, unfolded. How long he'd been staring at it wasn't clear, but it captivated him in a way which suggested something deeper than the words which were written on it:

Should I begin without you?

The man stuck his hand inside his pocket and removed his wallet. After opening it he took out a photograph about double the size of one required for a passport. Clenching the wallet between his teeth, he flipped the photo around and looked at the writing on the back, which had clearly been tarnished by time. Seemingly unable to look at it properly, he held both the paper and the photo up to the light above him. His head shifted left to right and vice-versa in a comparison of the two. Why he was doing it remained, once again, as unclear as the momentary darkroom one might mistake him to be standing in if they were found guilty of invading his personal space.

But neither her nor her mother had made any recognition of it. The look was merely a glance and an unregistered one at that. Whether through shame or perhaps denial, the girl's mother had simply tied a knot around her waist with the tassels of the coat. Through the blur of the girl's eyes her mother unlatched the lock and left without looking back, walking out into what the girl felt to be the darkest night she'd ever seen. The door slammed with a deadened thud. All the girl could do was listen on as the clickety-clack echoes of heels meeting toes began to fade with each smoothly taken stride...

-SMACK!-

The man, who was now standing on his tip-toes whilst inspecting the photo and note, flinched and tumbled backwards upon hearing the strange thump and fell to the ground like a tree chopped from its root. The wallet slipped out of his mouth, but the paper and picture stayed gripped in his hands. He got up and dusted himself off, then picked up his wallet. After sticking the note and photograph inside, he stuffed it into his pocket, then straightened himself in preparation to finally open the door. With a determined stride, he gripped his hand around the knob. But just as the hand began to twist, the faintest sound of crying could be distinguished from beyond the door, stunting him once more into a statue-esque pose.

Without realising it, the girl had been emulating how her mother strolled around in the same high-heels she was wearing, with grace, confidence and control, when the heel of one shoe had snapped. The result threw the girl to the ground at the same time the heel catapulted against the door. A montage of memories invaded her mind like parasites, of her mother clicking and clacking down the same hallway each and every night, the only difference being the shades of the clothes she wore. A flood of reluctant tears began to pour down the girl's cheeks. The silence which accompanied the house they shared during the early days of the separation was bad enough, but the one which followed, emphasised to the extreme by her mother's mysterious outings had only served to make it hellish. I never knew where she went. I never knew who she was with. I never knew what the fuck she was doing... I never knew anything about anything! It dawned on her at this moment that all she'd done by ending up in this place was reflect her own mother's actions during that period, as if by emulating her choices she'd finally understand her reasons, but no answers could become clear without questions being asked. A sadder realisation soon shone upon her mind, however. When her mother disappeared each night, she was the one who waited up for her, she was the one who worried about her and she was the one who even sometimes prayed for her. Something she hadn't done since being a child.

I was the only person in the entire world who was thinking about you, Mummy. Now here I am, alone in a fucking whorehouse... nobody knows where I am... nobody knows who I'm with... nobody knows what I'm getting up to. "And nobody fucking cares," she said to herself in a strained whisper, as the feeling cut through her with the promise of a scar that would never heal.

As the girl cried the man betrayed no emotion, except for the singular tear which ran down his cheek. It could've been the first time he heard such crying or the thousandth time, it didn't matter—palpable and heart-wrenching as it was. His head hung down as if he wanted it to fall away from his body and his eyes were firm shut like even his imagination was no place for him to be. He tied-up the buttons of his jacket and flicked the collar up, though he still glared at the door. As he slipped his hands into his coat pockets and pivoted as if to leave, his right hand thumbed around under the cloth, where he pulled out a handkerchief. Instead of wiping the solitary tear streaked across his face, he released the faintest, most tired of breaths and reached for the doorknob once again. What stopped him this time was the sound of a scream. A biting, teeth-clenched scream, muffled by some obstruction, which made it even more harrowing to the ear. What followed in between these desperate cries of hopeless eruptions were the harsh slaps of palms against cheeks. For the first time that evening the man's hands fell to his sides, until one of the cries betrayed the faintest hint of some sort of disturbed arousal.

The girl sat with her back against the bed-posts. A clump of hair was clenched between her teeth. A frantic, animalistic glare encased her eyes. Fingerprints appeared on both sides of her face, blotching in a shade of scarlet. Her left hand was lightly groping her breasts whilst the other shook around underneath her underwear, either violently from side to side, or running up and down in rabid fury. Moans of ambiguity scoffed and spewed their way out of her mouth as the tears continued to fall. She knew what she was doing, and that was what was making it so hard. Fucking the pain away didn't always work, but really seeing her world fall apart for the first time had sent her into a state of mania. Getting off seemed like the only thing her body was made for now and she didn't give a shit how she would make it happen. She grabbed the label-torn bottle of champagne by her side and began downing it whilst upping the tempo of her hand. Little eruptions of reluctant pleasure began to break away from her. Sweat began to form on her chest. Her hair became frizzier by the minute. Every little action began to work, as slow and frustrating as it was. Before long she couldn't even feel the hand that was so violently thrashing her clitoris. She hated her body. Hated her impulses. Hated her tits, her vagina, her biology, the men around her and the world at large. Fuelling this hate rose the pleasure. A reluctant charge brought about by seething rage. Her breathing became scattered and cut-off from each other. She switched hands, pressing down as hard as she could upon her swollen, reddening clit. It was already sore. It was already aching. It was already pulsing like it wanted to explode. Through her own force, she felt it begin to stir. She wanted to squirt acid. She could sense it about to erupt, a few more seconds and she'd have her relief, when the man behind the door sighed the most pathetic, creepy gawps she'd ever heard through the tiny slits around the handle of the door.

"*AAARRRGGGHHHH!*" she screamed. Gripping the neck of the bottle tightly and without thinking, she launched it at the door with such a force that it smashed into a thousand pieces. She pushed herself up by her fists, limp-paced towards the door because of the missing heel, then turned back, repeated the action, then finally snatched her cigarettes and stormed over to the window in the corner of the room, striding masterfully considering her impediment. After forcing it up, she lit a smoke with her raging hand trembling and leaned slightly over the windowsill, allowing the now spittle of rain to caress her face as she tried to calm herself down.

As her eyes regained clarity, she took in the view around her. Apart from the distant streetlights and the occasional car that drove by far down below, everything was at rest. A midnight-blue hue hung all around. The calming, distant sounds of rubber against wet tarmac served to put her at ease, whilst the rushing rivers of the gutters glistened in an unusual, almost ultra-violet manner. Even the lamp-posts seemed to have a surrounding aura about them, as if they would glow forever, if only left undisturbed. The sweet burning sound of the cigarette felt like the comfort of a steady fire, the trailing smoke like every lifeform, gone in the blink of an eye.

She followed the faraway current as it gushed along the side of one pavement, watched as it took the right turn into the long main road she was in alignment with, until it travelled under the bonnet of an antiquated grey car, where it stopped streaming. That must be where the trail ends, she thought, imagining the gutter underneath between the tires.

The front door had slammed whilst the girl was staring out of the window in her bedroom. For weeks her mother had been disappearing each night, always leaving around the same time, but never returning at one the girl could depend on. At first, she would wait for her, just to make sure she was still alive before she went to bed herself. But as the weeks wore on and the silence of avoidance surrounding the subject grew to an unbearable size, the girl had simply detached herself from the situation. It was only during the final week that she noticed him. Outside, across the street, her father had been sitting in his car, watching the house. All that was exchanged between them was a wave. She could never be sure, but she thoroughly believed that he'd been there ever since he'd left the house, watching over her, just to make sure she was there. She heard her mother stumbling up the stairs again, crashing her heels against the bannister, but this time she hadn't returned alone. A gruff sounding man alerted her of his presence by clearing his throat. Her mother had laughed and possibly slapped at his chest. As they rose from the stairs all she could do was stare at her father in the distance as he stared back, the two of them trapped inside the decision of her mother. The girl felt nothing as they clambered against her bedroom door, fumbling one another, her mother laughing in a manner that she'd never heard before. "If you want that, it'll cost this," she heard her mother say. The boots of the man soon walked across the corridor, whilst her mother turned the key in her door, locking the girl inside in case the stranger proved himself to be dangerous. The girl had turned as the lock clicked shut, picturing her mother beyond it. She heard the car struggling to start behind her, only for it to burst into life as she swung herself back around. The car moved forward without its lights on and her father remained in profile as he took a left and drove away from the house. He'd only just taught me to drive as well, echoed the thought from back then, and now there's not even a car for me to escape in. The noise of the engine drifted down the road and out of range, only to be replaced by her mother's feigned groans, as she began to fornicate with a stranger for money in the room next door.

She kept her up all night by doing that. After the deed was done the man stayed for an unknown number of hours. Her mother had been right to keep the door closed. During the deafening silence which followed the exchange, the stranger did make an attempt to open the girl's door. Whether he knew she was in there or not she'd never know, but the fear it instilled kept her awake until the early hours of the morning. It was only through exhaustion and stress that she finally fell unconscious. As if in the hope of it all being a dream, the girl slept until the time her mother was usually making her nightly exit. She got up with the same fear, not knowing who or what she might be confronted with on the other side of the door. It'd been unlocked without disturbing her, but all she found in the house was that it was empty. The home had already been taken apart, piece by furniture piece, but the cold, lonely atmosphere of the place instantly told her something else—her mother was gone. The fear of isolation quickly replaced the fear of danger. She checked her mother's room without any regard towards her safety, only to find it completely empty, all for the solitary bed still made with white sheets. In a trance induced by the dread of her abandonment, the girl checked the whole house, betraying no surprise when she found not even the slightest remnant of her mother's presence. All she managed to discover were the pair of high-heels her mother had been wearing during her travels of the night, sitting upright on a pile of overdue bills by the front door. Inside of one of them she could see a note sticking out. She picked up the shoes but decided not to unfold the note and read it there and then. Instead, she made her way back upstairs, back to her room and back to the window where she hoped her father could be seen, watching over the house, watching over her mother and most of all, watching over her. There she spent another sleepless night, but he never arrived. During the torturous wait she'd opened the note, but only managed to read it once the shock of its content ceased making the words blur inside of her eyes:

It's just a job. Remember that. It's just a job. I can't be here anymore. Tell your father that he doesn't need to sit in his car all night long. He can come home now. I'm going back to Vietnam, which, as my one and only daughter, you know is my only real home. Come visit me when you get the chance. I'm sorry. You'll understand this when you're a little bit older. I love you. Take care of your father for me.
Mummy X

What followed was a never-ending series of phone-calls made by the girl to a number that was no longer recognised. Her father, through observing what his wife had left him to do, had also made his own disappearance. As the old day broke into a new one and cast its wince-provoking glare upon the high-heels lying sprawled across her childhood desk, the girl realised, whether it was right, wrong or somewhere between the two, that the only way she was going to keep herself off the streets, was, ironically, by walking them. She knew, and accepted, what she was fated to do.

But he was there the whole time... why did he leave if he was only going to watch over us the whole time?... The whole time... the girl had thought then and was thinking it now, when she saw the man who'd spent his whole hour behind the door, in the corner of her eye.

"You're too late," said the girl without bothering to turn her head to look at him. "The next one's due any minute now." She continued staring out the window, specifically at the isolated grey car down below. Her brow creased as she gazed at it this time though. No, it can't be...

The man fell to the floor with a heavy slump like he'd just fainted. The girl turned to look and jumped up in shock at the sight, covering her exposed cleavage with a forearm and her crotch with a palm, squirming on the spot where she stood, as if she'd just seen a human-sized cockroach. But the man lay still with his eyelids down and his right hand over his chest. The girl, with hesitance, inched her way towards him, covering herself up as best she could.

"Daddy?" the girl asked for confirmation, despite knowing it was him. The man made no recognition of her presence and appeared to be unconscious. Shrugging her self-consciousness aside, she reached for his pulse and sighed upon feeling its strong beat, but its rapid nature instantly snapped her into a panic. She stood up straight and darted looks about the room. In the corner opposite the window, hidden behind the mirror, she located her handbag. After fishing out her phone she dialled the emergency services, limp-stomping back and forth in the centre of the room. But as the operator questioned the nature of her dilemma, the girl caught a glimpse of herself in the mirror, which caused the phone to slip away from her grip. There she was with perfect clarity: a seventeen-year-old prostitute. The voice kept calling through the speaker of the phone. The girl gave it a rabid look, then stamped over it with her remaining heel. The screen cracked as the last heel snapped, but the girl stayed upright this time and the operator offering help was silenced.

With lightning speed the girl got changed into her regular clothes and gathered her things, knowing it to be the last time she'd find herself in that room. She wanted to storm out of the place as fast as possible, but her concern for her father outweighed the judgment he may now have had of her. She re-checked his pulse. All seemed well, or in fact, even better, as the racing pulse had settled into a restful, almost comforting rhythm. But then a smell suddenly entered her nose. A smell she'd been all too acquainted with inside of this place. She sniffed at it displaying her suspicion, as her eyes moved across her father's pregnant-like stomach and betrayed her horror through its momentary wide-eyed alarm. A puddle of semen had formed around her father's groin. He'd ejaculated at the sight of his own daughter working as a prostitute. The intensity of the smell grew to an insufferable level. Its scent no longer only represented the situation she was forced into, or the mechanical actions she'd had to employ, which only ever ended with yet another whiff of its stench. What now infiltrated her senses was what she saw as the very source of her own creation. She kicked her father once, twice, then three times, all in that child-bearing imitation of a stomach of his, not caring whether he woke up to see his only daughter for the whore she'd become. She grabbed a pillow from the bed after the last kick and pressed it against her face. Muffled screams traced with agony shortly followed, not out of concern for her father, but so that she wouldn't arise suspicion, despite never once being bothered about that before. After she was done, breathless from her exhalations, she tossed it back on the bed. Upon turning towards her father again, she saw his wallet and car keys lying next to him. I don't want his fucking money, she thought, planting him with a final, hard toe-poke of a kick at his belly-button. She gathered her belongings in a haste and stormed out of the room, slamming the already open door behind her, which caused the light above it to flicker haphazardly through the disturbance.

As the anger-fuelled footsteps stomped across the corridor, the man lifted himself up by the waist and released an agonised breath; the postponed reaction to his beating. His widened eyes gazed about the room as if unaware of his surroundings, or simply horrified by the occurrences it had held. He made no effort to get up but caressed the wallet by his side like he was seeking the relief provided by a pet. He laughed when he saw the wet patch around his groin, smiling sweetly to himself over its provocation. "She really was perfect," he said, his memory private, but the elation evident by the tears streaming down his face. Without warning, the footsteps came crashing down the hallway again. The man quickly brushed his face with his sleeve and shoved his spine back to play dead, just as the girl barged back into the room.

She swooped the wallet and keys up from the shard-littered floor. After sticking the keys in her pocket, she flipped open the wallet. Her eyes immediately alarmed upon the sight of a wad of cash, which consequently made her scoff. How her father had managed to obtain such a sum was a mystery in itself, but that was a question she knew she'd never ask. Besides, it wasn't his anymore. It was hers. All hers. It was her ticket out. Out of that room. Out of the house no longer a home. Out of the country and into a jet-plane halfway across the world. She snatched the money and stuffed it down her crotch. Then she threw the wallet down at her father's chest. It landed in a sprawled, limp position, displaying the photograph from before. As if by instinct, she scooped it up once more and took it out for closer inspection. As she did, the note she'd written on the torn-off wine label came along with it, as if the two were part of the same piece. She glanced over at her father like he had just spoken to her, confessing to something she'd suspected since the light was shone upon her mother's past. But he remained as motionless as he was silent, once again giving nothing away.

"We met at work," her mother had once said in a dismissive tone, disregarding the girl's innocent, inquisitive nature whilst she brushed her hair with an antiquated hairbrush, notably upping the aggression as she tore through a knot and applied pressure to the girl's skull with its teeth. They were sitting in front of an oval-shaped mirror, the girl gazing into her mother's eyes with her own gleaming like the blood of a fresh wound, the mother looking at everything else about the girl, except for her eyeline. How others would see her, but not how she had once seen the world herself. It was back then and at that moment that the girl had learnt not to ask certain questions. And it was only here, back in the room that the girl, who was now a young woman, had ever recalled that specific recollection.

The photograph held the answer. Older than the girl herself and delicately tarnished by the inevitability of time, there they were, her mother and father, not much older than she was now. They were sat in a room not too dissimilar to the one she was standing in, except for the strong, Asiatic rays of sunlight beaming through the barred, windowless frame behind them. Her mother was dressed in her own version of what the girl was wearing underneath her regular clothes, sitting on the lap of her father, who had his arm around her waist, wearing nothing but a pair of outdated white pants. Her mother was wearing the trilby her father had seemingly glued to his head for his visit to that house of ill-repute. The price-tag was still dangling from the hem. The girl couldn't remember ever seeing her parents looking at each other like they were in that photograph. And she'd never welcomed tears like the ones which were now streaming down her cheeks.

She turned to look at her father and mistook the

tears formed around his eyes for her own. During which, the photograph slipped from her ungripped fingers and floated towards the carpet like a feather from a bird taking its first flight from the nest. As she turned back, the girl saw herself in the mirror. What she saw looking back at her finally made sense. It wasn't me he saw. It was Mummy. He'd worshipped her from the moment he first saw her and I'm the result of that glance.

This conjecture, which so palpably felt like a truth, confirmed its validity only a few moments later, when a reflective light from a shard of glass drew her attention back to the photograph, which was now resting between her feet, face down. Something was scribbled on the back. She knelt and picked it up with the same inquisitive nature she once had as a child, believing it to be the answer to her own existence. The handwriting was so similar it may as well have been written by her own hand.

You're my perfect client.

The girl became so awash with emotion that she felt like an entirely different person, like she was witnessing her very own re-birth. Barely containing the swelling of tears she was so eager to release, the young woman looked around the room until she located where she'd left the pen. After grabbing it she moved over to the door and pressed the photograph against it. Underneath the line, she quickly wrote:

Mine too.

Afterwards and with full composure, she inserted

the photograph back into the wallet and popped the button to ensure its closure. The note she'd written on the torn-off label of wine was still in her other hand. She looked at it for a second, shrugged, then placed it over her tongue and ate it. Satisfied with her midnight snack, she calmly strolled over to her father and slipped the wallet back into its regular home. Then, with a careful intensity, she peeled the trilby away from his head. It tore away from his skull with an ease quite unexpected, which served to delight the young woman even further as she planted it on her head. Whether her father would ever see the added addition to the photograph was an issue she'd dismissed before it was even pondered. The girl knew her father. She knew that even if he did see it one day, he'd never ask her about it. Then she kissed him on the forehead and blissfully made her exit, humming a tune to herself that she hadn't heard since she was a child. In silence and trying to make as little sound as possible, she pulled the door closed as if her father was in a deep and much-needed slumber.

The girl ran across the hallway by the tips of her toes, utterly unaffected by her surroundings. Instead of heading downstairs where the possibility of more johns could've been waiting, she pushed the bar of the fire escape down and shifted herself through it, closing it from the other side as if to make sure that the possibility of her return would be made impossible by doing so.

Out of nowhere, a tall, wide-shouldered man appeared from around the standard stairs of the hallway. With the look of a feral animal and inside his steel-capped boots he stomped down the corridor with what looked like a sick, lust-ridden desperation. Upon reaching the door he grabbed at the handle and practically shoulder-barged his way in. Upon seeing the man, who was still lying on the floor with his giddy-look of euphoric contentment, he said, "Right. Fuck off, old man. You've had your go. Where's the fucking whore?"

The man, as expected, stayed silent but betrayed no fear despite the brute standing over him. The thuggish man began looking around the room, knocking things over at whim, as if he owned them as well as the girl he'd paid for. After checking the bathroom, the half-closed closet and even under the bed, he finally concluded that there was no woman there.

"Oi! D'you fuckin' hear me or what?!"

Once again, the father of the young woman he was unknowingly searching for remained silent.

"Right. I'm gonna count—nah—fuck that. You're gonna tell me what you did with the whore or I'm gonna fuckin' beat it out of you. Last warning."

The silence that ensued lasted for only a few beats before the man unleashed his fury. "Okay. If that's how you wanna play this darling. So fucking be it," he said and smacked him square on the nose, fracturing the bone at the centre, splattering blood over his face instantly. The thug planted his knees on each side of his chest and continued launching him with a mixture of punches, slaps and backhands. More gushes of blood sprayed everywhere, but the man stayed quiet and docile, only making a sound when he gurgled on the build-up of saliva and blood. Pretty soon the thug grew tired of beating on what seemed like a mannequin of flesh and stopped hitting him. He swung his right leg back over and sat with his arms over his knees. As he caught his breath, sweating like he'd just finished what he'd originally walked in to do, he caught of whiff of something, then looked over to see the puddle around the man's groin.

"*Argh*, you filthy little cunt. You fuckin' loved that, didn't ya?" he said, pushing himself back up by his blood-soaked knuckles, which now had stained shards of glass pricked all about them.

He brushed himself off, readjusted his own groin, then headed into the bathroom and washed his hands. As he came out, he looked at the man on the floor and said, "If you tell anyone about this downstairs, I swear I'll fuckin' kill you." Then he tramped across the room again and spat at the man on the ground, who lay still like before despite his beating. The brutish man yanked the door open and glanced back over at the shadowed orgasm and shuddered. He winced as he walked away, neglecting to close the door behind him.

Rain soon began to patter against the window again, notably so against the exposed panel below it. Shortly afterwards, in the far distance, a car was heard, reluctantly breaking into life. The man lay as still as a sea on a breezeless day, with his arms outstretched. As the tires of the car peeled across the road more than several storeys down below, the light on the other side of the door began to buzz. Out in the hallway, the cockroach that'd scurried under the fire escape appeared, trudging its way towards the sound. As it reached the centre of the doorframe it turned and headed towards the man, whose face had flopped to the side upon noticing it. The streams of blood across his cheek matched the streaks of the walls either side of the now open door. As the cockroach neared, the light grew even brighter and buzzed even louder. It crackled and struggled, flickered and stuttered, but the intensity of its illuminance only grew stronger, as if it was fighting against the limitations of its own design. As the cockroach crept its way into the open palm of the now laughing man's hand, who welcomed it like a long-lost family member, the bulb exploded. Instead of bursts of the expected red, the brightest of pure white shone all around in what appeared to be a thousand separate pieces. They hung in the air for only a fraction of a second, but for the man they lasted a lifetime. Each individual one imploded just as they were at their brightest, like a star that follows a supernova. He gazed upon them as they twinkled inside his eyes with the wonder and awe of a child's imagination. With untouchable contentment he watched them each disappear until he was once again, shrouded in complete and utter darkness.

BLOODHOUND LUST

What sort of man would steal another man's dog? What kind of disgusting vile *parasite* would even *think* of taking a man's pup—*let alone carry the act out?!* My wife Helen insists that my boy Rex must have run away after the bloody baby was born but I don't buy it—it just doesn't make any sense. Throughout her whole pernicious pregnancy all she ever did was moan, groan and bitch about him; relentlessly attacking me about his odour. Well, what about her odour, huh? You think it's nice to wake up to the sound of your once attractive wife to hear and smell her vomiting into a toilet bowl? She must have been sticking her hands down her throat, I'm sure of it. There's no way one person can produce that much vomit! Not that she gives a toss now anyway, now she's finally got what *she* wants. All she's done since the baby was born is bark orders at me left, right and centre. She hated my boy Rex, my wonderful, trustworthy dog. She's been beaming a radiant, solar *glow* since he disappeared, whilst I've been cut out and cast aside for this bloody baby. And now, she wants to start trying for another one! Right off the bat! It's only been six or so bloody weeks! I'm exhausted enough as it is—let alone utterly dogless!

She kept pestering me to get him neutered a few weeks before he vanished as well—the poor bastard. All because she had this 'feeling' his natural impulses posed some kind of threat. As if my dear Rex would ever hurt anyone! Now all I hear each night is, 'Why don't you pop down the Man's Best Friend for a few? Rex might be down there'. So, yet again, here I am, aimlessly moping around with a pack of degenerate nowhere men, on the off chance that Rex might just pop in for a quick pint! I'm sure glad I never took him to the vet to get the snip now though. The only solace I get from his disappearance is the hope that he's out there somewhere, rutting about something silly.

It's this town I tell you... this wretched, scathing, bloodsucking hellhole of a place. It's so cursed that I wouldn't be surprised if it gobbled him up into the undergrowth of which it was founded upon.

"Hair of the dog again Mike? Been seeing you around here a lot lately," says the barman. One more snide, insinuating comment from that loathsome berk and I'll grab hold of the tongue that is forever flopping out of his mouth and butcher it right off!

"Just don't wanna get your hopes up mate, that's all. That dog's been gone for nearly what, a fortnight now? Plus, ain't you got a new-born to be worrying about?" says the barman, plonking down my pint with all the decorum of a junkie in withdrawal.

It's not that I do not have affection for my boy— the fleshy human one that is—it's just difficult for the untrained eye to see how much Rex means to me. He's the most loyal, loving and devoted creature I've ever had the pleasure of knowing. But this... *baby*, there's something so... *unnerving* about him. He's got my wife's self-aggrandizing eyes all right; always watching, staring and judging, hating me already because of my part in his creation. And I'm one hundred percent sure that he *never*, ever blinks! *He*—no, no, no—*It!* He's not a he—he's an it—it's an it—definitely an it all right! *It* glares at me as if I'm transparent. It's not my fault if Helen demanded that I penetrated her each and every night up until her water finally broke. Why doesn't it look at her the way it looks at me? Somehow though... It seems to know things about me. Don't ask me how I know that, but the feeling is beyond palpable and *yes,* I know how it sounds, but I'm absolutely, positively, cataclysmically sure of it! I'm disgusted to admit this, but sometimes... just for a second, when I look at its face for just a bit too long... it looks like—*oh god*—it looks like it's... *covered with semen!!!* Argh, Christ... I cannot bear this burden! And don't even get me started with the breastfeeding!

"Hey Mike," says the lady whose arse has been sniffed by every poor sap who once chose to frequent this abode.

"Oh hello... you," I say, apprehensive of her intentions.

"You wanna buy a lady a drink?"

"Yeah sure, where is she?"

"Oi, you cheeky cu—"

"I'm just playing with you darling. No, tonight isn't good. I'm gonna look for Rex in a bit."

"I dunno why you're still moping around about that, it's just a dog."

"Especially now he's got a real son," chimes in the barman.

"Ahh, so the mysterious wife we've all heard about but never actually seen has finally given up the goods. Congratulations Mike. I always wanted to have a child myself, but well... it wasn't meant to be. I am sorry about your dog though. If you ever need someone to talk to, you know where to find me," she says, making me shudder with a wink. And *yes,* okay, I admit it, I've been there. Only once! And never again! It only happened because during the past bloody year, Helen has managed to turn our sex life into some emasculating reproduction machine. I was dog drunk and the scrubber's sultry slurs whispered an illicit sexual release. Not just Helen's: 'No more masturbating!', 'Fill me up properly this time!', 'Only in the front hole!', 'We must do it *now, now, now!*' At *this* time and on *this* hour and in *this* position and *then this that and the other*, and immediately afterwards you have to hold my legs upwards to give my slow seed a better chance of piercing through your ageing eggs! Well, I needed a blowjob goddamnit! Guilty as charged. Oh, Christ. The trollop is still giving me the eye. One more for the road and I'm off.

The streets were dreary, desolate and deprived. Nothing to be found there but the dogged, desperate cries of bulldog-like males and their female counterparts, all howling out their mating cries at one another underneath a full moon. Put them all down I say. I'm sure every evening since Rex's disappearance the moon has been full... I'm not sure. Maybe. Or maybe I'm just imagining things...

Before I left Man's Best Friend, due to the slag's crude advances towards me, I threw up in the bathroom what could only be described as a cancerous bile. It hit the base of the bowl with an acid-like singe and oh, the smell. Positively disease-ridden I tell you. There were even specks of blood in it. Argh, doesn't the world see how I'm dying without my dog?!

Home was hardly better. Upon arrival, my wife insisted on another night of procreation. Three bloody times in one bloody night. She doesn't even let me warm myself up with a little anal or put her mouth to good use anymore. All she does is lay there like a ragdoll whilst I fiddle myself erect. And of course, *It* just stares at me, giggling the whole time! Oh, and just for measure, as soon as I climax, the bastard starts wailing for attention again. It's like it waits for me to feel the tiniest ounce of pleasure and then bang, swoop, *snatch!* Taken away from me in an instant. It's a thief of intimacy I tell you and I wish it'd never been born! No, I do not mean that... do I?

Of course, there was no rest for me. All night I tossed and turned with Rex galloping around in the back of my mind inside an abyss, cruelly reminding me of his unknown whereabouts. It made today's search for him particularly intolerable. I went to every park we once visited together and in each one I thought I saw him, only to see that it wasn't him at all. I must be so exhausted that I'm beginning to see things. Then, when I got back home, dog-tired from my scentless search around this shithole, as soon as I sat my sorry arse down, Helen woofed, 'Why don't you go down the Man's Best Friend for a few? I'm better with the baby than you are. Every time you get too close to him he bursts into tears. Go on, shoo! But be ready for another night of action when you get back, I'm ovulating!'

Charming! So here I am again! Evicted from my own home! My wife pays no attention to me now that It is here, and every time I try and talk to her about it she just switches the subject; sending me out on errands instead, getting me to fetch every little thing that she needs. Well what about *me*, huh? Don't I deserve something more than a little pat on the head? She has two other orifices you know! A man needs to eat out of a different bowl now and again! I'm sick to death of trotting around with my tail between my legs!

"Back again, 'eh Mike. How about that drink?" says the tart, barking up the same old bush. It must have been a while since the old mutt got any. She always whips her puppies out after too many rejections. In truth, Lilith ain't looking too bad tonight: Erect nipples. Drunken, dilated eyes. Eager jaw. Even her name came back to me. This must be a sign. Mmm... shouldn't really go there again... should I?

Seduced by her cleavage and for the lack of better judgment I indulged her request—*a few times in fact*—and now, low and behold, we're back at her place. I'll be in and out of here in a dash, as soon as I've mouthfucked her sober, the skanky little lush. "Don't unbuckle your belt just yet Mikey. If you want me to suck you off again, you better return the fucking favour this time. In fact, you can do the honours first," says Lilith, stumbling down over her creaky old bed. "Get on all fours and crawl over here," she says, spreading her legs wide open. "Turn off the light when you're ready and rip off my panties with your teeth. No hands. I'm waiting, Mike."

My spine shivered at her slurring request, but anything was better than pumping my dried-up, unfeeling wife. At least I thought so beforehand. Even in the dark it was grim. I don't know what is wrong with me... but I did it, I caved in! I got on my knees like a little bitch! I tell you, it was so vile, so, so, so disgusting! I'm sure she was on heat as well, the mangy old mare. I'll be picking out her pubic hair from my teeth for weeks. Sensing my disgust shortly after her climax, she began fellating me as an apology, but due to her ghastly, intoxicated state, she regurgitated when I came in the back of her hoarse throat. To her credit though, she still gulped it all down, but she could've left out the part when she swirled my penis around her vomit-filled mouth, that was just way too much! It seems no matter how many times I soap myself down, the smell just won't go away. My whole groin feels tainted with masticated pork scratchings, house gin and shepherd's pie.

"Hey Mike, are you awake in there? Don't be such a sensitive little pup, it was only a bit of vomit for Christ sake, come out here. I've got a little surprise for you."

I couldn't tell you how ominous that sounded to me at the time, but, to my surprise, immediately after opening the bathroom door, this beautiful dog started jumping up at me. It was the first time I've smiled since It came into existence. Only now as my teary eyes begin to clear do I fully clock-on to the fact that it isn't just any old dog, it's *my* goddamn dog.

"Rex?! It is you! Rex, oh my god where have you been, boy?"

"Woof, woof!" he says with dilated eyes, jumping up and down with pure elation, knowing that at last he's been rescued, as have I!

"Oh, I can't believe it. We're finally reunited! I've missed you so much boy, come here! I'm so sorry I lost you, it won't ever happen again, I promise. Life has been nothing without you."

"Mike?" says whatshername as Rex and I share another embrace. "Hate to break this to you, but I've had that dog for a few weeks now," she says, stunning me into sobriety. "He looked demonic when I found him, but it was just his amber eyes under the moonlight. He was in some bin, without a collar or a bone."

"Why didn't you tell me?! You saw how much of a wreck I've been during the last fortnight! Everyone in the pub knew about it."

"Yes. And everyone knew about our first fuck the minute you pulled out of me. You *used* me Mike. I was starting to have real feelings for you as well, wasn't I? Only to find out that you not only had a wife but also a baby on the way! After I did all of those disgusting, violating things for you, all for your putrid pleasure!"

"Alright Lilith, I'm so—"

"Ahh, so *now* you remember my name!"

"What do you want me to say?"

"Nothing, Mike. Nothing. I actually just miss you is all. In another life or in different circumstances we could've had a family together."

"We could've done, sure." In hell maybe.

"Well, let's just leave it like that. You're a lucky man, Mike. You're getting away with murder here. If you want me, I'm yours. There's just one little thing I'd like from you."

"And what's that?"

"I can't have children, Mike. I'm barren. Nothing's ever gonna live inside of me. I just want to know what it feels like to hold a baby, *your* baby in particular. If you can give me that, even just for an afternoon, I'll let you do whatever you want to me for as long as you want, or don't. There's no need to answer me right now, just go home and think about it. Your wife must be getting worried, it's nearly midnight."

Well, that sure made the drive back home rough, but at least I have my boy Rex back. He seems a little traumatised but then again, after fulfilling Lilith's little request, so am I. She's quite the loyal type though, if not somewhat psychotic. Maybe I will let her take It for a few hours one day—after things settle back down at home. Everything will be all right now Rex is back where he belongs.

I don't know what it was but an overshadowing, ominous feeling took shape inside of me as I approached the front door of my house. It'll sound odd, but the slicing jingle of my keys seemed to be the only thing making a sound. I looked out into the distance and even though everything was there like it always was, nothing felt concrete or structured or stable. It was just indifferent and... lifeless. For a period, it was as if the weather had ceased to exist. There was nothing: no wind, no sound, no atmosphere. Nothing. A certain, opaque stillness hung all around and the strangest conviction of being... swallowed overtook me. I looked up at the moon. It seemed to just sit there, with a vermillion circle spiralling around it, murdering the clouds. Before too long whilst absently staring at it a sudden, pungent smell of placenta hit my nose. I turned away and held my gaze on Rex, who just sat there, looking ahead without emotion, breathing like he'd just been chasing rabbits or bitches on heat—with his tongue dry but his teeth... sweating. Then Helen opened the door and threw her arms around me. Her touch reminded me to breathe.

"Mikey? Guess what?! We're pregnant again, hubby!" she said, clutching on the swab of another overpriced pregnancy kit. "Oh, look, you found Rex! What a happy day this has turned out to be!"

"One of the best," I said as we embraced, truly believing that things were going to improve from there on out. *Until it hit me.* If I thought it was bad enough when Helen got pregnant the first time around, what the hell was the second time going to be like? And who the hell is going to take care of It?

Me!?

"Oh Mike, I'm so delighted we're together again. I'm sorry for how everything's been recently. It's just the thought of our son growing up all alone really got to me for some reason and... I don't know, blame it on the hormones. We're good, aren't we?"

"Of course we are, Helen."

"You don't regret marrying me, do you?"

"Not at all, dear. Not at all."

Helen smiled at me, almost apologetically. "Good. I'm very glad to hear that Michael. I don't know what I'd do if I... found out something wasn't right between us. After all, we've built a home together now, haven't we?"

"We sure have, Helen. We sure have. Nothing is wrong my dear, quite the contrary. Everything's coming up roses."

"Ah, it's such a relief to hear you say that. Oh god, I don't know why I'm crying. I'm sorry."

"Don't be Helen, there's no need to apologise."

"Mike?" she asked, wiping her tears away, regaining her composure.

"Yes?"

"You couldn't go fetch me some baby oil, could you?"

***

It's been difficult to re-ingratiate Rex back into the family home. I'm beginning to wonder, for some bizarre reason, whether he is somewhat jealous of the baby. As if It is comparable to my dog. Rex is fine when it's just the two of us, which I'm sorry to say is seldom at best.

"Mike!"

Christ, what fresh hell is this now?

"Michael!"

It's only been a few weeks. Each day drags in another nuisance before yesterdays was even close to being resolved. Helen's constant bemoaning has made my skin come out in a rash. It's so itchy I want to scratch my own eyes out. How am I meant to undertake another nine months of this?

"Mike! Get up here! NOW!"

"What is it now *Hell*-en?" I ask, stepping into the bathroom. Helen's on her knees, but not in the manner which would've once provoked my arousal. She's vomiting into the toilet bowl again, for the third time this morning. I can feel its residue lingering around in the air, tainting everything with its stale stench of rot and decay, marking its territory. It's been like this every single day since the second coming began to take shape. There really is no wonder why Rex doesn't seem the same, he must be suffering something awful with that brilliant nose of his.

"Take Rex out with you, will you? He's done nothing but follow me around since he returned, like some *leech*," says Helen, spitting out further leftovers into the bowl.

"Hey, steady on. He's not doing anything wrong."

"Oh no? Look at him."

I do as she says. Rex looks up at me, the same way he's always done.

"Don't you see that?"

"See what?"

"His glare. He's not looking *at* me. He's looking *through* me."

"You're just imagining things, Helen. Probably because you can't stop throwing up. I'll take him down the pub, he hasn't been there since we got him back."

"Good. But it's not just my imagination. He's even worse with the baby. It's strange. I thought he would've improved after a week or so, but he's not the same dog as before. Remember what he used to be like?"

"Of course. I agree that he isn't quite all there, but he'll come back to us eventually. How long would it take you to recover from living out of bins for two weeks? Give him a chance."

"If memory serves, he started to act strangely the moment I gave birth. Don't you recall that, Michael? For weeks he just loitered around our baby, like he was waiting for his moment to pounce."

"That's just your overprotective, maternal nature, Helen. Rex wouldn't do a thing like that. Don't let your emotions blind you."

"Oh, get gone, will you? And bring me back something for my throat, it's throbbing terribly."

"Well, maybe you shouldn't use it so frequently."

"*Go!*"

Christ, the nerve of this woman. Just because she was once a beautiful young thing, she thinks she can demand anything she likes. She's not the woman I married. *It* took care of that all right. He made an abomination out of all of her redeeming attributes and now she's pregnant again, so that extra layer of fat isn't going anywhere anytime soon. Argh, even her lymph nodes seem to be gaining weight...

"Aye-aye, stranger!" says the barman, whose name I cannot ever seem to recall. "I see you've got your dog back. Good for you, Mike! Hello Rex, welcome back boy. Usual mate?"

"Please yeah and some water for the dog, he's had an unquenchable thirst since I found him."

"Coming right up!"

Finishing each day at the end of a bottle is beginning to take its toll on my mind, but it's the only thing that seems to give me any release anymore. Helen has taken on a completely different tact to her last pregnancy—bar the vomit. She was like a rabbit the first time around but this time all I get is: 'I'm sore!', 'Not so rough!', 'I know you know where my arsehole is Mike!' She won't let me do anything. I don't want to sleep with Lilith again, but Helen is giving me very little choice in the matter. I'd be better off if I just got neutered already. I'm sure it won't end this insufferable need to fornicate though. At least here, at Man's Best Friend, I am at peace.

"Hello Mike, ain't seen you around these parts for a while. And I should know, I'm here near enough every night."

"Oh hey, Lilith. Didn't notice you were here."

"That's because I only just arrived, like you Mike. Hello Rex, how's my favourite little tyke doing?" she says as Rex stands up on her legs.

"What you drinking?"

"Oh, how generous of you. I'll have my usual."

She stares into my eyes, expecting her statement to have some sort of meaning to me.

"A Bloody Mary, Mike," she says, patting Rex back down.

"You got it."

"So what do I owe for the pleasure of your company?" she asks.

"Helen's pregnant again."

"Oh. Congratulations Mike. Your boys are sure eager for life. Helen is one lucky woman."

Lilith keeps a close eye on the barkeep as he finishes serving us (once again forgetting to bring Rex some water) and waits for him to bugger off. She's a good lass deep down. There is something about her... she's so much more laid back than my wife. Tis a shame she's a skank.

"So Mike, now that we're all alone. Have you thought about my proposal? I presume now that Helen is back in the pudding club you could do with some relaxing *help*, if you know what I mean. What do you say, would you care to throw this gal a bone sometime soon?"

"That would depend. Is the tail wagging the dog?"

"It certainly seems that way to me, Mike. But I'll have to give you a thorough, rigorous check-up first, just to be sure. Nurse Lilith, at your service."

"You deserve more from this life, Lilith."

"And what about my other little request?"

"What other request?"

"You know, the baby one."

"Oh. You were serious about that?"

"Deadly, Michael."

"Fair enough. Actually, this Friday might work out well for you. Helen's going to the doctors for a check-up, so if you want to look after him for a while, he's all yours."

"Great. I'll see you then. But let's not waste any further time talking. I'll leave here after this drink and you'll follow behind me like a slave to his master." Lilith picks up her glass and gulps the entire drink down in one go. "Wait for five minutes." She wipes her lips dry with the back of her hand and walks out of here like we mean absolutely nothing to each other. She sure saw this sucker coming, I'm salivating more than Rex already...

***

Having a bit on the side certainly makes my marriage more bearable. Every man should have a mistress.

Lilith seems to have taken away the annoying, tinnitus-like ringing behind every word Helen utters. In fact, the last few days have been a dream. This 'family man' stuff is a puppy's first walk in a park! Helen stresses me out up until the point that I'm going to explode, and the ever-eager Lilith takes on the full load with her mouth wide open. God bless all barren women, for they truly learn how to fuck!

"'Ere you are Mike," says the barman, placing down my third pint of the afternoon. *It* is with Lilith and Helen is at the doctor's. This is the first time I've been alone with Rex again in about nine months. A man alone with his dog, the way things are meant to be.

"Cheers Rex," I say, making a toast to the two of us.

"Mike," says the barkeep. "Phone call for you."

"Oh Christ, let me guess, it's my wife?"

"No. Some bloke. Said it's important. Sounds personal, so I didn't ask," he says, handing over the phone.

"Hello?"

"Am I speaking to Michael, the husband of Mrs Mallory?"

"This is he. Who am I speaking to?"

"This is Doctor Tolbert. Your wife requested that I call you."

"Where's Tom? Urm, I mean, my wife normally sees Doctor Tom—"

"He referred your wife to me."

"Oh. Is there a problem?"

"No, no, nothing to worry about. It's all standard procedure. Better safe than sorry stuff really. I've sent your wife to the hospital at once for a full, routine check-up."

"Why?"

"It's too soon to say at the moment. I just noticed a few potential irregularities. Your wife complained of a few conditions which sound similar to the flu, but I've sent her to the hospital just to be safe. She may have to stay overnight."

"I'm on my way right now. I assume it's the main hospital, up Queen's Road?"

"That's correct, yes."

"Okay, thank you, doctor. Oh, one question. Can I bring my dog into the hospital? I know it sounds strange, but I lost him recently and really don't want him out of my sight again, just in case."

"I'm sorry Mr Mallory, the hospital has strict rules against such things. I'm afraid you'll have to make other arrangements."

"Alright fine, I'll work something out. Thanks for the call."

"Mr Mallory?"

"Yes?"

"I think you should come in for a check-up soon as well, just to be safe."

"Why do you think that?"

"I cannot say over the phone, Mr Mallory."

"Do you think I gave her... do you think I have this 'something' as well?"

"Again, I cannot say over the phone."

"Oh, bollocks to that. We're adults here, aren't we? Just give it to me straight doctor. I'm a big boy."

"I'm sorry, Mr Mallory. I cannot say."

"Oh, come on, this is farcical!"

"Goodbye, Mr Mallory."

"Tell me right now! Doctor? Doctor!?"

The coward hung up! *Fuck. Fuck. Fuck. What should I do?!* Okay, think Michael, think. I've got to get to the hospital as quickly as possible, but I'm not leaving Rex alone anywhere. *Lilith! Of course!* How could I be so blind?! "Come here boy, let's get moving!"

***

Wow, I've never seen Lilith glow like that before. She almost looked like a real woman with It cradled in her arms. Even the baby looked happy for a change. And Rex! He looked ecstatic to be back there with her. I wonder if she can cook. Life would certainly be easier with her. Lilith would be more than happy to look after It all day and then see to me all night long. Mind you, Helen used to do everything I wanted until she got a ring on her finger. The ulterior motives of women, 'eh? That's strange. The weather has stopped again. Probably just the alcohol or something. God, it feels like I only just left this bloody hospital. Helen was in labour for thirty-six goddamn hours last time. The mere memory of it makes me shudder. Hopefully she'll have to spend the night though. I could do with another evening at the end of Lilith's lubricated lips...

***

That woman has sure got a lot to answer for, let me tell you! Helen miscarried on her way to the hospital and when I got there, she flat out refused to see me! I waited there for hours, only for a fucking nurse to tell me to leave as I was 'taking up unnecessary space'—the bloody cheek of it! All of them in there kept throwing me their filthy-eyed looks every time they walked by. I nearly punched the woman at the reception desk as well, the cold-hearted *cunt*. She wouldn't answer *any* of my questions at all. Not one inkling of human decency in that one! I was pulling my hair out!

Right, time for me to get to the bottom of this!

"*LILITH!!!*" I scream at the house, slamming the car door shut behind me. Her front door is ajar. Is she *expecting* me? All right, Mike. Calm yourself down. I'm sure there's a reasonable explanation for all of this. No need to panic just yet. I nudge the door open and step inside.

"Lilith?" I say, locking the door behind me.

There's nobody here.

"Rex?"

No response.

I'm sure I can hear him breathing upstairs. He sounds like he's been feasting. Christ, it's freezing in this place. My breath leaves a trail behind me as I head up the stairs to Lilith's bedroom—the bane of my whole existence. I can hear her giggling... though it doesn't really sound like her.

"Lilith, is that you?" I ask, tentatively pushing the door open. She's sitting on the bed at an angle in her dressing gown, putting on white makeup like a Geisha. "Lilith? Are you okay?"

"Ahh, the guest of honour is here. I've been expecting you, Michael," she says, looking at me via the mirror of her cosmetic powder box. In the light, clouds of dust waft around her face as she pads her cheeks in an almost ritualistic rhythm.

"Where's Rex?" I ask.

Inside the mirror, she continues to glare at me, then suddenly clamps it shut and shifts her body around, facing me. She lifts her arm up like it belongs to another being, and points towards the next room. There's blood on her hand. She stares at my groin and licks her lips. I take a step back. She bites down hard on her bottom lip, piercing the skin until a teardrop of blood seeps out. Another step back. With her finger, she paints her lips with the blood. I'm fucking shaking with fear, yet beginning to get hard.

"Peek-a-boo, I see you, Mikey. Come here already, I've been aching to feel you all day."

"Oh, fucking hell Lilith, you're scaring me. What have you done!? Why is my wife refusing to see me?"

"Men get all the pleasure. Women get all the pain."

"Alright Lilith, this was a mistake. Where's my dog and It—I mean, where's the baby?"

"I told you. In there," she says, pointing again and laughing. "But come here first Mike, you need a little check-up." Lilith untangles the tassels of her dressing gown. She's wearing a nurse outfit... a very, very sexy one! Her breasts are pushed up to the heavens. She looks magnificent. I can't believe I'm still tempted by her!

She continues sitting there though, glaring into my nothingness. I step back until I'm out of the room. The same, ominous feeling from before invades my being as I head down the corridor. I never knew this room even existed before. It looks like a neglected closet from the outside. I turn the handle and with a sudden gust of wind it swings open and crashes against the wall. Cold sweat breaks out over my entire body. The room is coated in dust, with cobwebs in the corners and broken baby toys on the floor. In the middle sits a single crib, painted black, covered by a single bedsheet. It's a nursery for a child that was never born. There are more drops of blood trailing across the carpet. With my leg shaking and my stomach churning, I carefully approach it, terrified of what lies underneath the sheet, but unable to stop myself from looking. Slowly, I began to uncover the cot. The smell hits me too fast though, making me gag.

"Peek-a-boo, I see you, Mikey."

"*Argghh!! Fucking hell, Lilith. Just stop it, alright!? It's not funny anymore, stop acting like a freak.*"

"Go ahead, Michael. Take a look at what we made together," she says, standing in the doorway. She's holding a syringe—and her legs—there are huge patches of blood across her upper thighs and suspenders!

"Go on, don't be shy. Have a little looksie," she says.

My bowels are convulsing. I'm scared to look away from her, but her eyes are fixated on the crib. Eventually, my gaze is slowly drawn to it as well. "Go ahead Michael, look at our creation." My head shakes frantically—my eyes are slices of supersonic images—everything's turned a dullened auburn. I grip my shaking hand on the crib and lean over the cot to see... the baby... the baby has... no face... it's been... *eaten.* No eyes—no mouth—no nose—just blood—flesh—and bile—*It's been entirely eaten off!* I fall to my knees as projectile vomit shoots out of me, all over the floor. Lilith starts laughing and pointing at me—a cackling, tormented laugh. A stream of blood runs down her leg. I can see Rex behind her in the distance, creeping towards us. Droplets of blood hit his face as he crawls under the scissor-shape of Lilith's open legs. One side of his lip is quivering in a twitch. Lilith keeps on laughing, still pointing at my groin. "Unbuckle your belt, Mikey. Whip your monster out. You never asked me why I preferred fooling around in the dark. I bet you thought it was because I was self-conscious of my body, right? Like a typical woman, correct? Well, in a way that's true. You want to see me now, in the light?" she says. A blade of light suddenly beams through the window and moves up her legs as she rips off the suspender straps and unveils herself to me. She's shaved—or more—*slashed* herself. There are deep gashes and cuts, along with warts and bubonic blisters covering her entire genital area, which all look like they're breathing. Rex is foaming at the mouth, growling at me like I'm diseased! This can't be happening! Both him and Lilith start prowling towards me. I'm paralysed with fear and soaked to the bone!

"Oh no, Mikey had a little accident. Take off those soiled trousers of yours, you filthy little boy. Let's have some fun."

Rex hurls himself at me. I protect my face, but he's going for my groin! He bites down hard. I feel his teeth sinking into my shaft. I try to punch him off, but he won't budge! Lilith kicks me in the face, sending me flying backwards. My head crashes against the floor. She sticks the needle in me! Rex is gnawing on my foot. I go to kick him, but I can't move! All my muscles are tightening shut! Lilith laughs once more and stands over me. Slowly, she starts to squat down! As she gets closer and closer, her blisters hiss and pop over my face, spitting out into my eyes and mouth. She drops to her knees and clamps her thighs around my head. Oh god, the taste! She hasn't washed since last night! I'm eating my own bloodstained semen! My body betrays me, making me throw up again. Lilith pushes down even harder, making my jaw lock, forcing me to swallow it down again—but I heave it back up! Some if it bursts out and covers my eyes with blood. Lilith grabs my hair and thumps my head onto the floor. Again and again and again. She's riding my face! I can't breathe! I'm drowning in her blood! She spins around my face and starts unbuttoning my fly! Rex breathes in waiting. Fucking hell, how have I got an erection? My balls are exposed. My cock is the only thing I can feel in my whole body! Rex begins snarling, like he's been waiting for this his entire life. "One," says Lilith, caressing my testicles. Rex is going to castrate me—I can feel it. "Two," she screeches, laughing like a demon whilst violently pumping me away. Oh fuck, it's coming... he's sniffing... I can feel his saliva dripping from his tongue onto the head of my shaft... his jaw is wide open—with bits of baby flesh lodged inside his gums... "THREE!" *Oh god— HERE IT COMES!!!*

MOTHER NATURE
SENDS HER LOVE

A wet summer breeze wafted out of an engulfing forest along a darkening path into a field of green. Licks of dew hung from the tips of overgrown grass which were being scattered around in spraying puffs as a group of hormonal teenage boys tore through the blades. They were circling around their shelters, thrusting their feet down on tent pegs whilst teasing one another. The pathway, unnoticed by the lads thus far seemed to breathe a dank, lingering hot breath which would've normally gone by undisturbed, but was now sticking to the boys and creeping through the pores of their skins. Its influence had already begun to stir; the cause unknown, but the effect evident, going by the game the lads decided to play straight after they'd set up camp.

"Guess who I'm thinking about, Leander," said Danny, the first one to remove his trousers.

"Who?" he asked, his belt buckle jiggling along with the others, like a chorus line of tramps rattling their tins for spare change.

"Your milf of a mother," Danny replied, flopping to the ground.

"Fuck—"

"Shit, me too! How weird is that?" said Bruce, who was furthest away from the rest, but firmly in the lead. The boys were about twenty to thirty feet away from each other. It was dick-size (whether noteworthy or not) insurance.

"The tits or the arse?" asked Jez.

"She's seducing me. I popped over to see Leander. He wasn't at home. She's taking me to her room. She's making me jerk off in front of her. Now she's helping me."

"Is this a porn?"

"Shut it, Danny. Keep going Bruce, this is chubbin' me up," said Joey.

"Of course it's a porn. Every fantasy is!" said Bruce.

"No, I mean is it *actually* a porn, with Leander's mum in it?" asked Danny, "sounds hot."

"My mum never did porn! Shut the fuck up Danny," screamed Leander, his anger oddly egging him on.

"Guys, shut up," said Harry Buckleby as he half-humped the grass in the spooning position. Somehow, it appeared that the biscuit at the end of his cock was the one touching him.

"Now I'm thinking about your sister and all the drool that gathers up in those adorable braces of hers, Bucks," said Danny.

"Argh! Too much man," said Bruce.

Dude!" said Joey, "that's what I was thinking about!"

Be quiet guys, I need to concentrate," said Jez, "and don't talk about Harry's sister. She's like thirteen, isn't she?"

"Yeah guys, have a bit of respect," said Bucks, still trying to get an erection by thumbing the head of his penis around the edges of the cookie, but getting nowhere fast.

"So? We're only fifteen. There's no time to waste. Before we know it, we won't be able to fuck any sweet thirteen-year-old ass like Caitlin Buckleby. You should know Harry, you've been there."

"Danny. I've never touched my sister, alright? How many fucking times do I need to tell you!?" Bucks exclaimed, more frustrated by his still flaccid state than Danny's insinuation of incest.

With a sudden, spasming leg, Bruce cried out, "*Ahh-ahh*, I'm coming..."

"What!? Fuck off!" said Harry, with a hint of secret delight behind his outrage. He was the only one who had shifted upright to look, where he soon saw another set of legs tightening.

"Me too," cried Joey, "yeah, take it."

"Oh man, this digestive got owned. It's looking mighty tasty guys," said Bruce, giving it an over-zealous sniff as Joey skipped over to him, biscuit in hand. After admiring each other's loads, they placed the biscuits aside and lay down together.

Joey cracked the flint of his lighter, lit two cigarettes and laughingly said, "Two down, four to go," whilst Bruce admired the pinkening borders of the clouds above. Both guffawed as the moans of supposed pleasure transformed into that of doubt, fear, and throat-gulping dread.

Vvvvrrrmmm-vvvrrrmmm.

"Hey, who's watching porn?! That's against the rules," said Danny, worried that the stiffness he'd only just achieved was under threat.

"Not me," said Jez.

Vvvvrrrmmm-vvvrrrmmm.

"Nor me," said Bucks.

Vvvvrrrmmm-vvvrrrmmm.

"It's just Myra guys," said Leander.

"Funny, I was just thinking about her," said Danny.

"Come on guys, I could've finished twice by now," said Bruce, "get on with it, I'm getting hungry. Or more, I'm hungry to watch someone chow down on my fat load."

"Yeah guys, hurry up," Joey chimed in, "my biscuit's getting soggy over 'ere."

"I'm nearly there," said Leander.

"Same here," said Danny.

"And me," added Jez.

The only one who remained silent was Harry Buckleby, who had turned onto his side and looked to be whispering sweet nothings into the urethra of his unresponsive manhood.

"You're a bit quiet over there, Bucks," said Joey, nudging elbows with Bruce.

"Impotently quiet," said the latter. Joey slapped his knee and they both started choking on their own chuckles.

Vvvvrrrmmm-vvvrrrmmm.

"Argh! Leander," cried Bucks with an accusatory air, "turn that phone off, will you? It's impossible to concentrate—"

"*Argghhhh,* here it comes baby," cried Danny, ejaculating over his biscuit. A similar cry from Leander shortly followed.

"And then there were two," said Bruce, "who's going to be the lucky winner?"

"Bucks is. I finished ages ago. Just didn't feel like mentioning it," said Jez, zipping himself back up.

"What?! No way, no fucking way!" said Bucks, speeding up his hand-pumping despite its pointlessness, "someone must've cheated!"

"Guys, gather around. Every man needs to show some evidence before Bucks tucks into his dinner," said Bruce, skipping back to camp with Joey, almost crying with joy.

The rest all sprung up to their feet, except for the lucky winner. They buckled their belts back up and, with the caution of scientists, carried the now icing-glazed cookies towards the centre of their camp, using their fingers like pinchers.

"You know, this is still kind of gay," said Danny.

"Not as gay as Bucks is about to be," said Joey.

The boys chuckled and scoffed in victorious malevolence, mutually relieved that they wouldn't have to eat each other's semen yet delighted at the prospect of a close friend needing to because he couldn't ejaculate fast enough.

"Wow, Jez. Nice load man," said Leander.

"Why thank you. It's been a few days. Only took a few strokes. Easy. Bucks, why're you still jacking off?"

"Yeah, Bucks. Game's over dude. Get up and gobble down all five of your losses already," said Danny.

"I can't believe you guys. Someone must've cheated!" said Bucks. He got up with his head hanging low, annoyed with his lack of ability to masturbate, which normally came as so second nature. He shook his head at the limp dick in his hand like it was a child who had deliberately disobeyed him after years of dutiful subservience.

"I told you, Buckaroo. You should've thought about your sister, just like I did," said Danny.

"DANNY. HOW MANY TIMES DO I NEED TO TELL YOU THAT I NEVER TOUCHED MY FUCKING SISTER!?" Bucks screamed, crunching the cookie in his hand.

"Eat these up and I'll never mention her again," Danny said, pointing at the biscuits, then winking at him.

Vvvvrrrmmm-vvvrrrmmm.

"Fucking hell, Leander. Are you going to be texting Myra all night or what? Turn that phone off. You know the rules," said Jez.

"Sorry guys. I don't know why she's texting me so much," Leander replied, never moving his eyes away from the phone.

"Maybe she thinks you're with Bucker's sister."

"DANNY! SERIOUSLY! SHUT THE FUCK UP!"

"Get your arse over here, Bucks. There's nowhere to hide. Come and take your punishment like a man. We're all waiting, and our patience is beginning to wear thin," said Jez.

"A bit like your dinner," said Bruce, ripping open

a packet of paper plates.

The guys all laughingly gathered around in a circle and placed their biscuits on one of the disposable dishes brought along for supper. Leander broke out of the pack, glaring at his phone with widened eyes and a creased brow, whilst Joey skipped off and slipped inside his tent. The others all remained, watching Bucks, who was still staring at his flaccid cock, not caring that it was on full display. After another sigh, he zipped himself back up and walked slowly towards the rest of the lads.

"Myra, I don't know what you're talking about," Leander said. The boys all looked at each other with curious glee in their eyes. "I didn't do anything!" Leander said, unconsciously tugging on his hair. "Myra? Myra! Fuck!" he said, staring at his phone in shock. "She fucking hung up on me!"

"Everything alright?" asked Bruce, barely containing the ripples of laughter behind his pursed lips.

Leander ignored him and walked off instead, attempting to call Myra back.

"What was that all about?" asked Danny, to no one in particular.

"No idea," replied Jez.

"She must've found out," said Bruce, not looking at anyone.

"Found out what?" asked Buckleby as he joined the circle.

Joey came out of his tent, holding a BB gun in his hand. "I didn't wanna resort to this, Bucks, but if you're gonna be a massive pussy about it," he said, raising the gun at Buckleby's face, "eat those fuckin' biscuits."

Buckleby looked at everyone else in a panic for support, but nobody offered any. "Guys, come on," he said with his hands raised, trembling, "I'm sure we can come to some kind of agreement."

"The agreement was that the loser had to eat all of the biscuits, Bucks," said Bruce.

"Yeah, man. You know the rules. Eat up," said Joey, pointing the muzzle right between Buckleby's eyes.

"You don't really expect me to eat those fucking things, do you?" asked Buckleby, still looking imploringly at the others, his voice now shaking as much as his hands.

Nobody said anything. Joey cocked his gun. "Pick one of them up, or I'll shoot," he said, edging closer to Bucks.

"This is sick," he said, "what the fuck is wrong with you guys?!"

"You shouldn't have agreed to play if you weren't prepared to suffer the consequences, Bucks," said Danny. "Anyway, stop pretending you won't love it."

"As if! Please, guys, I'll do anything. Just don't make me eat those things. It's disgusting."

Leander returned, startling everyone with his sudden reappearance. His eyes were lightning struck with vermillion vessels and a slug-like slither of snot had gathered around his nose. "I know. Instead of eating the biscuits, each one of us gets to shoot you with the BB gun. How's that sound?" he said, ignoring all acknowledgement of his appearance.

"Urm. Yeah, that sounds fair," Buckleby replied.

"Mmm," said Danny, "it's not really the same though, is it? BB guns don't even hurt."

"No. They don't," said Bruce, crossing his arms.

"Neither does eating semen though," said Jeremy.

"Tell that to Myra," said Leander.

Everyone looked at each other, unsure whether they should laugh. Nobody did, except with their eyes. The glare of the sun tore across the scene, highlighting their hair into golden shades, whilst the sorry-looking biscuits remained in shadow because of their upright, developing bodies. Nobody realised it, but they were all staring at the cookies, each lost in similar, yet obscure thoughts.

"Just get it over with and shoot me with the gun," Buckleby pleaded, breaking the eerie silence, "that's my decision."

"Sounds good to me," said Joey, eager to pull the trigger.

"I know," said Jez, "we all get to shoot Buckleby. In the arse."

"Great suggestion, Jez," said Bruce.

"Why the arse?!" asked Buckleby.

"It's either that or you eat the fucking biscuits, Bucks," said Leander, with spittle flying out of his mouth.

"What's it gonna be Buckaroo? Biscuit Bukkake or Five Shots in the Arse?" asked Danny, giggling before all the others joined in.

Buckleby stood there, pondering his choice. He looked at the gun, then the cookies, then at the gun again. "Alright," he said, "I'll take the bullets. But nothing from close range. You guys need to be at least ten feet away from me."

"I'll go first," said Joey, waving the gun behind his back, signalling the others to form an orderly line.

The boys all started pissing themselves again, just as excited at the prospect of shooting Bucks in the butt as they were with him eating the biscuits. For the time being, it was enough to stop them asking Leander about Myra, but they were all wondering about it.

Danny grabbed a bottle of vodka from his tent. "Now seems a good a time as any to start drinking, wouldn't you say lads? A shot for a shot?"

They all agreed.

"None for me, thanks," said Bruce, second in line behind Joey. Jez quickly followed, taking the third position. Danny necked a few shots down and passed it over to Leander, who in return let Danny go ahead of him in the queue.

"Okay," said Buckleby, standing in front of his tent. "I'm ready."

Joey began to take aim, but Bruce pushed his arm back down. "You've gotta pull down your trousers first," he said, winking at the rest.

"What?! Nobody said anything about that."

"It's a fuckin' BB gun, Bucks. You won't feel anything with those cargo pants shielding the target. Take 'em down!" screamed Joey.

"Sounds fair," said Danny, chuckling away.

"Yeah. Pull those fucking pants down," said Leander.

"Are you serious?!" remarked Bucks, in a tone half horrified, half aroused.

"Deadly," said Jez, "what did you think I meant by 'in the arse?'"

To everyone's surprise, the expected and incessant protesting from Buckleby wasn't delivered, and before they knew what had hit them, he'd unbuckled his belt again and slowly revealed his pasty, pale arse.

"Fuck me, I felt a sea change. That thing is paler than the moon!" said Danny, guffawing away with Jez.

Even Buckleby began giggling until Joey wrapped his finger around the trigger and pulled.

-THWACK-

"ARGH!" Buckleby screamed like a five-year-old princess, scaring a flock of birds into flight. An instant red-patch arose on the right side of his buttocks. Joey high-fived all the rest of the guys like he'd achieved something, then took his shot of vodka. Bruce took the gun from his hand and lined up for his shot.

"I'm aiming straight for the centre," he said, stumbling at the end of his sentence.

Danny looked over his shoulder to see that Leander had drunk nearly half the bottle of vodka already. The latter just shrugged at his observation, took his phone from his pocket and handed it over to him. "Film my go," he whispered into his ear.

-PANG-

"Arghhhhh!" said Bucks, wriggling on the spot after the second blow, which hit him on the left side this time around. With uproarious laughter, Bruce went to pass the gun over to Jez, but Leander barged-in and snatched it.

"My turn," he demanded, pushing everyone else back.

"Hey, it's my go next!" said Jez in protest, but Leander dismissed him.

"How many rounds does this hold, Joey?" he asked.

"Urm. About fourteen," he replied.

"Was it fully-loaded before you started shooting?"

"Yeah..."

Leander didn't need any further information. After checking that Danny was filming, he just let rip. "Take this, Bucks," he said, -BANG- taking a step further -THWACK- towards him after unleashing -PING- each bullet. At first, Buckleby just screamed like a little girl playfully enjoying herself, but once Leander got within a few feet, blood began to seep out of his arse.

-BANG-SMACK-THOMP-

"What the fuck are you doing man?" said Buckleby, trying to move away, but falling face first to the ground due to the trousers around his ankles.

"Ah, no you don't," said Leander, pumping the eighth, ninth and tenth pellet at Buckleby's now sad and sorry-looking arse. He wriggled on the floor as the others looked on in shock at Leander with a mischievous look of perverted enjoyment behind their apparent disbelief.

"Please, no more," begged Bucks, "it really fucking hurts!"

"Shut the fuck up," said Leander, thrusting the gun between Buckleby's buttcheeks and pumping him with the remaining bullets. Two dead thuds were heard along with the ripping of clumped grass inside of Buckleby's hands. His body convulsed as his head hit the floor. The blades of grass fell from his clenched fists like the blood slithering down his arse-crack. Muffled sobbing soon followed. "That's what you get for not playing by the rules, faggot," said Leander, dropping the gun to the ground. It seemed like he was going to walk away whilst swigging on the bottle again, but as his foot brushed past the plate of biscuits, an idea gleamed across his eyes.

He scooped up the dish and stormed back over to Buckleby, who was still crying into the earth. The rest all watched on as their friend seemingly lost his mind.

"Time for dinner," said Leander. "Open wide, bitch."

"Don't!" protested Buckleby, but it was all in vain. Leander slammed the biscuits onto his face. Cum-layered crumbles appeared around the still visible sides of Buckleby's cheeks almost instantly, as Leander spread the plate around in a circular motion, pressing down as hard as he could until the plate crunched in half around Buckleby's nose. Leander pushed himself back upright from his forehead, leaving the plate behind. He marched through the crowd of onlookers without looking back. The plate slowly peeled away from Buckleby's face. His eyes were half-shut, already pinkened and swollen. His nose looked like it was dribbling with translucent white snot whilst the crumbles on his forehead twinkled under the setting sun.

"D'you get all that, Danny?" Leander suddenly asked. Danny nodded, still watching Bucks, who was weakly spitting and spluttering out his dinner. Leander grabbed the phone from Danny's hand without him even noticing.

"What the fuck was that man?!" asked Jez, appalled.

"Dude. That was brutal," said Joey.

"Yeah man, I mean come on. I know he lost and everything, but I don't think he deserved that," said Bruce.

"Oh, shut the fuck up you guys. It's not my fault if he doesn't stick to the rules. You know the drill.

You all loved it anyway. Didn't see anyone trying to stop me."

"Yeah but dude, look at Bucks. You destroyed him," said Danny.

"Oh, fuck you guys. He's fine. It won't be the first time he takes it in the arse," said Leander, checking his phone again.

"What's up with you man? Is something wrong?" asked Jez.

"Nothing. I'm fine," Leander said, walking away.

"Where are you going?" asked Bruce.

"Away from here. I need some space," he replied, walking towards the darkened path that trailed into the belly of the forest.

"Come back man," said Bruce. "You shouldn't go into the woods alone."

The others all pleaded along with Bruce, all to the unhearing ears of Leander. He began running straight into the forest, never once looking back to see if anyone was following him and darted along the thin, leaf-covered path into the darkness.

"Let's go get him," said Bruce, already running.

"Alright," said Joey, "wait a sec though, I'll get some more ammo and a torch." He dashed in and out of his tent again and quickly followed behind Bruce, snatching the gun from the ground beforehand. Danny and Jez just stood there, dumbfounded, looking at one another like they saw no reason to go after Leander. It went unnoticed, as Bruce and Joey were already gone.

"What the hell was that all about?" asked Jez.

"No idea," Danny replied. "Must've had something to do with that phone call though. You alright Bucks?"

They both looked over at him. He was still lying on the ground, unmoving, making no effort to wipe away the semen-seasoned crumbs glazed over his countenance.

Leander ran through the forest, away from the pleading cries of Bruce and Joey, which grew in distance the more he sprinted. The remaining light of day was enough to help him see where he was going, despite being noticeably darker than before. Everything around him felt dank and sticky. However, these observations were disregarded. He needed to speak to Myra, but as she hadn't picked up after a lost-count amount of calls, he knew she wasn't going to answer. She had found out what he did, but how, Leander had no clue.

Distracted by the unchanging glare of the screen, Leander was stopped in his tracks by a sign blocking the path. It stood askew in the growing thickness of the mud he was trekking through. He put away his phone and went to shove the sign out of the way, but noticed some scribbling on the plank of wood nailed onto the post:

NO TRESPASSERS BEYOND THIS POINT
persecutors will be violated!

Leander stared at it, a little scared, but mostly confused, as beyond the sign there was nothing but shrubs, pools of thick mud and an endless stream of trees.

Vvvvrrrrmmm-Vvvvrrrmmmmmmm.

"Myra?! Myra. What's happened? Please tell me. I don't understand why're you're so upset."

"I'm only calling because I just got my period, Leander."

"What does that mean?" he asked, "you thought you were pregnant?"

"For a while, yes. I thought I was. Then I thought, *how can I be pregnant? Leander always uses a condom*, don't you Leander?!"

"What?! Yeah, of course I do!" he pleaded.

"Then how come I found an empty condom at the end of my bed, stuffed behind the mattress, Lee?"

"What? I don't know what you're talking about."

"Don't give me that. You fucking stealthed me! There was nothing in the condom! Nothing! Not even a drop—"

"I don't know—"

"Oh, don't pretend! I know it's all the rage to whip it off when we're not looking! I could get you done for rape!"

"That condom could just be old, Myra, come on. Think about it, please. I'm begging you here," he said, his voice shivering.

"Yes, I thought that too, but then I remembered. That disgusting smell of semen never goes away, no matter how old. You did it, didn't you!? Just admit it!"

Leander paused.

"Oh my God! You did do it!! I knew it! What the fuck is wrong—"

"No, I didn't! Well, not intentionally! Please, I promise. It was an accident," Leander pleaded.

"An accident? A fucking accident? *'Oh look, the condom fell off. Must've been too big for me. Oh well, might as well fuck her anyway.'* I bet that's what you thought—is that what you thought Leander? Come on, tell me!"

"No. I don't know, alright? It must've just come off. I don't know!"

"How could you not know?! You always complained about using them, always! Argh, god, you so did do it on purpose! Don't think for one second that you're going to get away with this!"

"Myra, I don't know what to say. Please. I'm sorry—"

"*Don't ever speak to me again!* We're done!"

"MYRA!" Leander screamed, but it was all too late. He'd heard that tone before. She was gone. He frantically tried to call her back, but she'd already turned off her phone.

"Leander! Leander," he heard, this time not too far away. Unable to face his friends for now, the tear-ridden Leander booted the sign over and decided to take his chances. Using the branches of trees to keep himself upright, he carried on moving forward with mucous and tears once again spewing out of his face. After around twenty or thirty paces, he was confronted with a set of three pathways. The one on the right, his first choice by instinct, looked to be the best lit, but as Leander walked down it he noticed the footprints he was leaving behind. Fearing an easy detection, he walked another twenty or so paces, then carefully, but as quickly as he could, trailed back on himself. Once back in front of the paths, he grabbed as many leaves as he could, skipped down the trail on the left and covered his footprints with the gathered leaves. After a few minutes, he had disappeared.

"Leander!" cried Bruce upon reaching the sign, which had fallen face first into the dirt, concealing its written warning.

"LEANDER!" Joey shouted behind. They both looked at the sign and Joey went to pick it up.

"Joe, look," Bruce said, pointing at the footprints in the mud. "They must be Leander's."

Joey, distracted, forgot about the sign and peered at the tracks. He got up to his feet again and started following Bruce, who had already made some decent ground on him. He struggled a bit through the mud, annoyed his trainers were ruined and came up behind Bruce again, who was staring at the pathways.

"Look!" said Joey, taking his turn to point at the prints on the right path. "Let's go man."

"Wait. You didn't think I came out here for Leander, did you?" asked Bruce, facing Joey.

"What d'you mean?" asked the latter.

"You know," said Bruce. "Look. There's a tree trunk down the middle path. Why don't we head down there? At least we can sit down then."

"Alright. Sounds good. We'll be able to hear Leander when he comes back either way then too."

"Exactly," said Bruce. "You got any weed on you?"

"Already ahead of you mate," Joey said, taking a tin out of his pocket. "Let's get baked while we wait," he said, laughing.

"Let's," replied Bruce, winking at Joey and placing his arm around his shoulder as they headed for the stump.

Back at camp, Danny had got busy by getting a bonfire going and Jez begun cooking some sausages. Buckleby had finally gotten up to his feet, but when Jez tried to speak with him, he just gave him the finger and dived into his tent.

"Those smell fucking good," said Danny, tearing open a packet of buns. "Think I might eat the lot."

"Me too," replied Jez, passing the joint they were smoking back over. "You think we should go looking for the others?"

"Fuck no," Danny retorted, taking the spliff.

Jez slapped the sausages into some buns, "here you go, dude."

Danny took his hotdog and looked it over. "Cheers man, but this isn't done enough for me. I like my food cooked," he said, taking it out of the bun and sticking it back over the fire.

"They look fine to me," said Jez, eagerly munching away. "Shall we offer Bucks one?"

"Yeah. Hey, Buckleby! You want a hotdog?!" asked Danny.

The crackling of the fire was all that could be heard. Danny spun his sausage around whilst Jez carried on eating. They cracked open a couple of beers, courtesy of Danny. The zip of Buckleby's tent slowly came up and out he stepped, clutching a large, cylinder-shaped object.

"Is that a water gun?" asked Jez.

"Looks like it to me," said Danny.

"This isn't just any old water gun, lads. This," he said, holding it up for admiration, "is a Super Soaker Constant Pressure System 2000. Banned in thirty-nine states across the U.S. and considered too dangerous for retail here in the U.K. I only brought it along in case somebody fucked up with the fire. Now I have it for a much better purpose. Check this out," he said, pointing it at Leander's tent. In a terminator pose, Buckleby thrust-pumped the gun three times, causing his grip on it to shake and vibrate, looking as if it might explode. He pulled the trigger. With a singeing hiss, a gush of yellowish liquid blasted away from the nozzle with such a force that Leander's tent lifted from the ground, popping some of the pegs out of the grass along with it.

"Woah," said Danny, marvelling the mechanism of the rifle.

"That is fucking sick," said Jez in awe.

"Told you. Now, I hope both of you need a piss. I've only got half a tank of ammo left here. There's a dead man wondering around the woods out there begging for a good soaking."

Danny and Jez looked at each other and smiled. The former's sausages were done. He tossed them both into buns, threw one in his mouth and gave the other to Buckleby, which he swallowed down in practically one gulp. Danny and Jez unbuckled their belts for the second time that evening, as the nocturnal tweeting of an owl could be heard from the ever-darkening forest.

Leander stood by the swing of a tree, glaring up at an owl perched upon one of its branches. It had gotten darker, but the red paint on the wooden seat of the swing was still visible. He figured he had about an hour of natural light left. Everything looked tinged with midnight blue, except for the still-rising moon, which glowed with a sickening yellow.

He wiped away the last rivulets of tears from his face and sat down on the swing. The branch above him creaked, but only ever-so-slightly. He began thinking about Myra again as he slowly rocked. He knew what he did to Bucks was wrong, but something had overtaken him after Myra called. She'd accused him of being a monster, and then he acted just like one. But he shrugged it off, knowing that Bucks probably enjoyed the attention in secret anyway, and vowed to apologise to him after a quick swing and smoke. He lit his cigarette, checked his phone one more time to see nothing had changed, then pushed himself back with his feet and started swaying. After a few swings, he realised he could get quite high if he wanted to, so he did. He wanted to feel like he was floating in mid-air, away from everything the world was offering, to be in a place where what he did didn't matter, as he was just floating through life like he was meant to. As he relaxed, taking in the heat-filled air, swinging higher than he could've ever imagined, the rope snapped.

"ARRRRGGGHHHHH," echoed an agonising scream through the central path of the forest Bruce and Joey were sitting in. "What was that?" asked Joey, breaking away from Bruce.

"What was what?" the latter asked, going in to kiss him again. Joey refused his advance, so Bruce moved around to his ear instead.

"That sounded like Leander man, but like he was hurt. Real hurt," said Joey, staring at the swaying leaves and branches.

"Well," Bruce said, nibbling on Joey's earlobe, "maybe he deserves a little pain."

"What?" asked Joey, pushing Bruce back again.

"Oh, come on, Joe. You must know as well. You're just as close to him as I am."

"Know what?" Joey asked honestly, placing his hand on Bruce's chest.

"You really don't know why Myra called?"

"No. Why should I?"

"Because Leander stealthed her, that's why."

"*Ahhh, shit.* I didn't know. That's fucked up... what's stealthing?"

"Seriously?" Bruce asked, ruffling his hair. "You don't know?"

"Never heard of it," he said.

"You sure you want to know?" asked Bruce.

"If you know, I should know."

"Good point," remarked Bruce. They shared another kiss.

"Come on, tell me already. I'm dying to know now."

"Alright. So, this is done intentionally, okay?"

"Okay..."

"Okay. Basically, 'stealthing', as it's called, is when a guy wears a condom when he starts having sex, but who only does so because he knows, at some point, he'll remove it without the girl knowing and carry on anyway till the end."

"Without telling the girl?"

"Without telling the girl."

"Wow. That's sick. Wait, that's what Leander did to Myra?" asked Joey, shocked.

"That's what he told me. He bragged about it."

"What's there to brag about? She could've got pregnant or something. No, wait. Do you think that's why she called? She's up the duff?!" Joey asked, giggling.

"Who knows."

"Were you the one who told her?"

"Nope. Wasn't me. Who knows how—"

"Come on Bruce, you can tell me," said Joey.

"I would if I did. It wasn't even that long ago. Leander told me about it a couple of weeks back."

"Shit. Do you think he really did it on purpose?"

"No idea. Could've been an accident I guess."

"You haven't told anyone about us, have you?" asked Joey.

"Course not. Why would I?"

"I dunno. People talk," said Joey.

Bruce put his arm around him. "Don't worry about that."

"I think we should go find Leander and ask him."

"Alright, yeah. It's starting to get dark now anyway. Don't want to be out here all night."

They shared another kiss, then both stood up. "I hope the other guys are still at camp. There's something funny about this place," said Joey.

"Are you scared?" asked Bruce, teasing, going in to tickle him.

"No. Just saying. We're supposed to be hanging out together. Hey, stop that!" he said.

"Or what?" Bruce asked, aroused.

"Come on, I'm serious. Let's go."

"Alright, alright. Beat you there," Bruce said and started running.

"Oi!" Joey exclaimed. He ripped his shoes out from the mud and began to chase him. Within a few seconds, he'd nearly caught up.

"The sound came from over there," Bruce said, turning back at Joey. "We should find him in no time—"

"Bruce!" Joey cried, watching him go flying over, but, having failed to see what had caused it, soon tripped over the same fallen branch that sent Bruce tumbling. They both landed face-first into a pile of thick, sludgy mud. Joey pushed himself back up and checked to see if Bruce was okay. After lifting him, he saw that he was. They were both covered in dense, brown sludge, practically from head to toe. The two of them started laughing. "Oh well," said Joey, "I've got some spare clothes back at camp."

"Yeah, same here. Never mind," said Bruce, laughing.

"What the fuck is that?" asked Joey, pointing behind Bruce.

They both looked. Hanging from a branch was a group of six used tampons, all dangling there like a set of wind chimes. A sudden looming sensation overtook the two of them. They looked at one another. The whiteness of their eyes was still visible, but the gleam in both was gone. Before they got up again, an exchange of smiles occurred, but neither realised that their cheeks had never creased in such a manner before.

"Hurry up, Danny," said Bucks, "Leander's nearby. I can taste him."

Danny had just chucked away the beer can that he brought along with him and was looking for a decent place to piss. "Just be a second mate, take it easy," he said, "no one can ignore a call from mother nature."

"Just get it done. I wanna see Leander's sorry fucking face when I blast him with this beauty."

"Yeah, we know Bucks. You've said it a thousand times already."

"Don't get shirty with me Jez," said Bucks. "I should shoot both of you for doing nothing back there."

"You should've eaten the biscuits," said Danny,

accompanied by the soundtrack of his flowing piss, "none of us would be here otherwise."

"He's got a point, Bucks," said Jez.

"Like any of you would've eaten those things."

"You'll never know now," said Jez, unexpectedly letting out a burp, surprising even himself.

"You done yet Dan?!" asked Bucks.

"Getting there."

"Fucking hell, you're like a horse."

"Not the first time someone's said that to me," Danny replied, turning towards them yet laughing to himself. "You two wanna hold it?"

"No thanks," Jez replied. One of his hands never seemed to move away from his stomach.

Danny shook away the last drops. As he did, his dick caressed a large, bristling leaf. "Arghhh, *fuck*," he said, tucking his manhood away.

"What happened?" asked Bucks.

"Nothing, nothing. *Ahh, shit man*," said Danny, the urge to itch instantly taking over him.

"Dude, what's going on?" asked Jez, his voice carrying a frog-like belch behind it.

"Nothing. It's just my cock. I touched some fucking leaf with it. Stung like shit. *Ouch, Jesus*. Any of you guys got some water?"

"Only the piss-water in this gun. Come on Danny, don't be such a puss," said Bucks.

"It really fucking stings man! I'm burning up."

"Man, my stomach doesn't feel so hot," said Jez.

"Listen up you two fags. Leander's out there, waiting for his punishment. If you two don't help me find him, I'll assume you're siding with him over me. And guess what that means?" he asked, pointing the pistol at Jez.

"Come on dude. Of course we're with you. Look! We're with you right now! *Argh*," he said.

"Yeah, come on man," said Danny, breaking out of the shrubs, scratching around his groin. "Let's just get this over with and get back to camp. I've got some cream back there that should take care of this."

"Guys. I don't feel so good," said Jez.

"Not you as well," said Harry, "the fuck's wrong with you?"

"It's that sausage," Danny replied for him, "I told you it wasn't cooked. You should throw it up. I knew a guy once who ate a bad sausage, ended up with six months of food poisoning."

"You serious?" asked Jeremy.

"Yup. He could've been exaggerating to get out of work though. I know I would."

"Bullshit," said Buckleby, "food poisoning doesn't last that long. A week tops. Guys! Come on! We've got a mission to do here. Stop being such pussies."

Jeremy stuffed some fingers into his mouth, tried to throw up, but only managed to cover his hand with saliva. "Nothing will come up."

"You gotta force it down there. Gag on that shit. Then you'll heave," said Danny, still scratching away.

"I did. Nothing happened. D'you think it's too late?"

"To what?"

"To throw up," said Jez.

"Is it ever too late to throw up?" asked Danny.

"I don't know," said Jeremy, letting spit fall from his mouth, "that's why I'm asking."

Danny shrugged and continued scratching his

balls. "Maybe when it's turned to shit."

"Oh, fuck this!" said Buckleby, limping away due to his injuries. "Who needs you guys anyway? I've got the gun. I'm going solo."

"No way, dude. I wanna see this," said Jeremy.

"Same here," said Danny.

"Well let's get fucking moving, shall we?" said Buckleby, "we haven't got all night."

"Actually, we do," replied Danny, "we're camping here, in case you forgot."

Buckleby sliced his gun through the air, halting at Danny's nose. "Any more lip from you and you'll get a blast, Danny. I'm sick of your shit."

"Calm down Bucks," said Jeremy, "you're not powerful with that fucking water-pistol. You look like a grown-up with the mental capacity of a five-year-old who's just shat his pants."

"Both of you shut the fuck up! Danny, don't think I didn't see you filming Leander whilst he attacked me. And you, Jez, with your big snarling grin. You did nothing. Both of you watched whilst I was being violated! I should spray the fuck out of you both."

The leaves above their heads suddenly ruffled inside a thrust of wind. They all looked at one another. Singular tweets from scowling birds rang around the damp, darkening forest, then a loud, agonising scream caused a flurry of wings to flutter all around. The guys looked up and watched as a set of crows disappeared from the underbelly they occupied. In unison, they cried: "Leander."

"That's him. I know that little girl's scream any-where! Right. This is happening. No more pissing about. Let's go! Danny, take your hands away from your cock for a change. You better fucking film this too. Jez, if you're going to throw up, do it now or keep it down. We've got a little faggot to find," said Buckleby, kicking the wayward shrubs out of the way without looking back, feeling masculine, yet looking feeble and somewhat deranged.

"I always forget what a massive twat he can be," said Danny.

"Yeah, I know what you mean. How's your dick?"

"Still stinging, but not too bad thanks. And your stomach?"

"Iffy."

"Smoke?"

"You've got more weed?"

"Yup. Brought some along just for me and you. The rest of those guys never fucking buy their own," said Danny, whipping out some pre-rolled joints. He gave one to Jez and slipped another into his mouth. "Can't wait to see Leander's face blasted with piss though."

"Same. But I bet Bucks finds a way of fucking it up."

"True," replied Danny, sparking up Jez's spliff and then his own. They both watched Buckleby, who was trying to avoid deep patches of mud like he was playing a special needs game of hopscotch all to himself. "D'you reckon the rumour about his sister is true?"

Jeremy shrugged. "I doubt it."

"Same. But you never know what people get up to behind closed doors," said Danny. "Some teacher once told me that for every hundred or so houses you drive by there'll be somebody inside one of them, fucking their dog. If that's true, which for some reason I think it probably is, then a sister doesn't sound so far-fetched." They shared a look. Jeremy said, "Fetch," and they both started giggling at the unintended pun. Afterwards, they recommenced following Buckleby's lead, a tad tentative about getting too close to him.

Leander lay on the ground, rolling from side to side. Whether the fall had made him pass out, or the vodka had put him to sleep he didn't know, but the throbbing pulse inside his swollen ankle had woken him up. His foot had landed right on top of a large, curved rock, instantly twisting his ankle. He didn't even remember screaming. His foot had swung back into place by itself. The swelling was instantaneous though and seemed to be worsening. He'd tried to check it, but even the slightest touch caused a thunder-bolt of pain to shoot up his spine, crushing any hope of getting back on his feet alone. Instead, he lay back on a bed of moistened leaves. The comforting warmth of sunlight was gone. Starlight twinkled behind the blur of his eyes. Their mysteriousness mocked him, but blanketed him all the same, until a strange, familiar scent made his nose twitch. Amongst the decaying leaves, half-hidden behind his medium-length chestnut hair, there was a condom, that had evidently been used.

Bruce and Joey made their way along the path, the latter with the dangling tampons in his hand, the former with the BB gun.

"Oh man. Bruce, wait a sec. I've still got mud in my eye," said Joey, stopping and trying to wipe his eye clean with the t-shirt underneath his jacket.

"We're both caked in mud man. What did you take

those tampons for anyway?"

"Just a little house warming gift for Buckleby's tent when we get back," he said, laughing, with one eye pinkening as he clawed at it. "I'm going to plant them inside his sleeping bag during the night."

"Great idea," said Bruce. "You ready?"

"Yeah. Let's go. Leander could be back at camp for all we know by now though."

"Nah, I know him too well. When he's this upset, he's liable to do just about anything," said Bruce.

They continued clambering through the muddy, moistened path, with their feet tearing off the mud like the tongue of a drunk's mouth away from his palette the morning after a heavy night. Everything was filtered in a neon, midnight blue and the moon was so huge and full, that the outline of the dark-side was clearly visible. The skittering of mice or rats caused each of them to flinch, but neither mentioned it to the other. Moss on the trees glistened in an opaque fashion, dripping and appearing to breathe whenever a gust of wind passed through the leafless, limb-bent trees. Though the forest appeared to hold nothing edible, it left a taste of something old and rotten in their mouths, of a food that had once been sweet. Neither Bruce nor Joey said anything, but they both couldn't wait to get back to camp, Leander or no Leander.

"Wait!" Bruce whispered to Joey. "I can see the other guys!"

"Where?" asked Joey, skipping forward to reach Bruce.

"Over there," he said pointing, "keep your voice down."

Joey turned and saw Harry limping and charging

through the trees, whilst Danny and Jez followed behind, looking like lepers.

"Ha! Two minutes in the forest and look at them, they're all nearly dead!" said Bruce in delight.

They both laughed in a hushed manner.

"Should we follow 'em?" asked Joey.

"Course we should. Who do you think that water-gun is for?"

Once again, they laughed, then scurried around the left side of the path to get behind them.

Leander, still unable to get up after a few unsuccessful attempts, lay on the ground with the blurred constellations above beaming inside his eyes. His phone had died from trying to call Myra so much and without assistance, he knew he'd struggle to get back to camp. Something about him didn't care though. An object directly above him in front of the stars had taken his attention, despite him not knowing what it was. To Leander, it looked like an old pillow-case that'd been ripped open and tossed up on the branch, or possibly part of a puffy, child-sized jacket. It hung there, without moving, even when a strong breeze passed through the frozen-claw like branches of the time-chiselled trees. The tree which he had swung and fallen from, was now mocking him with a cruel inscription:

M & L Forever

It wasn't something Myra and Leander had done, but there it was, a couple with the same initials staring back at him, reminding him of what he'd just lost.

"Well, well, well," said Buckleby, tearing through a couple of matching bushes. "What's the matter dude, need a helping hand?"

"Oh, thank fuck for that. Here," said Leander, "I twisted my ankle real fucking bad man. Help me up." He tried to push himself up with one hand whilst reaching out the other, but Bucks didn't even acknowledge it.

The light of Danny's phone soon shone upon the scene. Buckleby looked down at Leander with one side of his lip raised. Danny took a step closer whilst Leander threw Bucks and the lens looks of disconcertion. Jeremy stepped into the circular stage, gagging every minute or so, his skin now a perfect camouflage in the surrounding foliage. Buckleby aimed the gun.

"No! Don't man! I'm sorry—"

"Fuck you!" said Buckleby. He glanced at his tank. Only half a barrel of piss remained. He shook it. "Danny, wait a sec. I need to refill this quick."

"I'll be waiting."

"Oh god. Hurry up, Bucks. I'm dying over here," said Jeremy, blinking rapidly in a futile attempt to feel normal again.

"I told you, man. You gotta throw that shit up," said Danny.

Buckleby ignored them both, pivoted, whipped his cock out again for the third time that night and started pissing into the tank. Leander then realised what he was about to be shot with.

"You can't be serious!" he screamed, in such a panic his legs moved of their own accord. "*Arrgghhh! My fucking foot!*" he screamed, struggling. "This is sick! Danny, what are you filming this for, man?!"

Buckleby let out a scoff. "Every standard he has is doubled, I swear to god," he said, shaking out the final drops of his piss. "Danny, you still rolling?"

"Yep. Ready when you are, Bucks."

"Good," he said, popping the cap back on as he lifted the pistol for focus, "I'm aiming for the middle of those beady-little eyes of his."

"Bucks! Don't do this man!" Leander pleaded.

Buckleby pumped the barrel.

"Please, dude! I can't even run away. This isn't fair."

A second thrust. "What? And I could when I had my trousers around my ankles?" Bucks asked.

Danny scoffed.

"Shut up Danny or you'll be next," said Bucks, thrusting number three, "you see how this baby shakes, Leander? It fires at sixty miles per hour from this range. ONE!"

"No! For fuck sake! I'm an injured man—"

"TWO!" Bucks screamed.

"Danny. Do something, man. What did I ever do to you?! Jez! Come on. This isn't right!"

"THR—"

A sudden flash of torch-light beamed into Buckleby's eyes, blinding everything around him.

-THWACK-

"ARRRRRGHHHHH!!!!!!!!" Buckleby screamed, clutching the side of his face. "You cunts! What the hell was that?"

Danny and Jez looked at one another, perplexed. Bucks dabbed his cheek with his fingers. Instead of his buttcheeks now the cheeks of his face were bleeding. He grabbed the gun, pointed and said,

"Which one of you did that?"

"Wasn't me man. I'm filming this shit," said Danny.

"Dude. I couldn't throw something if I wanted to. I feel like I've eaten a rat!"

"He's right, Bucks. It wasn't him. I was watching the whole thing," said Danny, holding his phone up.

"Bullshit," replied Bucks. "It must have been one of you—"

Another beam of blinding light pierced through his eyes.

-PING-

"ARGHH!! My fucking head!"

"Look! It couldn't have been us!" said Danny.

"Joey..." Bucks said, his voice trailing off.

"And Bruce," said Danny.

"Right. If you two don't come out here this instant, Leander's not the only one who's gonna get a face full of piss!" Buckleby screamed. He took a few steps closer to Leander, leaning right over him.

"Bucks man, it's not me doing the shooting, is it? Why not give them a little payback? It was Bruce's idea to smother you with the biscuits, not mine! He and Joey both talked me into it—I didn't even want to do it—I was angry—Myra broke up with me! Please, my ankle's killing me—I don't have any spare clothes. Be reasonable, dude."

"Be reasonable? Be fucking reasonable!? You shot me from point-blank range in the arse!" Buckleby screamed, stomping his foot into the ground.

"It was all Bruce's and Joey's idea. You know what they're like! If they're not bumming each other, they're both stirring shit around about us!" Leander pleaded.

The forest fell silent. Danny looked at Jez. Jez looked at Bucks. Leander at Danny. Back and forth they switched, never once seeing eye to eye. Each rustle of leaves, slither of moss or crunching of twigs seemed to point to where Bruce and Joey were hiding, but no one could detect them.

"Shoot," a voice called out from behind one of the shrubs.

"We didn't tell Leander to do shit, Bucks," another one called.

"No! That's bulls—"

"I knew it!" Bucks screamed. "Time for your payback, Leander! ONE!"

"No!!!"

"TWO!!!"

"FUCK YOU BUCKS!"

"THREE!!! TAKE MY PISS!"

Bucks went to pull the trigger, but another flash of light blinded him. Through desperation Leander grabbed a chunk of leaves behind him, feeling around for the rubber. Buckleby blocked the light out with his hand. A trail of piss pathetically sprayed out of the gun, reaching only between Leander's widespread legs. The BB gun went off. Leander's fingers tightened around the ring of the used condom. Buckleby smiled as he realised the bullet had missed him this time around and lifted the water-gun once more, pumping it again. From Danny's view behind the lens, Buckleby appeared to have an erection. The latter watched the crippled Leander scrambling on the ground and scoffed, relishing the power he had over him. With the gun upright again, he circled the muzzle around in a slow tease, taking his time over which part of

Leander's body to strike first. Suddenly, Leander stopped moving. The stand-off was seconds away from completion. Confused, Buckleby's eyebrow arched and he went to pull the trigger. "Oh, no you don't!" Leander screamed, tossing his arm forward.

-*SMACK!*-

Before Buckleby had time to react, the used condom flew straight into his open mouth and struck him in the back of the throat—causing him to jump back as he crashed to the ground, choking like a turtle on plastic.

"C H H H H A A A A A A A A A A A A A A A R R R R G G G G G-GEEEEEE!!!!!!!!!!" Joey and Bruce screamed, jumping through some shrubs like a couple of sasquatches on the hunt. Everybody screamed. Joey spun a tampon around his head like a pair of nun-chucks, tossing one straight at Jeremy. It hit his collarbone and slipped inside his shirt.

"Argh god, what the fuck is that?" Jeremy shouted, but Joey just tossed another one into his face. Bruce shot the BB gun at Leander's other foot, but he didn't even seem to notice. He was too preoccupied watching Buckleby trying to cough up the condom, fearing what he'd do when he did.

"That's what you get for blaming your dirty little deeds on us, faggot," said Bruce, shooting him again, but this time on the head.

"*Argh!*" Leander cried.

Danny, busy enjoying the view from his phone, nearly pissed himself as Bruce turned around and took aim at him. "Bruce! What the fuck have I done?!" he pleaded.

"Nothing. But I'm gonna shoot you anyway," said Bruce.

"No, please—"

-THWACK-

"ARGHHHOOUCCH! My cock! Never in the cock man!" cried Danny, falling to the ground. A tampon shortly whacked him on the head as Joey ran around like a bellowing Red Indian in delirium.

Jeremy wriggled like he'd just been laced with itching powder, whilst Buckleby lay on the ground, suffocating; until he finally managed to cough up the unknown object lodged in his throat. It flew out of his mouth, landing on the tip of a twig near the centre of the circle they were fighting in. Buckleby coughed until the pain in his lungs was felt by everyone. As he came to a stop, so had everybody else. Dangling in the middle of their warfare was a used condom, which had stopped each member of the group in their tracks—apart from Buckleby. He looked up. The abject terror of what had just been inside his mouth left him paralysed. Nobody could look at each other. The tampon finally fell from under Jeremy's jacket. As he saw it bounce and land on the bladder-browned leaves by his feet and realised what the rancid smell really was, his cheeks filled up like a balloon, but nothing more. Bruce laughed and shot Danny again, but he, ignoring the pain, began running towards him. With his head down, he charged forward and threw himself at Bruce, catching him in the chest and forcing them both down into a huge splodge of mud. As they fell, the wide-eyed horror inside Buckleby's eyes had morphed into a demonic-like rage of the most maniacal psychopath. Behind him, Joey was whacking the remaining tampons over his skull, but Buckleby didn't even flinch. Across his countenance bore the stoicism of the most methodical, thought-out plan of vengeance. He lifted the water-gun, pointing it over his shoulder. Joey, still in pandemonium, began mocking the supposed power of the pistol, with a cacophony of chirping laughter. "Go on then Bucks, fire your little girl's gun if it makes you happy!"

"This is for Leander," Buckleby said. He spun his legs around in a full circle, catching Joey's legs halfway. He fell back, tossing the remaining tampons in the air as he did, and landed on top of Bruce and Danny as they continued trying to kill each other.

Buckleby got up to his feet. He looked at Leander like he'd just murdered his mother. "You sick, twisted cunt," he said. "That condom could be riddled with all sorts of fucking diseases. And you threw it at me!"

"Bucks! I didn't mean to throw it in your mouth, I promise! It was just a lucky shot!" cried Leander with both his hands shaking in protest.

Bruce, Danny and Joey all started pissing themselves laughing. Jeremy leant forward with his hands on his knees, breathing like he was suffering from the worst type of constipation imaginable.

"Jez!" pleaded Leander, "please! Tell Bucks to put the gun down! This has got way out of hand!"

"Bucks," Jeremy mumbled, "don't you think we should get back... oh god..." he said upon the sight of another tampon, a few feet away from Leander's head. Mumbled gags soon followed.

"No, Jez, no, don't do it man!" cried Leander with his hands imploring. Danny, Joey and Bruce stopped fighting and watched eagerly as Jeremy struggled to fight back the onslaught of impending puke. He tried to move away from Leander, but

Buckleby forced him to stay static by threatening him with the water-pistol. With nowhere else to go, Jeremy looked at everyone except for Leander with pleading eyes, all to no reaction. Then it happened. Jeremy swung himself around, tried to run away, but simply couldn't manage to in time. Vomit erupted out of him with such a force that everybody flinched. Between his fingers, Leander saw a long stream of neon-yellow, layered with streaks of half-digested mayonnaise and clumps of pinkish offal. It crashed upon his groin with an acid singe, permanently destroying his trousers. Jeremy finally stopped, but a foaming of white bile had formed around his mouth. "Ahh fuck, I'm sorry man," he said whilst chunks were still falling from his mouth.

"Jez, you fucking cunt!" said Leander, fighting himself back from breathing as the acrid smell began to linger.

"Are you alright man?" asked Danny, at Jeremy rather than Leander.

Jeremy put up his hand, burped a couple of times between spits and settled on simply nodding his head. The others weren't quite sure whether what they'd just witnessed was hilarious or somewhat terrifying.

"Move aside, Jez," said Buckleby, "and stop trying to steal my thunder. Leander's my bitch now. Thanks for warming him up for me. Leander, open your mouth. I've got a little something I want you to swallow."

Leander didn't even protest.

"Jez. Did you hear me? Get out of the way or you'll get it too," said Bucks, lining up his shot.

"Dude, did you see what just came out of him?

Give him a minute man," said Bruce.

"Yeah Bucks," backed up Danny and Joey.

"*I don't care.* He didn't fucking shoot the BB gun into your arses, did he? This fucker's only getting half of what he deserves."

"Well, if you ate the biscuits like we agreed, we wouldn't be in this position, would we?" said Danny, taking his chances.

"If you thought I was going to eat all your sperm, you had another thing coming."

"Interesting choice of words," remarked Danny.

"Shut the fuck up. Jez. Move."

Jeremy stumbled away until he found a log and sat down. Licks of sweat appeared in patches all around his scarlet-blotched skin, like a woman who'd just given birth in the olden days.

"Actually," said Buckleby, "it looks like you just got my revenge for me, Jez. I've had a sudden change of heart. Shooting Leander now will only clean him up. So, I guess," he said, turning towards Bruce, Joey and Danny, "you guys will have to take my load instead."

"Bucks! Come on man," said Joey.

"Yeah man, what did we do?!" asked Bruce.

"Dude, don't even think about it!" said Danny.

"It's what you didn't do you fucking arseholes," said Bucks. He began pumping away on his gun again until it physically hurt him to pump anymore. The guys looked at each other, knowing nothing was going to change Buckleby's mind now.

"Drink my piss," were Buckleby's signature choice of words just before pulling the trigger. The guys all winced and held up their hands. They waited inside the blackness of their eyes—but nothing happened.

"What the fuck now?!" shouted Bucks, shaking the unfired water-gun. The trigger pulled back, but no liquid had released. Buckleby stopped shaking it around and examined it instead. He checked the barrel, which was obviously still full. Then he put his ear to it. Nothing unusual there. Finally, he gave it one more pump, but again nothing happened. "This doesn't make any sense. The one time I want nothing more than to blast this thing," he said, placing the gun upright between his legs to check the nozzle, "and it doesn't fucking work—"

-SWWWWIIIIIIIIIISSSSSSSSSSSSSHHHHHHHHHHHH-HHHHH-

A torrent of teenage urine blasted Buckleby, soaking his entire face before it escaped from the grip of his dangly legs. The gun spun in a frenzy, spraying everywhere and hitting everyone. Each lad, except for Leander and Bucks, all threw themselves behind any makeshift barricade they could find, ducking behind the fallen trunks of trees and the bushiest shrubs around. They didn't manage to avoid getting hit, but they took far less damage than the two men they left behind. Through quick glances sneaked in whilst the water-gun continued spinning, Buckleby stamped his foot down on it. Whilst it carried on spitting out urine, he pointed it straight at Leander, but just as he did, the gun stopped spurting.

"Oh, for fuck sake!" screamed Buckleby in a tantrum. He checked the barrel, which somehow still had about a third of piss remaining. So, once again, he began to pump. Whilst he did, his back was turned to Bruce, Danny and Joey, whose heads were all peering over a log. They each saw Leander, looking helpless in the face of his fate until Bruce noticed the BB gun by the side of his hand. Whilst Buckleby grunted out his frustration, Bruce tossed the gun to Leander, who caught it clean through his desperation. Without a second of hesitation, he let rip, for the second time that night, at Buckleby's backside.

-THWACK-PING-THOMP-SMACK-POW-DINK-

The scattered pellets pierced into Buckleby's back, sending him falling to his knees again, but he swiftly turned around with the water-gun ready.

"Bucks! This is getting way out of hand. Let's call a truce dude! We're going to fucking kill each other if we don't stop soon," said Leander, holding his hands up in surrender.

"Yeah Bucks, this is getting dull now," Jeremy said, coming out of his shelter.

"Dude, Jeremy's right. We should be having a blast, not blasting each other with piss," said Danny, following his lead, finding his phone in the mud, half-covered in vomit. The rest came out shortly. Buckleby looked at them, with drops of urine falling from his hair. He looked exhausted, beaten, and on the brink of tears.

"I wanted to have a good time as well you know," he said, "but that fucker ruined a perfectly good night for me. Don't you guys think he deserves some retribution?!"

"Look at him, Bucks," said Danny.

"Yeah man," said Bruce, "he's had his comeuppance. He's covered in puke for fuck sake. And look, it's nearly dark. We need to get out of this forest soon."

"If I put this down, he'll shoot me again," said Buckleby, keeping his sights on Leander.

"No, he won't," said Joey, "will you, Lee?"

"No. I've had enough too. I just want to go back to camp. Or maybe even home. The gun is out of bullets anyway."

"Prove it," demanded Bucks.

"Fine," said Leander, pointing it above his head. He pulled the trigger. A pellet flung out and hit the branch above him. All the others looked up, except for Bucks.

"You see guys? He was fucking lying again."

"I didn't think there was any left man," Leander said. "Look." He fired again. The chamber was empty. But Bruce, Danny, Joey and Jez weren't paying attention. Under the moonlight, they watched the strange, white-flaps Leander noticed before, twisting around the twig that was keeping it up there. A chilling, death-like gust of wind brushed over the mysterious object. As it passed, everything turned still. It seemed to drain away the arguing voices of Buckleby and Leander, who both soon noticed what was keeping the attention of the others. Leander craned his neck upwards to see what was so fascinating, only for the twig to snap. The flappy object fell directly downwards, opening itself up before landing straight on Leander's face. It wasn't a soft, comforting pillow as he had first thought, or a weather-worn blanket, nor a child's puffy jacket. It was a nappy. A thoroughly and recently used nappy. It crashed onto Leander like an industrial boot to wet, thick mud, covering his entire face with shit. He didn't move. None of the boys did. They all just stood around, feeling sorry for their friend, but more relieved that it wasn't them it'd happened to.

After a few minutes, Leander peeled off the nappy

and began to cough and splutter, attempting to vomit himself, but couldn't. "Bruce... Joey... anyone, just please, help me up."

All the boys assisted him except for Buckleby. After directing them to put him up against a tree, Leander scurried them away and told Buckleby to fire his gun.

"Are you sure?" Bucks asked, turning towards him with a worsened limp.

"I'm covered in shit and vomit. My ankle is killing me. I just want to get back to camp. One of you guys must have some spare clothes, right?"

A few heads nodded.

"But you'll be soaked," said Bucks.

"Not as soaked as your sister was when you fingered her," Leander replied. It worked. Before he could even flash Bucks a smile, a huge gush of piss-water hit him directly in the face. He cleaned himself up the best he could. The battle, if it could be called as such, was over.

In silence, the boys all walked back to camp together, taking turns to help Leander stay upright. Along the way, they found a suitably sized stick for him to use as a makeshift crutch. Jeremy, though still feeling rather ill, managed to keep himself in check. With enough weed, Danny forgot about the reddening rash around his groin. The mud on Bruce and Joey's faces eventually dried and, though unknown to the rest of the lads, they both felt very comfortable with the masks they were wearing. Buckleby, unable to tolerate the taste in his mouth, excused himself for a piss as they neared the camp, to urinate into his hand and wash out his mouth. Using the torch as a guide, they managed the task with surprising ease. Joey and Danny passed around the spliffs they'd brought with them. Despite not making any jokes, each one of the lads let out an occasional chuckle as they recalled the maddening events of the evening. They couldn't tell if they were laughing at the horror, or at what had happened to each of them as they entered the forest, but they all felt it had a strange knowingness about it, which baffled their teenage minds. As Leander stepped over the warning sign he came upon so shortly after entering the woods, the sudden dread of what happened after he ignored it sent a shudder through his spine. He felt no need to tell the others about it though.

"Guys. Just so we're clear," said Jeremy as they neared the end of the path, "what happened in the forest—"

"Stays in the forest," said Danny, finishing off his sentence.

The rest nodded or vocalised their approval. As Bruce broke through the final shrub, Joey's torchlight touched upon the camp. It had changed since they left it, not in a metaphorical way, but a literal one.

"What the fuck," said Bruce. The others all rushed over to join him by his side.

"Great," said Danny.

"Perfect," said Jez.

"I can't believe this," said Bucks.

They each stared ahead at the flattened tents before them, visible only through the torch. There was no exception; every shelter for the night had crashed down into a pathetic heap. After a few minutes of staring at the camp in silence, they made their way over to it and briefly attempted to put their tents back up, but it proved to be too tough of a task. The gusts of wind were too strong and most of the pegs had either vanished or were impossible to find amongst the overgrown grass. After a discussion about whether to go home or not, the boys soon concluded that it'd take them just as long to walk back than it would to simply spend a sleepless night where they were. So, they collected what comforters they could find from their pancaked tents and gathered around the remaining embers of the fire from earlier. Once huddled, they lay down together and hugged one another in the spooning position. Buckleby, who was at the front, hugged no one. Leander, who was at the back, was hugged by no one. Nobody really slept, as the blankets they used couldn't possibly conceal the amalgamated stench of their closed-in, foul-smelling bodies. The only positive, from Buckleby's point of view at least, was that he finally managed to get an erection. The rest of the boys all listened, but kept silent, as he masturbated until completion.

They spent the night wrapped in each other's arms and legs, determined yet terrified, whilst the gaping, angular hole of the forest they'd entered and returned from, breathed over them. An abstract thought crossed through each of their minds during the night, but it was too opaque for them to properly conceptualise. Mother nature had exploited them all during the course of the evening, but had it simply exploited what it previously instilled? Whether any of them would ever come to question that, remained, like the future's that lay before all of them, and like all things in the world most dreaded—inside the blackness of the unknown.

SQUIRM

They were just your typical teenage boys who didn't even know they were born, as unimportant to the world as they were self-entitled towards it. Sure, they were aware of its foreboding outlook, but they were too busy diluting its intimidating glare with whatever drugs they could get their filthy virgin hands on. Fine, they'd been laid, but each one of them remained as clueless about the vagina as when they fell out of one. If a member of the group did happen to get lucky with whatever female he'd managed to trick, the rest of the herd heard about it before he'd even zipped up his fly. They were in the prime of their youth and, much like many others, they were pissing it all away with reckless abandon.

"You got any scissors, Jez?" asked Leander, running his hand through his fringe.

Ahh, Leander. If he wasn't playing with his pristine hair, rolling joints or ripping off the labels on beer bottles, he'd be masturbating in the corner of the dark room, usually over one of the groups' mothers—as he told it anyway. His mother, on the other hand, was a self-confessed entertainer in the performing arts. You know, the type to piss in a cup on stage and then drink it. Rumour had it around the time she was pregnant with him she'd moved on to the adult industry and in private would treat her more financially advantageous clientele by laying them under a glass table, squatting over it and... well, you get the picture. It was no surprise most of the group thought Leander had shit for brains.

"I'll go fetch some," said Jez as he skipped up the stairs like a kid on Christmas morning.

The rest of the flock, Bruce, Danny and Joey, took off their jackets and tossed them across the unmade bed or into the dark room beside it.

Jeremy's bedroom was situated in the basement, made up of two rooms of exactly the same size, separated by a single wall through the middle. It was coined the dark room because there was barely any light coming through the overgrown, foliage-blocked window. It had a lamp, a bucket and a single, beat-up old mattress inside and that was pretty much it. A modern-day, Eastern-European pimp would probably view it as ideal for his next trafficked beauty queen, as it had no exit. The boys generally avoided it unless they were too wasted to give a shit. The room they usually spent most of their time doing nothing wasn't much of an upgrade, but at least it had a small side toilet and a way out.

"Where's the special cocktail mixer?" Bruce enquired, peering his eyes down at everyone else. Joey giggled with a wide-eyed smile and eagerly showed him the contents of the white paper bag he was holding. "We got about a pint's worth of the stuff," he said. "This is gonna be fuckin' funny!" he guffawed, resembling an anorexic rat sniffing out cheese, but each member of the gang shared his enthusiasm—they couldn't wait for their guest of honour to arrive. Murmurs of 'sweet' and 'wicked' ricocheted between the formed huddle of their faces as they marvelled at the contents of the paper bag.

"Titboy's definitely coming, right?" Danny asked without looking up.

"Yup. He's got work till about eight. Gives us plenty of time," said Leander.

"We should order an Indian," said Danny, barely getting the words out of his mouth.

They all chuckled away like devilish schoolgirls as Jeremy returned, clutching a pair of scissors. He seemed to take his time, but it was assumed that he was telling his mother not to disturb them during the night, not that she ever did anyway. As luck would have it, she'd decided to spend the weekend at her own mother's, so the boys had the place all to themselves, but Jeremy decided to keep that quiet. He held the clippers in the air with a look of fervent joy in his eyes. "Here we go guys," he said. "Who wants to do the honours first?"

Leander raised his hand and snatched the scissors from Jez. "I'll go first," he said with pride, unbuckling his belt whilst propping himself up against the door. For a second it looked like he was about to urinate, but once the shrilling sound of a complete scissor cut rang around the room, the boys rip-roared into an explosive, uncontrollable paroxysm of laughter.

"Here you are, lads. In all its glory," Leander said, victoriously holding up a clump of his own pubic hair.

"Fuck me, you've got a black man's pubes," said Joey, smirking along with his rodent cackle.

"Shame they don't match up," said Bruce.

"These are man's pubes, my friends. Danny, you're up, man."

Leander threw him the scissors. Danny took his turn without any of his theatrics and before long the clippers had trimmed the whole bunch. Each one of the lad's pubic hair lay in a pile together on the floor like a burnt clump of satanic candy floss. Leander then took it upon himself to roll a few cigarettes, inserting the pubes inside with a disconcerting ease. He stored them away for later after he was done, inside an empty packet of tobacco he foraged from the lint-ridden floor of the dark room.

Then they bummed around smoking cigarettes, much like they did on most evenings, trying to make small talk over a few drinks but all that was really on their minds was Titboy's imminent arrival. After what felt like a lifetime, the doorbell rang. Each of the boys took a final glance at each other, but none of them said a word. The doorbell rang again. With a big Cheshire cat grin, Bruce made his way up the stairs.

"Let the party begin guys," he said, rattling the top hinge of the door as he left. The rest of the group now averted their eyes away from each other whenever their glances met. They listened on as Bruce's size thirteens stomped across the corridor. The Yale lock clicked and the front door swung open.

"How's it going, Jimbo?" asked Bruce, projecting his deep, sonorous voice down the corridor.

"Not bad. Just had work. Was shit."

"It's good to see you again man, been too long. How's life treating you?"

"Alright I guess, going to uni this Sept to study computer programming. In a few years, I'll be richer than all you chumps."

The flock then all locked their eyes upon one another, one by one, all nodding like what they were about to do was heroic. They continued listening as Bruce reeled Titboy in via the hallway.

"Haha, that's great, man," said Bruce. "You've always been pretty good with computers, haven't you?"

"Yeah. If that doesn't work out I can always become an accountant. I'm good with numbers too."

"I've always thought I was pretty good at calculating. Maybe I'll look into that myself," said Bruce.

"Really, *you?* You didn't even go to college, how're you gonna do that?"

"Plenty of ways these days," Bruce remarked.

"But you went travelling *straight after school*, I don't think you'll have too many options," said Titboy.

Bruce entered through the door with wild eyes and raised his eyebrows, "Hey guys! *Jim* is here."

"How's it going dude?" asked Leander.

"Alright dick heads? Long time," said Titboy, glancing around the room for somewhere to put his duffle coat.

"Good to see you, man," said Jez.

Joey made a fart sound with his mouth. The gang tried not to laugh but a couple of them couldn't contain themselves.

"I see your sense of humour hasn't changed much. Have you guys been drinking without *me*?" asked Titboy.

"Only just started. You know what a lightweight Joey is."

"I'm no lightweight, Danny boy. I could drink you all under the table."

"Yeah, yeah. Only if you're allowed to throw up every half an hour."

"That was one time lads, one time."

"Yeah, sure."

"Jim, you want a drink mate?" asked Bruce, eager to get the proceedings underway. Jez sprung up like a rabbit being hunted, "I'll help you man," and dashed behind Bruce. Before anyone had even said what they wanted to drink, they were gone.

"What we drinking then?" asked Titboy.

"Vodka. We got bucket loads of the stuff," said Joey.

"Sweet. Smirnoff, I hope."

"Only the best for an old friend," said Leander, rounding it off with a double-click of the mouth.

"Nice. Come on then Lee, budge up will you, you want me to stand here all night?"

"Sorry man, didn't realise you wanted to sit down. Here, this cushion's the best. Plant your arse over here," said Leander, slapping down twice on an old withered cushion. Titboy removed his coat and threw it onto the mattress inside the dark room. He then dumped himself on top of the pillow with all the finesse of a baboon. "Any pussy here tonight?" he asked.

"Nah. I wanted to get Harry's sister over here but nobody else did," said Danny.

"Harry? What, *Harry Buckleby*?"

"The one and only," Danny confirmed.

"What, his downy-looking sister? Didn't he finger her or something?" asked Titboy.

"Hence why I wanted her over. Easy pickings," said Danny, winking at Titboy.

"You can have her for yourself, thanks. Wouldn't touch anything he's had, especially his own sister. Oh well, boys' night in. Can't complain. Harry isn't coming though, is he? *I fucking hate that cunt.*"

"Dunno. Anyone invite him?"

They all looked around at each other, but no one said anything.

Bruce and Jez returned with a tray of half-pint glasses filled to the brim except for one, which was a full pint. Bruce handed them out.

"Here we go, guys. Jim, I made you a larger one so you can catch up with us."

"*Too right.* Cheers man," he said, grabbing hold of the juice and gulping it down in an instant. "Ahh. Sweet as. This is the life. Which one of you fags got a spare rollie then?" he asked.

"I've got some spare Jimbo," said Leander, reaching into his pocket and taking out one of the special cigarettes. "Here you go, man."

"Cheers dude," said Titboy, snapping his fingers at the rest for a lighter with the *spliff-de-la-pube* dangling from his mouth. Everyone patted their pockets in a frenzy—but Leander beat them to it. He cracked down the flint and held out the flame for Titboy. The rest all watched with sickening eagerness. "It's my pleasure man," said Leander. "Suck hard on this bad boy though, I think I might've rolled it a little tight." Titboy rolled his eyes but obeyed his orders and vacuumed up such a long drag that only two-thirds of the cigarette remained after he was done. He let the smoke hang in the air briefly before sucking it all back in through his mouth and nose, expanding his impressive chest to its fullest for the utmost enjoyment. He exhaled and through the floating smoke exclaimed, "Ahh, tastes sweet as," until all of it began wafting around the room. "This is just what I needed."

Joey, who was sitting directly opposite where Titboy blew, started laughing himself into near agony until his words resembled nothing but the squeals of a retarded pig. The rest soon found out why. The rancid stench suddenly hit them at full force, invading their noses with all the gases of Auschwitz. During the concocting and scheming phase of Operation Pube Smoke, they'd neglected to anticipate what the smell of burning hair would be like. Now there was a plague in the room, but the boys weren't disgusted by it—they were elated.

"Joey, is that you mate?" asked Titboy, "It fucking stinks."

"Wasn't me man. I'm not even smoking."

"What? That doesn't even make sense—"

"Come on guys, drink up," Bruce interjected, "let's get this party started."

"You're not even drinking, *Bruce*," said Titboy.

"You know Bruce doesn't drink man," said Leander.

"What? What are you, some kind of pussy? Why

the fuck not?"

"Just don't. I prefer smoking, man," said Bruce.

"Fair enough. More for me then."

"Yes indeed, Jimbo. Yes indeed," said Danny.

Bruce could run but he could never hide from the drunk elephant in the room that was his father. Titboy knew all about Bruce's alcoholic daddy, but the rest of the group knew that he knew as well. Silence locked them between the four walls. Titboy continued sucking-up smoke like he'd just discovered his favourite brand, oblivious to the smegma-like stench it was giving birth to and carried on gulping his vodka down like it was an elixir. Joey, losing himself in a premature frenzy of hysteria, started giggling like he'd become stoned from the second-hand, pubic hashish.

"The fuck's wrong with you man?" asked Titboy.

Joey attempted to speak, but couldn't even open his mouth without screeching.

"So, how's your love life Jim?" said Danny, stepping in.

"Non-existent man. You?"

"Not too bad, not enough sluts in this town though."

"Tell me about it. Sucks."

"Yup. I thought you were knocking around with that Asian chick?" Danny asked.

"Yeah, I'm still seeing her. She's frigid as fuck though."

"Ahh, that sucks. My first bit of action was a bit like that. Just tell her you love her. It's the easiest way to get laid."

"You reckon?"

"Yeah, without a doubt. Chicks love to think they

are living out that fairy tale bullshit, especially the young ones. Plus, if she thinks you love her and all that crap it'll guilt trip her into the sack anyway. It's a complete no-brainer."

"I'll keep that in mind."

"Speaking of chicks, where the fuck's *Jane*?" asked Jez, directing it at Leander.

"Ahh, she couldn't make it. Busy," he replied.

"Flaked out on you again, has she?" wise-cracked Jez.

"I saw her a while back, with that long streak of piss," said Titboy. "The lanky guy—what's his name—*Markus*. You guys remember him, don't you? Used to cry about his daddy all the time," he said, holding his eyes on Bruce.

"Jane told me about him," said Leander.

The group paused. Bruce once had a thing with Jane, so they were unsure of what to say, as none of them had a clue why they'd broken up. If there was ever a town bike in their social circle, Jane was the one who came rolling in with her stabilisers still attached. Leander was put in the waiting line when it came to her and oh-my-me, was he willing to keep his mouth shut and wait. It drove him crazy that he'd been cast out to the friend zone with her whilst she fell for a fresh narcissist every other fortnight.

"Well, what she say then dick head? Don't keep us waiting," said Titboy.

"Yeah come on Leanderthal. Dish out the dirt, dude," supported Jez. Leander sat there, parting his straightened fringe. After a moment of basking in the only limelight he'd ever get, he finally broke his silence.

"Apparently... this is according to Jane, alright

guys—"

"Yeah, yeah, yeah," they all said.

"Alright. Apparently, Markus told her to stop using tampons 'cause he reckons he should be the only thing to go inside her."

"Fuck *off!*" said Danny, delighted to hear anything transgressive.

"I swear that's what she said."

"So, did she? I bet she did. Bruce, you'd know. What do you reckon?" asked Jez.

"Yeah, maybe. She's quite impressionable."

"Her pussy must stink," said Titboy.

The group all laughed, except Leander.

Then the moment finally came. The time everyone (aside from Titboy) was secretly waiting for. In anticipation, Danny had decided to use the facilities just before Titboy realised how desperately his bowels were beginning to beg.

"*Danny?!* Get the fuck out of the toilet man, I'm gonna shit myself if you don't get out of there soon," said Titboy, squirming like a worm without a head whilst frantically knocking on the toilet door.

"You want another smoke, Jimbo? I've heard that can stop a man from shitting his pants."

"Fuck off Bruce. *Danny. Come on!*" The toilet flushed. Seconds went by. Danny stepped out. "Out the way, move aside," demanded Titboy, thrusting himself through the small gap between Danny and the door.

"Calm down, Sugar Tits. The toilet ain't going anywhere," said Danny.

The group all began laughing but Bruce hushed them down. They all looked at one another, biting their lips and gritting their teeth. Joey, still barely containing himself as it was, crept closer to the toilet door, but just before he peered through the keyhole, a huge rip-roar of uncontrolled, mismatched flatulence exploded behind it. The guys fell onto their hands and knees, marvelling in their perfect prank, bellowing out in a wild, high-pitched and hormonally-charged cacophony of blistering laughter as the basement morphed into a menagerie of the deranged. Leander spewed out a fountain of vodka and coke, Bruce choked on his cigarette smoke, whilst Danny and Jez fell on top of discarded beer cans and knocked over makeshift ashtrays.

"Arrggghhhhh, arrrggghhhhhhhh!!" Titboy screamed through the wails and cackles. A long series of violent, disconcerting squirts shat out from his anal passage like his arsehole was intoxicated and slobbering down the mouthpiece of an unfortunate saxophone. Some were long and resonant, others short and mouse-like in pitch, but the majority were just out of tune and off-colour. Titboy's buttocks screeched up and down the toilet seat back and forth several times before he made an agonising final push—squealing like swine in a slaughterhouse—until the explosion of shit came to a stop. The lads fell silent and listened to Titboy as he panted heavily behind the door. Even the toilet seemed to choke as it flushed. Joey, chortled to the point of mania now, lay crying to himself on the floor, tossing and turning like he was having an epileptic fit. "Ahh man, that's fucking disgusting!" he said, clenching his arms around his torso. Tears streamed down from his bloodshot eyes and his skin appeared to be yellowing. "I can't take it—it smells like an abortion." He got up, stumbling from left to right, completely disorientated and one hundred percent *fucked*. "I'm gonna puke," he cried.

"There's a bucket in the other room. Go in there. Quickly," Jez insisted, pushing him into the dark room. The rest of the group followed behind and watched as Joey fell onto his hands and knees and vomited, in a similar violence to Titboy's arsehole. Leander flicked on a lamp. The group burst into an unexpected, second round of animalistic indecency—except for Jeremy. Bruce took out his phone and held it up, "Joey, could you do that again, please? I completely missed it," he said.

"Why the hell did you throw up on the floor?!" asked Jez, "the bucket is right next to you!"

"Argghhh, man," said Joey. "I'm sorry Jez. It's just that smell... I can taste it on the back of my throat," he said, still spitting out bile onto the carpet. "I'm really sorry dude."

"*Don't* call me *dude*," said Jez.

The toilet flushed again, reminding the group that Titboy was still in there.

"I'll take care of Joey, guys. He's just had too much to drink. Nothing serious. You guys keep watch over Sugar Tits," said Bruce, picking up Titboy's jacket and tossing it over the pile of vomit.

In acquiescence, they all nodded and walked back into the main room. Bruce closed the door behind them, which Leander seemed to take notice of but left the others nonplussed. The toilet door had opened and after a minute or so, Titboy walked out, hunched over like a Neanderthal, his entire face pink and licked with sweat. He removed his cardigan and threw it onto the unmade bed. He now resembled a man who had been placed in a wet t-shirt competition against his consent. "Oh man, my stomach. Guys, I don't know what's happened but, I think I need to go to hospital or something," he said, flopping onto the bed with his arms clutched around his brutalised stomach.

The doorbell rang. Everyone looked at each other in an accusatory panic, like they'd been caught trespassing on private property and one of them was the idiot who'd given them away. It rang again.

"I'll get it," said Leander, hastily heading towards the door. Jez quickly caught up with him and pulled him back by the hood of his jumper.

"Expecting anyone Leander?" he asked.

"It's obviously that cock-hungry slut otherwise known as Jane," said Danny.

"Don't call her that Danny you prick," said Leander. "Yeah, so what if it is her anyway. Jez, you don't mind, do you? She texted me earlier. She needs a friend. So I invited her over. It's no big deal, is it?" The doorbell rang once more.

"No, I suppose not, but you could've asked me first. What are we going to do about him though?" asked Jez.

"Oh, he'll be fine. Won't you Jimbo?" said Leander.

"*My stomach...*"

"Oh, man up will you? Don't get your titties in a twist. You just had a little too much to drink, right guys?" insisted Leander, flicking looks between Jez and Danny for back-up.

"Yeah I'm sure it's nothing Jimbo," said the latter.

"What about Bruce? Should we tell him that Jane is here?" asked Jeremy.

"Nah, I know Bruce too well. He'll be with Joey for the rest of the night," said Leander as he double-paced up the stairs, leaving Jez and Danny alone with Titboy, who lay on the bed like his water just broke. They listened as Leander opened the front door to hear Jane barge in, fully engaged in a state of teenage turmoil. They both rolled their eyes at one another and eavesdropped in on Jane: "I just can't believe it Lee, that fuckin' bastard. He said he'd never do something like that and I really believed him! How could I be so stupid? Oh, *god!* Why are all men such fucking scum?"

"I'm sure it's not as bad as you think, Jane. Have you tried calling him?" asked Leander, changing his normal voice into the one he reserved for females, much like how adults address children when they want to fuck them.

"Of course it's as bad as I think, I saw him picking up a girl on his motorbike who was still in her school uniform for fuck sake! How much worse could it get than that?"

Jez and Danny laughed amongst themselves as Jane and Leander walked down the stairs and entered the room. Jane's mascara had run down her cheeks and her hair was dishevelled and unkempt. She wore a denim skirt with a matching jacket and a white tank top in need of a wash. "Oh, hey guys. Leander, you didn't tell me there was anyone else here," said Jane, tying up her hair. "God, it stinks in here, what the hell have you guys been doing? Jesus, what's wrong with him?" she asked, pointing at Sugar Tits.

"Oh nothing, he just drank a bit too much poison that's all," said Danny.

"You guys got something to drink then?" plucked up Jane.

"Yeah," said Leander. "Vodka. You want some Jane?"

"*Obviously.*"

Leander picked up a bottle from the floor and looked around for an empty glass but Jane just snatched it out of his hand. She necked it a few times with the ease of future dependency. "Any of you losers got a smoke for me then?" she asked. Leander patted the side of his pockets but failed to find anything on his person. He looked at the door of the dark room, suspecting that his tobacco was in there. "Nope, sorry Jane," he said.

"*Typical,*" she replied.

"So, what happened Jane? Been tossed aside for a fresh piece of meat, have you? I wouldn't worry about it, happens to the best of us after a while. No one can resist a bit of jailbait."

"Fuck off Danny, what would you know about it?"

"Yeah leave off, man, can't you see she's upset?"

"Oh, shut up Leander, I don't need you kissing my arse all the time," said Jane.

Danny and Jez laughed as Jane's phone started ringing, to which she tut-sighed in feigned disappointment before answering.

"Hello, Markus. I thought you might call. Got anything to say for yourself? I saw you earlier today with that *slut*. Yeah, that's right. Huh-uh, yep. Oh, she's your *niece*. You really expect me to believe— well, that makes sense. Oh. That's nice of you, I guess. Actually, that's really rather sweet. Yeah, babe. I'm just at Jez's house, hanging out with the losers. Yeah, okay. I'll see you in a bit, babe. Love you." She hung up the phone.

"You hear that guys? Markus was just picking up

his niece, so there was nothing *perverted* about it after all. Oh, that's such a relief. Sorry for being so mental."

"You really believe that bullshit?" asked Titboy. Danny burst out laughing at his sudden interjection. Jez asked if he was okay, to which he nodded but without much conviction. Leander just stood there, mouth agape, staring at Jane.

"Who asked you, Titboy? Keep your little lightweight faggoty virgin tits out of my business," said Jane.

"What did Markus say, Jane?"

"What I just said, Leander. You need to learn how to listen more. Hasn't one of you guys got a spare rollie for Christ sake? Can't you lot tell when a girl's in need?"

"My tobacco's in there," said Leander, pointing at the door of the dark room whilst taking a seat next to Titboy, who had his eyes closed and breathed in and out like an act of erotic asphyxiation gone wrong.

"Fine," said Jane and walked over to the door. Danny smiled in terrible glee. Jez looked worryingly at Leander, but he avoided receiving his gaze by looking at the floor in a sulk, nibbling away on his bottom lip.

Jane swung the door open, to a sight that she was all too acquainted with, but to which the rest of the group was completely nescient. Bruce stood with his trousers around his knees in front of a barely conscious Joey, with his phone in one hand and his cock in the other, trying to find the right angle for the perfect shot. Joey, upright, swayed around in circles mumbling the occasional vowel. To the others, it wasn't clear if he even knew that Bruce's cock was right in front of his face.

"Oh for fuck sake!" Jane screamed. "Why am I always walking in on you with your cock in another man's mouth?"

Bruce just stood there. "Guys, it's not what it looks like. I thought... I thought I might have a genital wart... and, and Joey generously offered to check it out for me. There's nothing gay going on here."

"*Yeah right!* What the fuck are you filming it for then?" asked Danny.

"Yeah, Bruce," said Jez.

"Is that true, Joey?" asked Leander.

Joey tried to speak but all that came out of him was a series of unintelligible blurbs. Bruce buckled himself back up. Danny and Jez watched him with their mouths wide open, dumbstruck. Leander crossed his arms and went to speak to Jane, but she burst into the room, snatched the tobacco from the floor and slammed the door shut on her way back out. She began crying as she walked across the main room towards the stairs. "Jez, I'm going to smoke in your garden. Sorry for bursting in on your fag party."

"It's not a fag party, Jane," he said, but she was already up the stairs and passing through the kitchen.

"Nice one, Lee. What the hell did you invite her for anyway?"

"Oh, fuck off Jez, it's not my fault. How was I supposed to know she'd go mental?"

"Urm, I dunno, by not being a blind retard maybe?"

"Eat shit."

"You're never going to fuck her, Lee."

"I'm getting closer than you'll ever get, *Jez*."

Whilst Jeremy and Leander flirted, Danny saw a window of opportunity and sneaked out of the room, taking the bottle of vodka with him. He walked through the kitchen and saw Jane in the little garden summer house, possibly smoking each one of the losers' pubic hair. Danny entered the springhouse and offered the vodka to Jane.

"Thanks," she said and took a gulp. Danny sat down next to her and she lay her leg over his lap.

"Not the first time you've seen Bruce buck naked with another man 'eh?" asked Danny.

"No. Didn't Leander say anything to you guys then?"

"Not a word."

"I shouldn't say anything but well, the cat's out of the bag now. Bruce convinced me to have a threesome with him and another man. He said he just wanted to see somebody else fucking me, so I thought, why the hell not, you know. You only live once right?"

"Right."

"So anyway," she said, handing the bottle back, "he found this guy online who was up for it. He came over whilst my parents were away. We had a threesome, which was okay at first, but then it just got weird. Bruce kept asking me if I wanted to see him suck his cock and before I knew it he was gobbling the guy up like no tomorrow. The guy was clearly gay as well, so I thought, would they even notice if I wasn't here? So, I excused myself, went downstairs and watched TV instead. I fell asleep and woke up at about two or three in the morning. I was knackered, so I went straight up to bed, but when I got there, Bruce and this guy were still going at it. It was so disgusting Danny, the whole room stank of semen, lubricant and faeces. So yeah, after that night we broke up. I'm surprised Bruce hasn't just come out of the closet, to be honest. I guess he'll have to now."

"I guess so," replied Danny, handing the bottle over to her again.

Jane's phone beeped. She looked at a message and then sighed.

"Bad news?" asked Danny.

"Nothing bad. Markus is just running late. Oh, I just know he's cheating on me, Dan. What should I do?"

"Get revenge," he said, taking the bottle out of Jane's hand and swigging a bit for himself before once again gesturing for her to take it.

"What do you mean?"

"What do you think, stupid? Cheat back."

"What? You mean, with you?"

"Why not?" said Danny, putting his arm around her shoulder, "I love you," he whispered in her ear. "Fuck off," said Jane, smiling, but Danny just ignored her and placed his hand firmly on her right breast. She looked at him groping her with indifference and took another swig from the bottle. Danny was now moving her breast around in a circular motion. Jane shrugged, then grabbed his other hand and moved it under her skirt.

Meanwhile downstairs, Jeremy and Leander's dispute had progressed into a full-on blowout. They were now rolling around on the floor taking pop-shots at one another, whilst Titboy sat upright on the bed with his hands clutched around his stomach, witnessing the spectacle despite the pangs of discomfort his enjoyment derived.

"You always were such a selfish cunt," said Jeremy, tightening his arm around Leander's neck in a headlock.

"Get the fuck off me faggot," Leander cried, thrusting his elbow into Jez's balls.

"Argghh!!" Jeremy screamed, losing his grip on Leander and falling to the floor with his hands on his groin. The blow brought tears to his eyes and for the moment, the whole room was a blur. They both lay on the ground, breathing heavily inside the shit-scented sauna of their own making. Leander got up and approached Titboy.

"*My stomach... feels like it's been ripped to shreds*," said Titboy, barely getting the words out of his mouth.

"Are you alright Jimbo?" asked Leander, putting his hand on his shoulder. Titboy nodded, trying to keep his composure and a measure of his pride. The pain in Jeremy's testicles subsided and as his vision returned he noticed the pair of scissors from earlier, inches away from his head. After the initial shock of having come so close to landing on them, he picked them up and crept slowly over to Leander, who had his back to him.

During the whole two-minute battle between Jeremy and Leander downstairs, Danny had slipped himself inside Jane, who was now quite tipsy and flushed. She was on top of him, sloppily swirling her hips. His eager head was buried between her breasts and his hands were squeezing her arse, with a curious middle finger inching towards her anus.

"Just fuck me, Danny, fuck me," she demanded, slapping down hard on his back until his finger got stage fright.

"Argh, you've got the wettest pussy I've ever felt Jane."

"Shut up and fuck me then," she said, guzzling down more vodka. Danny proceeded to hump her with all his might, which only provoked Jane to roll her eyes, sensing his impending climax. "No, not yet Danny for fuck sake, I'm nearly there myself. Just wait—"

"Argghhhh," he cried, prompting Jane to huff and drumroll punch his back as he orgasmed. Shortly afterwards, he went in for a kiss to shut her up, but she slapped him across the face, grabbed his hand and shoved it between her legs.

"Finish me off Danny," she said. He poked around for her sweet spot with a nervous hand and began to rub. "No, just finger-fuck me you idiot," she demanded. He did what he was told. Jane closed her eyes for the first time as his cock flopped out and his fingers slid inside. She scrunched his hair with one hand and started rubbing her clit with the other. Danny couldn't believe it. In his mind, he was already fucking her again. He started trying to thumb his cock into her arsehole but froze when a peculiar, metallic scent hit his nose. He looked for the source whilst Jane moaned with further intensity, but before he could blink, she screamed, "That's it, you prick!" and climaxed, squeezing his face with her slap-friendly hand. Seconds later he felt her thick juices ooze down his fingers, accompanied by the strangest fart he'd ever heard. Jane, breathing hard and oblivious, avoided looking at Danny and cherished the moment in solitude. But it was soon interrupted by the obnoxious sound of a moped in the distance. Jane lifted herself up and began to look for her underwear. That's when Danny saw it. His entire hand was covered in blood, with a trail of his own semen running down the palm. The sound of the moped came closer. Jane cleansed her vagina with a few splashes of vodka and frantically slid her panties back on. Then she saw Danny's hand for herself. "Oh, that's a relief, I've been due for nearly a week now. Thanks, Danny," she said and kissed him on the cheek. "Say bye to the losers for me." She took out a stick of gum from her pocket and threw it in her mouth as she walked off. Danny didn't notice. He just sat there, staring at his hand, gobsmacked at the sight before him.

Jeremy delicately spread the scissors apart, reached around the base of Leander's head, caught a clump of his hair between the blades and in one quick slash, sheared-off Leander's neatly straightened, side-parted fringe. It fell down in front of his eyes and he watched in agony as it landed on Titboy's lap.

"There's your faggoty fringe, Lee," said Jez.

Leander, paralysed in shock, moved his hand through the ghost of his hairstyle, already close to tears. Titboy, in agony now, got up to his feet and started making his way to the toilet again in baby steps.

"My hair! My fucking hair! Jez you *cunt*," Leander cried, as Jeremy made his way to the staircase for a quick escape. Leander, too lost in his own vanity, dashed for the bathroom instead, shoulder-barging Titboy out of the way just before he was about to walk through. The shock of the blow threw him against the wall and knocked him straight back down to the floor.

"Lee, you bastard. I'm desperate here. It's only your fucking hair—oh god—it feels like I've eaten razorblades," said Titboy. His stomach now bore the burden of purgatory. Cries of endless torture and eternal rape echoed behind the walls of his skin. He desperately tried to keep the brown-stained lips of his pressured arsehole shut. "I'm sorry, dude," he said, on the verge of giving in.

"No, don't dude! Lee! Lee, get out of the fucking bathroom you vain prick, Jimbo needs it more than you!" Jez screamed, banging on the door. "*Leander!*"

"Yeah, get out of the toilet, shit for brains!" said Titboy.

The door suddenly, yet slowly opened.

"About fuckin' time," said Titboy, getting up to his feet in a struggle.

Leander stood in the doorway, motionless, staring at Titboy. "What did you call me, Sugar Tits?" he said.

"Move aside Lee, I'm bursting here," said Titboy.

"What did you say faggot?"

"What me? I didn't say anything, man. I just need the bathroom—"

"Yes, you did. I fucking heard you."

"I didn't fucking say anything, Shit for Brains," said Titboy, plucking up his courage and taking a step closer to Leander.

"Guys, let's not let this get out of hand," said Jez.

"What's the matter sweet tits? You gonna shit yourself? You wanna know why you're so desperate for a dump, melon chest? You drank half a pint of laxatives, that's why. How does that make you feel faggot? Oh yeah, that rollie from earlier, it was full of our pubes. Mine were full of dried-up cum. You smoked my seed fat tits. How does that make you feel?" asked Leander, crossing his arms like a bouncer in front of a garrulous drunk.

Mortified, Titboy looked at Jeremy. "Tell me that's not true, Jez."

"Oh, it's true, Titty-Titty Bang-Bang," said Leander.

Titboy looked at them both as the truth sank in. Jeremy looked at Leander for the rat that he was. Leander stood there like his confession had earnt him a medal.

"You guys are fucking cunts..." cried Titboy.

He held onto his stomach, close to tears. Leander moved to the side and held his arm out as if to welcome him home to the toilet. Jeremy looked at Leander in disbelief. Titboy unbuckled his belt and unbuttoned his fly. He looked at Leander as the sound of a moped starting up could be heard in the distance.

"Wait," said Leander, "where's Jane gone?"

They all looked around the room.

"And where's Danny?" asked Jez, directing it Leander with coyness.

"I bet he's busy bangin' her right now, Lee," said Titboy, smiling directly at him and thrusting his pelvis in violent motions until it hurt his stomach.

"That slimy toad," said Leander. He went to walk towards the door, but Titboy's arm flew out in front of his face, barricading Leander's exit.

Danny ran through the garden screaming, holding his hand in the air like it was contagious and attracting all sorts of lethal bacteria. He dashed through the kitchen, across the hall and in a mindless panic, lost his bearings and fell down the stairs.

"Eat my shit," said Titboy. With a tightly-breasted left hook, Titboy took the air out of Leander's lungs. Sensing his weakness, he went for the kill by jumping up in the air as high as he could and let the gravity of his tits speed-up the fall upon Leander's sorry spine. He crashed onto a plate in Leander's back, but so did Titboy's elbow. Leander lay on the floor in terrible agony along with Titboy, who was struggling to pull down his trousers. Jez, standing on the second step of the stairs, watched on in amazement. He then looked up and saw Danny heading straight for him. Danny reached out his hands to protect himself but caught Jez on the way down. They both smashed into the door, which broke off one of its hinges, and landed on the floor. After a moment, they regathered their surroundings, to a sight they weren't quite prepared to see.

Titboy's bare arse was showing like a full moon, ready to expose its dark side to Leander's face. He struggled and strained, but instead of shooting straight out of him like the first time, it could only stream down his arse cheeks like a polluted Bangladeshi river. As it slowly made its way down the crevices of Titboy's crack, Leander screamed out like a terrified little bitch. He squirmed with all his might to wriggle free from the forced sixty-nine position he found himself in. Leander struggled whilst Titboy tried to sit on his face. Danny and Jez pretended they were both knocked out when in actuality they were peering through the shuttered gaps of their eyelids like lonely men with fancy telescopes. They both looked at each other in complete and utter joy as Titboy's arse was about to crash land home. Leander, knowing his fate was imminent, did what all little bitches do: he found a faeces free-zone on Titboy's flabby buttcheeks and clamped down as hard as he could. Titboy screamed as Leander's teeth pierced through his skin. Blood circled around Leander's lips. Danny and Jez, both looked on in horror, unable to avert their eyes. Leander finally stopped gnashing on Titboy's sorry arse and kicked himself free. Titboy fell to his side, crying angry tears. He began to crawl for the toilet door again but Leander, returning the favour, jumped on top of his back and finished him off. He got up and looked at Danny and Jez. They continued to feign unconsciousness but saw Leander spit on Titboy's arse before he went back into the bathroom again. Titboy buried his face in his right arm, letting out an occasional, pitiful, wet fart between cries of shame and humiliation.

The dark room door opened out of nowhere. Out stepped Joey, wearing nothing but his boxer shorts. He looked down at the half-naked and soiled Titboy, went to laugh but stopped himself, perturbed by the blood. He looked for answers in the faces of Jez and Danny, but they both carried on pretending to be knocked out. So, he did what all good friends do and shut the door again, pretending that he saw nothing.

A minute or two passed by. Jez and Danny looked at each other, perplexed and unsure of what to do next. The toilet flushed. Leander walked out with his hood up. His eyes were red raw, with a cold malevolence that darted out frantic glances. He looked down at Titboy, who began crawling for the bathroom again, then at Jez, who appeared to be out of it. Leander noticed the scissors from earlier, on the floor near the bed. He walked around the circle of corpses and picked them up, tiptoed slowly towards Jez and, with the blades completely widespread, grabbed Jeremy by the neck and held them up to his throat. "If you ever, ever do anything like that again," he said, "I'll slit your mother's throat in her sleep."

Danny sat up. Jez looked at him, terrified. Danny held his hand up at Leander, trying to make him stay cool. Leander double-took at the sight of his hand and raised an eyebrow at him.

"Oh, that," said Danny. "This is what you've been after for months now Lee. You know, I've been with bitches when they've been on heat before, but none ever tasted quite as sweet as Jane," he said, "Mmm, mmm, mmm," he added and then began to suck on his crimsoned fingers.

"You *FUCK!!!*" Leander screamed. He threw his arm back behind his shoulder and hurled the scissors towards Danny. They missed, but only by an inch and landed on the wall like a dart. Danny looked at the blades that came so close to slashing him. He made to turn back to Leander, but he, in a full fit of rage, bulldozed straight into him. "You know how long I've been trying to get with her Danny, you slimy pisshead cunt!" Leander thumped down on Danny like a chimpanzee short a banana. Then Jez joined in on the action. With his elbows up, he bombed into Leander's spine again. It made a disturbingly clean hit, popping like a cricket ball to a bat.

Before it had even begun it was over. They all just lay there, exhausted, unwilling and unable to move,

234

breathing in and out like sufferers of emphysema. After a moment, they sourly sat up. No one looked at each other. Titboy tried to get up as well, but it proved to be too much effort. Each one of the lads helped him up onto his feet and guided him into the toilet. They apologised to each other in the accustomed way that they did. Then Leander knocked on the door of the dark room.

A brief pause ensued. The door opened, but only slightly ajar. The smell of marijuana broke free. Leander turned to Jez and Danny. "You coming in?" he asked. He didn't wait for a reply.

Jez looked at Danny. "You wanna go in there, after what we saw?" he asked.

"We'll probably all end up in a stinkin' cell at some point. Might as well get used to it now."

"All right. Let's go. Wait, where's Jane gone?"

"Ahh, that paedophile Markus turned up. Jane fucked off as soon as she heard his moped outside."

"Ahh right. Fair enough. How was she?"

Danny waited a moment. "Disturbing," was his reply.

They went into the dark room. A few mumbled greetings could be heard going on behind the door. Then a long silence. Laughter began to erupt, and small traces of smoke drifted out of the gaps around the door. The knocker twisted, and it opened. Titboy's duffle coat was tossed out. It landed in a clump. The bile glistened in the light. The boys started laughing again. Titboy came out of the toilet. He saw his jacket on the floor and betrayed no look of surprise. He limped over to the door of the dark room and knocked.

"Guys, the toilet's fucking blocked. Let me in."

The door opened, but all that came out was the unused bucket. Titboy stared at it as it spun around like a top until it eventually landed. It appeared different to him in the light when it stopped. An idea began brewing inside his laxative-drenched brain. He unbuttoned his fly and urinated into the bucket. Then his stomach growled again, so he turned, squatted and shat into it as well. He stood up and stared at its contents. He knew what to do but felt like there was one thing missing. He started touching himself, thinking about the wankers in the room next door. The rush of impending revenge raced through his now morbid mind. He was going to make them taste everything that came out of him. Sweat poured out from his temples. Every mumble or cackle behind the door made him pump himself closer and closer to release, fuelling his animalistic desire. He began laughing to himself with glee with the single thought of seeing their faces when he walked in, bucket in hand, filled to the brim with the juices of every orifice he had to offer. Titboy envisioned them, shrieking and screaming out like terrified children. He was going to tease them, make them all beg and plead. He would show no mercy. One by one, he was going to make them all squirm.

THE
LAST LAUGH

Lowlife. Drunkard. Piece of shit.

Oh, don't mind her, that's just Sandra. She used to love heckling me moments before a gig and despite our recent departure, the aftershock of our downfall is still ricocheting around the inside walls of my mind. *I hate you, I really fucking hate you. You're scum.* Charming, isn't she? Don't worry, I'll drown her out as soon as the barman comes back with some courage. *Arsehole.* She keeps on trying, the persistent little minx, I've got to give her that. We broke up about a week back. Or maybe yesterday; or somewhere in between. To be honest I can't remember. The last few months of our relationship was spent in a perpetual state of on again, off again, so much so that I'd often forget if we'd split up that week or just got back together. Seeing that we met here after my first gig about three years ago probably doesn't help matters much. For what I can only assume was the giggles, insomnia turned up at my door during the early stages of our decline, just to make things that bit more hellish. The funny thing is that not sleeping for months has made everything feel like a dream. It's like I'm trapped inside a bubble that only ever pops to reveal itself trapped inside another.

"Isaac," says the bartender as the hinges behind him squeak, "sorry to have kept you waiting, mate. The place is a tip downstairs. Wow, you really can't get enough of that stage, can ya? Here, I brought ya your favourite." He gives the bottle of rum in his hand a shake and places two glasses down on the edge of the stage.

"Let's drink," I say.

The ice crackles as he pours and gentle, ashen clouds float around the rim of each glass. Beautiful. He hands it over to me and gestures at the wall behind him. "So, what d'ya reckon? Look good don't they?"

"When did you have them painted again?" I ask.

"Yesterday, like I told you before. They needed a bit of a brush-up. Thought I'd add a couple more for effect."

Go on, pretend you were looking at them like you pretended to listen to me you f—

"Well," I say, taking a decent, Sandra-silencing hit of rum. There are three pink elephants on the wall opposite the stage with blurry eyes and bubbles around their mouths, which I guess is something to do with the martinis at the end of their trunks. "You'll have to change the name of the place, you know. Pluralise it."

"To what, The Pink Elephants?"

"Yeah, you've got a trio up there now."

"Nah, you're looking at it all wrong mate. That's the same elephant. He's already half-cut so he's seeing two other versions of himself."

"Oh. Which one's the real one then?" I ask.

"Which indeed," he replies. "How you feeling anyway?"

"Me? Right as rum."

"Rum's the word," he says, gesturing for a toast.

He stretches up whilst I kneel down. Our glasses chink and we share a laugh, though I'm not sure why.

"Glad to hear that, Isaac. Things took a pretty shaky turn last night. Surprised to see you turn up here again."

"Last night?" I ask, but just as he goes to answer, the lights all cut out in a fatal swoop, shrouding us in darkness.

"Argh, fucking hell not again. Sorry about this, Isaac. The fuse has been playing up over the past few days. I'll just be a minute. You'll be alright here, won't you?"

"'Course I will."

The creaking door suggests that he left before he heard me. It's funny really. Most nights I need to drink myself into a blackout, but the blackout's come early tonight, just to say hi. *You're a fucking blackout.*

As I knock back the rest of my drink in the dark, the stage lights already begin to flicker on. And here I am in the centre. Where it all began. A small, dank smelling square stage with a gleaming solitary mic. I check my watch to see I've still got five minutes before I'm due to begin, which, if things remain as they are, will be to an audience of none. *A nobody performing to no one. Story of your life.* To drown Sandra out for good tonight, I pour myself another, much larger rum. After a swig, I tap the mic a few times to find out that it's off, then get behind the deplorable, makeshift curtain (that looks more like a bedsheet announcing the end of some poor woman's virginal worth) designed to create a wing and wait there. It might seem stupid, but I really prefer not to be seen before a performance. It ruins the intrigue, the mysteriousness of the persona I'm about to portray if they see me beforehand. The sound system is by my feet amongst an assortment of dust-laden cables. I bend down to flick it on... but my nose begins to—*ahh-choo!*—twitch—*ahh-choo!*— so I take out some tissues from my pocket, which for some reason I—*ahh-choo!*—knew were going to be there. After blowing my nose under a blur of bright lights, I flick the switch.

Feedback pierces through me in a whiplash of harsh electrical currents. *I can't believe you.* It lingers as I wince. *What the hell is wrong with you?* Shifts pitches as I grind my teeth. *Why would you joke about that?!* And almost makes me gag...

"What the fuck are you joking about my vagina for Isaac?!" said Sandra, splashing rum over my face. "I don't want people knowing that I squirt when I come you impotent prick!" Then she threw the glass that only just missed my head. It smashed behind me and the small crowd in front of us burst into a round of laughter far bigger than any of my jokes did that evening. They cheered as she stormed out, leaving me standing there dumbfounded. All I could think about was when she saw the joke she was referring to scribbled down on a note back at home. She said nothing about it at the time, even laughed... maybe. I guess seeing me mock-ride the surfboard across the wave of her ejaculation hit a nerve. But the words were still the same. She knew about the joke but saved her protest for when I was on stage... that's when I should've cut her loose. Sliced her out of my life. Summoned the guillotine blade down between the centre of our already volatile relationship.

"Isaac?!" says the barman, his head peeping around the door. "Are you alright mate?"

"Oh yeah. I'm fine."

"You ain't been hitting the sniff again have ya?"

"What?"

"Those tissues there on the floor," he says, pointing a finger. "There's blood all over them."

"Sorry mate they must've fallen out of my pocket without me realising it. Don't worry, they've all dried up now—"

"Go easy on yourself mate. I'm not being funny or nothing, but you look like a man who's seen something he can't," he says, twisting his wrist to check his watch. "Ah, shit. The time got away from me again."

He needs to start ushering people in now, late as always. As his eyes glance back up, he holds an open-palmed five fingers in the air and gives me a nod before disappearing back down the stairs. It feels good to see that again, the little cue. In five minutes I can finally try and resurrect the career I had before it was torn to shreds. It shouldn't be too hard. I was only popular for a very brief spell and now nobody knows who I am. Being anonymous might even help in some ways. There's no pressure to stick with what worked before. I hope the bartender didn't think I was shaking due to pre-stage jitters. It's the lack of alcohol in my system which is causing that, or possibly the shell-shock known as Sandra. I hope I can't be seen behind this curtain. *Sure, blame me for all your downfalls, Isaac. As always. Sandra this, Sandra that. You sack of—*

The hinges creak. Footsteps shuffle. Seats are scraped.

My second chance is here.

Second? More like zillionth—

And with this swig, I silence thee. *Ahh.* I can feel it reaching all the way to the bottom of my core, the place where she lurks and plots and machinates. No more tonight baby. See you in the morning. The sweet sound of mumbling strangers has replaced her voice. My heart is beating again. Adrenaline is already on the rise. It's a reminder that I'm not done with the game of life just yet. This time I've just got to make it count.

Just as I check my own watch the second-hand ticks towards the minute, at the same place it was exactly five minutes ago. Perfect timing. This is a good sign. With a deep intake of breath and my best American announcer voice, I say, "Ladies and gentlemen, please welcome to the stage, the one and lonely, ISSAAAAAAAAAAAAAAAAAAAAAAAAAAAAAAAAA AAAAACCCCCCCC EEEEEEENNNNEEEEEERRR-

RRSSSSSSSOOOOOOOOOOOOOOOONNNN!!!"

I sweep the curtain to the side, feeling like a superhero. The lights above me are blinding yet euphoric, whilst the audience welcomes me with an unexpected thunder of applause, almost as if they know me. The faces are familiar yet unknown, expectant though dubious, hopeful but cautious.

With a liquor-kissed swagger, I swoop the mic out of the stand and spin the latter off to the side. I play it silent for the first half a minute or so, just to distort the levels of confidence in my audience. Winning people over once you've created doubt in them awakens their sympathy, doubling-down their appreciation and making them more likely to remember you, as you come across as a real human being instead of a fantastical one. It took me nearly three years to learn that. Whilst keeping them waiting as a few more make their way in and settle down, I pour myself another rum and make a toast to one of the pink elephants on the wall, who seems to be staring right at me. The glare and twinkle in his eye gives me an idea though. Cheers, Dumbo. I'm gonna wing it.

"Relationships, to me, are a lot like eye contact," I say. It triggers a few chortles. Beat. Continue. "You see, both start out very pleasant, endearing and mysterious. You don't know the person and the person looking back doesn't know you. All things are equal. But, as time lingers on, the unforgivable mistake of getting to know each other inevitably takes place." More chuckles. A few audible ha-ha's. Another beat. Proceed. "Just like with eye contact, the longer a relationship goes on, the more clearly you begin to see the other person," I say, freezing my glance on an unsuspecting, cute little blonde, who stands out amongst this sea of blurs. I hold no gender bias with this joke. I just look for whom I deem to be the most compliable spectator, much like how a hypnotist scans a room for those who are especially eager to be hypnotised. The blonde's got eyes as innocent as they are timid, meaning her resistance looks likely to be lacking. She'll squirm waiting for me to move on to the next victim, which I'll do after the bit without looking back, but I can't let her think that now. The illusion is dependent on fear. "But the scariest thing about relationships, as with eye contact... isn't what you discover or learn or even see in the other person. It's the person rarely noticed, the one who hides in the dark and doesn't want to be found... and that person... the one you've been avoiding all these years without even realising it, who lurks behind the impression of the person you thought was the real deal," I say, holding my gaze until I see myself staring back inside this stranger's eyes, "is of course... yourself."

It's met with a better reception than I'd expected. Maybe there was more truth to the bit than I first anticipated. Chuckles of a relieved acceptance breeze over my head like a laugh-track. Now it's time to get into the regular bits, with perhaps a few call-backs to the opener now I can trust they'll understand and appreciate it. The girl I stared at is still laughing, buying me time. I'm currently the weirdo—*currently? You are a fucking weirdo*—and that's just fine by me. Time for another rum, it seems. As I pour I can hear the door weeping amongst the mild cries of awkward, diminishing laughter. That's it, laugh at the freak. I take a large gulp of rum, wondering why certain crowds seem to unite as one whilst others only ever seem to—

Sandra.

Hello Isaac. Happy to see me? Don't I look extra fuckable tonight? Oh look, I'm wearing the same dress I seduced you with. I bet you want me back now, don't you?

"Right, where was I?!" I say, but my mind draws a blank. How did she—why is she—what the hell is she doing here?! She made me double-take, nearly giving myself away. "I'm sure I was somewhere..." Fuck. She's making me bomb. That dress. Fully black with slits at the hips. She's matched it up with a pair of large-rimmed sunglasses. It's as if I sensed her presence coming, which was what inspired my opening bit! She takes a seat at the front. The seat creaks like a rusted bedspring.

Okay. Shit. Shit. Shit. Wing it, "Sorry, the comedian is experiencing a strange influx of déjà vu. He'll be with you shortly once it passes. We apologise for any inconvenience this may cause," I say, stalling as well as I can. The crowd doesn't seem to mind or take notice of my sudden discomfiture.

Okay. Breathe Isaac, breathe. Everything's fine. You can handle this. Sometimes you've got to be cruel for the greater good. Just keep it professional. Speak to her through the jokes. Make sure she gets the message this time. This isn't the first time she's seen you perform. Just make sure it's the last!

I need to shake it off. Avoid looking at her. She's only here to see me stumble and fall. If she thinks she can just follow me around and continue to make hell out of my existence, she's got another thing coming! I finish my glass of rum and feel the surge of warmth shoot through my veins. Right. Let's do this.

"Sorry about the delay. It's just that I've been a bit sick recently... it was a real *bitch* of a flu, you know? One of those ones which kept lingering around, forever threatening a comeback. Outstaying its welcome by a good three or so... years. Don't worry. Not all jokes will surround an unstable, energy-zapping relationship that *I cannot seem to ever shake off no matter how hard I fucking try...*"

I clear my throat. Feign a smile. Walk along the tightrope of madness. Sandra hasn't even flinched yet. She's just glaring at me, following my movements by the neck. Well, two can play at that game. If she wants to continue this shit-show we've created for ourselves, let's see how she handles what I've got in store for her. I know the next section like the back of my hand...

"I always get really horny when I'm sick. I'm not sure why, but I have a theory. I think it's because I feel disgusting and personally degraded... a bit like the pornography I watch."

Pause. Shuffle. Continue.

"I'll be lounging around at home, panting and sweating myself into a death wish, and my cock, already lubricated by my own sweat, must think a vagina is nearby or something. Then my stalking psychopath of a girlfriend will just storm into the room out of nowhere and ask me if I want anything," I say, sliding into the material like it's all gobbledegook...

"I cannot believe you, Isaac," said Sandra. "After everything I've done for you! You have to go and joke about that. I landed you this gig, and this is how you thank me. It's not my fault if I can't control my temper. Oh god! I can't believe you. Now everybody in there thinks that I'm abusing you!" she screamed, making everybody else around us aware of her violent tendencies too. I couldn't believe she'd still make herself out as the victim. The intention of the joke was to highlight that it didn't matter much to me, that it was something we could make light of and hopefully address. It's not like I said her name or referenced that she was my current girlfriend or anything. But there she was, announcing it to everyone else around us. Her crying over it was like a soldier balling his eyes out over a war ending, not through relief of the terror he'd suffered, but because he could no longer rape and kill.

"What are you talking about?" I genuinely asked. "It was just an aside. It is kinda funny when you think about it—"

"Funny? What the fuck is funny about it? You can't joke about stuff like that."

"Of course I can. You know what I think when it comes to this stuff. When it comes to jokes, or any form of expression for that matter, *anything* goes."

"But there's a line, Isaac—"

"No there isn't, Sandra. I have total freedom to say what I please up there. It's only ever up to the people watching me whether it works or not."

"But Isaac, you were joking about our relationship! About things that should only be between us. I don't want the whole world thinking we're a couple of loonies."

"Sandra," I said, "seriously, look around you, at where I'm performing. I mean, don't get me wrong, I'm grateful for the gig and all, but this place is a shithole. Look at it. It's a pub in the middle of nowhere-ville. Nobody is going to remember. We're all walking dead men anyway."

"You don't know that Isaac. Anything could come back to us eventually. What if someone was filming it?!"

"Even if they were, what does it matter? It was a joke. If anyone asks me, which they never will, I'll just lie and say it was made up."

"But it wasn't made up!"

"I know. That's why it was funny."

"Oh, god. That's all that matters to you, isn't it?! As long as it gets a laugh then it's all okay. Well, it's not—"

"Would you listen to yourself? Don't you realise that everybody around you is a nobody? That we are nobodies? Nobody fucking cares about a twenty-second joke about a flailing-armed woman losing her shit once in a while."

"But I don't want people to know that. I don't want people knowing that my vagina gushes like the Niagara Falls, as you so *romantically* put it. I don't want them knowing that I've taken the morning after pill because you 'forgot' to pull out. I don't want them fucking knowing that I fucking hit you because you're a massive cunt!"

"You're absurd. Why are you with me? Did you think I'd just tell a bunch of jokes about, I dunno, toilet seats being left upright or forgetting to buy flowers on an anniversary?"

"I still haven't forgiven you for that."

"Oh, don't I know!"

"That isn't the point, anyway. I don't want people knowing that I've hit you."

"Well, maybe you should stop fucking hitting me then."

"I can't help it."

"Funny. I can't help making jokes about it either."

"Ha-*fucking*-ha. It's not funny Isaac. These are personal things between me and you—"

"And?! It's not like I'm entirely truthful, is it? It's a joke. The performance is a persona. Nothing is meant to be taken as real. It's only idiots who believe that. Why can't you just accept that this is what I do!? I've been working at it for years and I refuse to let anyone tell me what I can and cannot say whilst I'm up there. This is art—"

"Art? You call making cunt jokes art? What are you on? You're a clown, simple as that. If people aren't laughing with you, then they're laughing at you. Freak."

"All the better! You think I care? With or at me, they're laughing. It's all good. My job is being done and done well. No complaints from me."

"Well, your job with *me* isn't being done."

"That's because you're a bitch."

-*SMACK!*-

I glance back over at the crowd, specifically searching for Sandra and say, "And that's when she, punches me in the face."

The eruption of laughter waves over me. She's still sitting there, unmoving, staring straight ahead. Inside her frames I see myself shaking my head. An inside joke just for the two of us. She won't think so, but it's pretty romantic, in a sort of tragic sense at least.

It seems the shame is with me this time. Sandra didn't flinch throughout the entire bit. In fact, she even half-chuckled on occasion. The rest of the crowd is out of focus because of her. They resemble nothing more than bobbing heads without any difference between their faces, whilst Sandra sits there, with the faintest crack of a smile forever resting on the side of her mouth. I don't know what I did to deserve that woman. Funny how ambiguous such a thought is... a couple of years ago I think I thought the same thing, but in reverse, before hate's patient tumour started to grow, waiting for its moment of exponential growth. I'm currently raising a toast to the pink elephant on the wall, which is being lapped up by this easy crowd. They're in delirium. I guess they've all had a psychopath for a partner at one time or another.

I think I might be drunk.

"You wanna hear more, miss?" I ask.

Sandra stares. Sandra feigns surprise. Sandra nods.

"The woman I'm speaking of... the one who sees me as her own personal punching bag... she's recently, in fact very recently, walked back into my life. Admittedly, I did sleep with her a week ago, but believe me when I say that I had *no intention of ever seeing her again.* I considered it a fair trade for all the uppercuts she blessed me with and, most importantly, for ruining my one shot at the big time.

"There I was, in the limelight, rocking, and I mean rocking the place apart. The lights were shining bright, heaven-like in their illuminance, filtering the uproarious, *better-looking crowd than this one* into a blurred landscape of contented, trouble-free chuckles. Every joke was hitting the right note and even when it didn't, I had the comebacks to save them with. It was one of those rare nights where the crowd was eating out of the palm of my hand. I had them. The competition was mine. Here's the bit:

"I love it when blokes say to me, '*I could drink you under the table mate, I could drink you under the fucking table.*' Really? Dude, I drink so much that I often wake up in the morning, wondering why I ever stopped wearing a nappy..."

Take in the guffaws, speak just as it lessens.

"I drink so much, that I often have trouble maintaining an erection," I say, letting the mic drop away from my hand like it went limp on me.

"I drink so much, that I once woke up with a cock in my mouth! Have you ever drunk yourself gay? *Drink me under the table...* I'll drink you under the fucking covers mate!"

It worked. The audience was laughing just like this crowd is now. If a laughometer was there, I was surely going to be The Last Man Laughing. That was the name of the competition... wasn't it? Well, what does that matter now? As the chuckles began to wither, I took an intake of breath. Just before I went to speak again, Sandra decided to intervene with her contribution by *heckling* me. Proper, hate-filled heckles as well. I couldn't believe it. She chimed in with a loud, tinnitus-inducing round of boos and jeers. I just froze. I couldn't speak. All I could do was watch as Sandra screamed at me in disgust, proclaiming that I was nothing but a piece of shit. It was so extreme that the security team had to escort her out. I was left standing there, looking forward at the previously pleased faces, who now all glared at me with suspicion. She sabotaged the finest set of my career, for a reason I couldn't fathom, and that had left me utterly paralysed on top of the only place I'd ever felt to be home. By the time the announcements were made for the final round (I was in the semi-final when Sandra pissed all over my chances) I was pretty half-cut. Well, steaming actually. Steaming from the fumes of too much booze and the anger I was trying to repress with it. The names were announced as if I hadn't even performed. No comedy club wants a loudmouth, unstable comedian with equally unpredictable audience members. Sandra had known that and exploited it. The thing that was killing me the most, was why. As I stumbled away with everybody around me avoiding my glance, I knew I wouldn't be able to enter the competition as Isaac Enerson again for a few years at best.

Sandra was stood across the street smoking a cigarette as I crept through the doors with my head hanging low. I was a little surprised she waited for me to leave and through my refusal to learn from the past, I actually thought she'd realised the error of her ways and wanted to apologise. But as soon as I saw her smile—*that knowing, revenge-delighted sneer that always rose on the left side of her upper-lip only*—I saw that she still thought of herself as in the right.

That's when I realised there was no hope for us. I could no longer tolerate the merry-go-round of our relationship. I needed her gone. Out of my life. But I didn't want to cause a scene. I'd had my fair share of those and always forgiven her and that had only served to encourage her to push it even further. I couldn't understand it. I didn't want to understand it. There was no logical way of ever possibly understanding it!

Luckily then the cold breeze in the air served to soothe the stampede of thoughts shattering my mind. It ran across my face to cast a new world view of Sandra, something I'd been ignoring and avoiding for some time—reality. As my foot switched from pavement to tarmac and I took in a breath of that clarifying air, a blonde woman broke-free from an until then unnoticed, huddled group. "Excuse me?" she called out, appearing on the right side of my peripheral vision to save me from making a further ass of myself. I turned to look at her and heard Sandra scoff. "You're the comedian who just performed right?" the stranger asked.

"Urm, yeah. That was me," I replied, tutting as I spoke.

"Oh wow! This is so cool. I'm sorry to bother you, but would you mind signing this for me?" she asked, removing the programme for the competition that was tucked under her arm. Despite the night being a fairly damaging event, here was this person, who'd appreciated the effort I'd made. Sometimes that's all you want: a tiny, fleeting recognition.

"Sure thing. I'd be happy to," I said. Sandra had moved closer without my notice. Her back was turned, and her arms were crossed with her fingers already drum-rolling over her elbows.

"Here you go," the woman said, handing me the mag and a pen she dished-out from her bag. I scribbled my signature on the cover and handed it back.

"Thank you so much!" she said. "Oh, I just wanted to say that I really loved that bit about Utterly Butterly and I Can't Believe it's not Butter. It's a riot! My husband and I always go for the two-for-one deals as well, and he always opens the second tub of Utterly Butterly before the first one's anywhere near finished!"

"Ha!" Sandra blurted, immediately taking more pleasure from the stranger's mistake of my identity than she ever had from one of my jokes. The woman had confused me for some other comic, who in fairness had a similar, goofy style and haircut, but who also had the most obnoxious, pun-fuelled jokes I'd heard in years.

"Thanks," I replied. "You wouldn't believe the fights we've got into over the smallest, most pointless things you could imagine. Isn't that right, sweetheart?" I asked, throwing my voice over Sandra's shoulder.

The shaking of her head was my reply. The woman in front of us detected the tension steadfast. She quickly smiled and thanked me again, then dashed towards the entrance on her tiptoes. Sure, I wasn't the person she thought I was, but to me it didn't matter. Sandra soon made her opinion of it known though. She'd started walking back and forth, pacing from side to side at all angles like she was trapped inside a loose, transparent knot. "That's more important to you," she kept muttering to herself, scuffing her shoes along the ground, her dismay threatening an onslaught. It appeared that she'd already absolved herself of any guilt she might've possessed over the sabotage of my set.

"What is it now?" I asked, facing her.

"You. You're un-*fucking*-believable. That woman didn't have a clue who you were, but instead of correcting her, you went along with it."

"Sandra, you're being a bit over-irrational here. Come on—"

"No, I'm not! It's true, isn't it? I heard that shit joke about I Can't Believe it's not Butter and I saw you rolling your eyes over it. *And now you're taking credit for it?!*"

"Hey, calm down. I don't see the problem with her believing it was me. Didn't you see her? It made her day."

"No, it made your day, you phoney loser piece of shit. You're willing to be somebody completely different just for a few seconds of fame. Fake fame at that! You're so unbelievable. I don't even know who you are. How can I trust you?"

"How many times do I need to tell you, Sandra?! It's just a performance, an alter-ego."

"Oh, sure. Whatever. Who are you!? What's wrong with you? What's wrong with me? Why aren't I good enough for you? What's the matter with me? Why am I not enough!?!"

I should've realised why she held back from her attack. She was waiting for the crowd of people to go back inside for the final round.

"I love how you're making this all about you," I said, trying to keep as calm as possible. "That's what's un-fucking-believable here. You ruined my chances tonight and now you've got the temerity to make yourself out as the victim—"

"No, Isaac. That was just the half of it. I did it because you're a counterfeit parasite, that's why! You told me about that ladyboy who face-fucked you whilst you cried in my arms. I was really touched that you told me about it. I thought you were confiding in me. You said you were frightened and only did it because you didn't know what else to do... I thought it was just between us."

"Did you hear me mention anything about a ladyboy up there Sandra?" I asked with my hands open. "Well, did you?"

Sandra screamed, "They're not supposed to know what I fucking know, Isaac. I'm the one who's supposed to know these things, not a room full of strangers or anyone else for that matter! D'you get that? Those are our secrets! My things to know, not theirs! *Why can't you understand that?!*"

"Alright. Jesus Christ Sandra, calm down."

"I'll calm down when you apologise."

"Apologise?!" I spluttered, laughing in the face of adversity. "You want me to apologise? You're the only one around here who should be apologising!"

"Stop laughing you dick. I hate it when you laugh. I always have. You always need to laugh longer and louder than anyone else, don't you? Say sorry!"

I don't know what it was, but everything Sandra said at that moment was like comedy gold to me. Maybe it was exhaustion. Maybe I was just drunk. Maybe it was the realisation that our relationship was the very definition of insanity. I don't know. But I just couldn't stop.

"I trusted what you told me would only be between me and you and once again you betrayed me—*stop fucking laughing!*"

"Ah, you know what?" I said, out of breath from my chuckles, but Sandra's last grunted scream made it sound like she was shitting herself. I thought she was going to give herself a hernia or give birth to her spleen. Through my laughter, I said, "This is ridiculous. We've been going around like this in circles for longer than I can remember now. I'm done. If you're not on my side, what's the point?"

"What!? What are you saying?"

"I'm saying that I've had enough, Sandra," I said, fully sober. "You humiliated me up there tonight. And do you care? No. I never know what's gonna trigger you next. You don't even want to address it. I guess playing the victim is the only way you know how to get attention. I wanted us to work. I really did. It's not the first time my ambitions have collided with my personal life and I'm sure it won't be the last."

"But Isaac..."

"But nothing Sandra. You've had your chances. More than enough in fact. You don't even like me. Let alone love me."

"Of course I love you—I need you—you said you wouldn't ever leave me..."

"Well, like you said, I lie all the time, so how can you ever believe what comes out of my stupid, lying mouth?"

"Isaac. Let's just forget about it and go home. We can spend the day together. Please. I'm sorry about everything, okay? I'll try to be a better girlfriend. I know I can. You can joke about anything you want. I'm sorry."

"How many times have we been here, Sandra? This is the web we weaved for ourselves. Neither can wriggle out of it by helping the other," I said and began to walk away.

"Isaac! Please, just come home with me now. I need you. I've just been upset. I hardly ever see you anymore. You're always working, and that's fine. But you don't even sleep most of the time. Please, you can forgive me. I know you can. I just miss you is all. I dunno what I'll do without you. What about us?"

"So do I, Sandra. But I'm not sure if what I miss is even there anymore. Feels like I'm conjuring it up in my head to fool myself. We're just not compatible. It happens. I don't think we can change how we see each other anymore. There's no going back."

"Hey, where are you going?! You're not going to leave me here, are you?" she cried out, slumping her handbag and body to the ground.

I had nothing left to say. Even turning to look at her felt too hard. I knew it would carve me with guilt and I'd go crawling back. It wouldn't have been the first time. My body still shook despite my motionlessness. I could hear her behind me, gagging between shaken, petrified sobs like the unwanted child she always believed herself to be, who cries despite knowing nobody will come. Nobody, except me, if I turned around to face her.

I forced myself forwards.

"NO! Please don't—don't leave me Isaac—please— I'm sorry—I'm nothing without you—please, please—say something—don't leave me here," she said, stuttering and choking on her words. Her anger and sadness had never made me cry before, but her despair at that moment had me in streams. The unknown road ahead of me was nothing but a blur. Despite knowing it was the right and only thing to do there was still something inside tearing me apart. It was the first moment I realised sympathy had its limitations. The relationship was going to destroy one, if not both of us. Maybe not physically, but mentally and spiritually for sure—if it hadn't already. Resigned to this thought, I turned to check on Sandra. She'd already gone. I stood on the street, entirely alone. All except for a floating bubble. It seemed to hold an answer to a question I had yet to ask. An impossible glimmer surrounded it like a sphere. As it drifted closer I saw my reflection. My eyes were pinkened. Bloodshot. I had a terrible feeling that it wasn't my reflection at all but more... a revelation of my being. My chest heaved like the tightening of a knot. I was trapped inside that bubble. Forever a slave to the limits of a knowledge I had no part in assimilating. As this trailing thought ran through my mind, the bubble, as ludicrous as it sounds, seemed to detect it, to *know* it. My reflection crackled into an unsightly red. Lightning strikes of broken capillaries formed across my entire face. Embers of my frame began to shed that I tried to grapple, but every swift movement made further dust of myself. The particles formed and took shape inside the same bubble from before. It grew bigger, louder somehow, reflecting everything around it through some unknowable force as if the opposite of some terrible black hole. The light suddenly snapped into an impossible strength. It began to eat what was left of me, whilst piercing through my sightline... until I saw nothing... which is all I can see right now.

Sandra's gone.

Everybody's gone.

I'm alone on the stage. There's a microphone in my hand, unplugged and lifeless. All the seats have been stacked in front of the pink elephants... the bottle of rum from earlier is empty. Where did I go? Did I continue my gig without realising what I was even saying? It's happened before... but I always remember the crowd leaving, whether they enjoyed the show or not. Could I be so used to performing certain bits that I can slip in and out of them at any time, without even realising it? Yes, it must be that. I just drifted off somewhere. Somewhere with Sandra. But now, for the first time in living memory, I do not know where she is.

I need a drink.

The barman looks surprised, even slightly relieved to see me. "Isaac, there you are. Sorry for leaving you up there so long. The cleaner went and pulled a sickie on me, so I had to stay down here. The place was in a right state after last night. You wanna drink, mate?"

"Rum please."

"Rum! Yeah, of course. Coming right up. Sorry again, my mind's been all over the place this morning."

"I think I know the feeling."

"So," he says, placing my drink down. "How're you and Sandra doing?"

"I have no idea."

"She looked awful upset last night."

"Last night..."

"Yeah she stormed out during your set, so I guess you must've made a joke she didn't like or whatever. I tried to speak to her—"

"Last night?"

"Yes, Isaac. Last night. You. On stage. Sandra. Running. Screaming."

"I was here, last night? Performing? Sandra came too?"

"I think you've been hitting the sauce a bit too much mate. How're things at home? You sleeping alright?"

"And what about tonight?" I ask.

"What about it? It's Tuesday. It's always dead in 'ere on a Tuesday. Not even sure I'll open up. So, did you and Sandra get your shit sorted or what? She ain't half a livewire, that one, but she sure has a thing for you. Bad 'n all. I'd watch myself if I was you."

"What's the time?"

"It's about six."

"And no one's here?"

"What? No, why would they be? You're the only bloke around here who turns up at six in the morning."

"What the fuck are you talking about?"

"Last night. We had a lock-in. You must remember. I thought you'd gone home after we'd finished off the sniff I had but you turned up just as everyone left. Said you needed a nightcap. You know I can't sleep after a night on the blow, so I let you in. You looked pretty worse for wear. Shaken up. I guessed you and Sandra had it out and she'd kicked you to the curb for the night. Didn't seem right to probe you about it straight away, you know?"

I dozed off through exhaustion or something. Yes, that must be it. I've been working too hard and hitting the bottle too much. Don't remember any coke. Doesn't do my sleep pattern any good. Or lack of one. I need to go home and sleep. Sleep for eternity. Yes. That's what I need to do.

"Isaac? You there?"

"What? Oh, yeah. I'm here. Listen, mate, you couldn't call me a cab and give me one for the road, could you?"

"Well, I was hoping to hear about what happened

with you and Sandra, but I guess that can wait. You look like fucking shit if I'm honest mate," he says, sticking the phone up to his ear. "Alright mate. Yeah, I need a cab. Yep, The Pink Elephant. Two minutes? Sweet as. Cheers."

"Thanks for that."

"No problem, Isaac. Your nose is bleeding by the way."

"Is it?" I ask, reaching my hand up. It's soaked.

"You ain't got any more sniff have ya?"

"No, nothing. Only did it last night because..." I say, reaching into my pockets for a tissue. I always keep some in there in case of a tough crowd breaking me into a sweat. After yanking out a few, I go to wipe my nose, but stop.

"Sure as hell looks like it to me mate. You ain't holding out on me are ya?" the barman asks.

The tissues in my hand are already covered with dried-up crimson. I used to get pretty bad nosebleeds when I was younger, especially when under a lot of stress. My mother always said it happens to people who lie to themselves.

"'Ere you are. Some fresh ones for the cab. You don't wanna grub up his seats now, do ya?"

"Cheers mate," I say, taking some serviettes from his hand.

"No problem pal. You just take it easy on yourself. You ain't Sandra's age, after all. No point in acting like you are. Too tough on the body and mind, let me tell you. In the long run, they just aren't worth it. 'Specially the mental ones, if you don't mind me saying."

"Wait," I say, mopping up my nose. "So what happened last night?"

Honk-honk!

"That's your cab, mate. Don't you go worrying about last night. It was nothing any different from you and Sandra's usual antics. I'll let you know tomorrow if you're still up for doing five minutes."

"Tomorrow? Yeah, why not," I say, necking down my rum for the road.

"Good. Thought you might've wanted to quit after last night. I tell you, nobody has ever bombed like that before. It was epic, let me tell you. Well, more tragic I suppose but fuck me did it get people talking and drinking and having a good old time. I think you should do it on purpose in the future. People seem to like seeing others fail miserably rather than entertain them. They're a bunch of fickle c—"

-Honk-honk!-

"Yeah... cheers for that. I'll be sure to bring in a bouquet of lead balloons tomorrow, just for you."

"Lead balloons? You sure you're not on something?"

"Never mind. Take care. Cheers for the rum."

"Anytime mate."

The cabbie already knows where I'm going, as I usually end up getting a taxi after a night at The Pink Elephants. He keeps flashing me looks inside the rear-view mirror with suspicious, untrusting eyes.

"Mind your nose for me, will ya?" he asks, stopping at a red light. "Don't get any blood on me sheets."

"What sheets?"

"Seats. I said, 'Seats', not 'Sheets.'"

"Oh. Sorry yeah, I'll be careful not—"

"Do I know you from anywhere?" he asks, taking longer glances into the mirror now, appearing closer to it as well.

"Maybe. I'm a comedian."

"Oh! A funny man, are ya? What's your name then?"

"Isaac Enerson."

"Isaac wot?"

"Enerson."

"Enerson... Isaac Enerson. Mmm. Never heard of ya."

"That's okay—"

"You sure look familiar though. You're not that bloke who does the Utterly Butterly gag are ya? You look like him. That one didn't half have me in stitches the other week. He got a two-for-one deal on some Utterly Butterly, but he only went and opened the second one before the first one was finished. I couldn't believe it! I did the very same thing. The missus was on my case for weeks after that. We both still can't believe it's not butter 'n all! Ha! That weren't you by any chance?"

"No," I reply, "it wasn't me. I know the gag though. Very TV friendly. Shame it doesn't make sense."

"What d'you mean? It makes perfect sense."

"Utterly Butterly and I Can't Believe it's not Butter are not only separate brands but also separate products. Utterly Butterly is *butter,* hence the word *utterly* going before it. I Can't Believe it's not Butter, on the other hand, is *not* butter, hence the words *I can't believe it's not* going in front of it. I'm guessing it's some sort of vegetable spread instead, not to be confused with, but encouragingly compared to its counterpart of butter."

"You sure you're a comic? Just say it out loud. *Utterly Butterly.* It's funny!" he says, pulling over to the side. "Christ. They let any twat drive nowadays.

Look at the parking job on that one."

"Tragic," I say, handing over a twenty. After a shuffle, he starts scooping up some coins out of his money belt. I wave him off. "Don't worry about the change mate."

"You sure? That's nearly a tenner."

"Yeah, I'm sure," I say, cracking the lock open, "I don't want it."

"Suit yourself. I guess you are a funny man after all, only in the wrong way!"

To that, I simply sweep the door closed.

He swings around, but slows down as I'm taking out my keys.

"Listen mate," he says, "I'm not being funny or anything, so don't take this the wrong way or nothing, but I've picked up chemo patients who looked healthier than you. From one man to another, I think you should really get yourself some rest."

"That's what everyone keeps telling me, so that's what I plan to do."

"Oh, and another thing. Find out who drove that fucking thing and report him. If he ain't driving drunk, he's driving blind. Twats like that make these streets dangerous for the likes of us cabbies. And besides, only arseholes get their windows tinted. Bollocks to that bloke."

"Will do," I say, almost laughing. If you haven't guessed it, he's talking about my car.

"Ta-*ta!*" he cries, finally driving away. He could've just said ta-ta like a normal person, but he said it like the ending soundbite of a punchline reveal. Everyone who meets a comedian instantly transforms into one themselves. There's part of me that really fucking despises this profession.

The comedian I was confused for must've won that competition with his dairy related material. Maybe Sandra didn't sabotage my chances after all if that's what people are looking for. What the world wants these days Utterly Butterly escapes me.

He was exaggerating the failure of my parking ability. The car looks fine to me. Well, it's still a beaten-up old hunk of metal which nobody in their right mind would want to possess, but the parking job isn't that bad. It's only the trunk that's poking out a bit. I had the windows tinted black like an idiot because other idiots kept waking me up in the middle of the night when they saw me sleeping in there. Couldn't afford hotels whilst I worked on the road. Didn't help much mind you. It only made other morons knock thinking I had drugs to sell.

The lights in the house aren't working. Before I'm even in the flat I'm pissing about with the fuse above the door next to my neighbours. It wouldn't surprise me if Sandra did this. Yes, there it is. The switch for the lights. Turned off. Flick. Finally, I can rest. A little midnight tipple should ease me into a sweet, peaceful slumber. The flat is unusually quiet, even for this hour. Sandra normally has something playing in the background. If not the TV, then the radio, or something on her phone or laptop. Helps her sleep, she says. The silence, though somewhat eerie because of its long absence, is still rather welcome. I'm not sure why I'm so certain she's here though. My mind is a slideshow of déjà vu, coupled with amnesia.

At the top of the stairs, there's a trail of tissues leading towards the bathroom, soaked in blood like the ones in my pocket. The light is on. The only other one that's on is behind me, piercing through the slit of the ajar door; the living room we converted into our bedroom.

I follow the trail in a haze as if I'm being dragged by a time I did it before. I stagger and stumble, feel queasy and nauseous. The rum sure took its time to take effect. I haven't felt this giddy in... oh god— *blllllluuurrrghhhh!!!*—years. Nor have I thrown up in that time either. Everything's doubling around me. The toilet basin is cold against my cheek. Comforting. I hold myself there, letting the bile fall from the side of my mouth. Throwing up helped. The room is merging back into...

Sandra ran a bath. Sandra filled it with a whole bottle of body wash. Sandra stuck my microphone stand in it, with the unplugged mic still attached. It's poking out through the large bushes of bubbles.

Bubbles...

"I'm really glad you're back home babe," Sandra said, flicking a clump of suds at me with her foot, pressing it against my chest. I'd been away for two or three weeks. As soon as I arrived she suggested we took a bath together, mostly because I stunk but also because back in our early days it was a thing we did a lot together. We'd play around in the foam, drink cheap wine in extravagant glasses and fool around. We're laughing right now, over a joke I don't remember. She went for a sip of wine, her auburn hair darkened from the moisture, yet still tinted red, much like the peppered freckles of her pale skin.

"Why do you always do that?" she asked.

"Do what?" I replied, the chuckles still echoing from my mouth.

"You know what I mean."

"No, I honestly don't," I said as the base of her glass hit the porcelain on the side like a clamp. I tried to ignore what I took to be a switch of her tone. "What do I always do?"

"Every time we share a laugh, you always have to have the last one."

"Meaning?" I asked. Sandra just rolled her eyes and flicked a wet lock of hair to the side. A silence of stillness took over us. Our limbs remained still under the hot, steaming water.

"Don't pretend you don't know," she snapped out of nowhere. "You're always getting in the last one, like someone who keeps clapping when everyone else has stopped. I don't know why you never let me have it."

"Hey, come on," I said, reaching for her knee but she pulled it back. "Don't be like that Sandra. I just got back. I've barely slept in the last few weeks. I don't even know what you're talking about."

"Yes, you do. If we're both laughing, you're always the one who has to finish it. You never let me have the last laugh."

I should've known better, but I couldn't help it. I started laughing. Then I said, "I didn't realise it was an issue, Sandra. I'll try not to be the last one laughing?"

"But you're doing it right now, you dick," she said, crossing her arms. The water rose in a disturbing wave. "Why did you say 'issue' of mine?"

"What?"

"Stop laughing!" she screamed, her hand slapping the water, destroying the bubbles layered over the surface.

"Okay, okay. I'm sorry. I didn't mean anything by

it. It's just a turn of phrase. I didn't say it was an issue of yours—"

"Do you think I have a lot of issues then? I bet you didn't think that about your ex's, did you? No, just me—"

"Woah, time out. Relax. Come on. This is crazy. We're having a romantic moment here, you know? Did I tell you how delicious you look draped in bubbles?"

"No. And don't. I'm not crazy. I don't want you perving over me," she said, turning away. "You didn't even notice what I did for you."

"What d'you mean? How could I? You covered my eyes and brought me straight in here, to the bath. Are you talking about the bath?"

"No, of course I'm not talking about the bath. Try opening your eyes instead."

I looked at her quizzically, but she turned away from my glance and flipped her crossed arms around. This was our entire relationship at this point. One minute we'd be sharing a laugh, the next we'd be arguing over the laughter. The stress of these moments had started to make my thoughts jagger and slice. They quite literally felt as if they were cutting each other apart.

"Well?" she asked, diminishing the bubbles covering her cleavage through the huff that followed her question. Although I sensed an attack coming, she still looked fatally sexy, especially clouded in steam. Even the water felt hotter, stickier somehow.

Ignoring my arousal through fear of dismissing her question, I began to look around the bathroom. Nothing appeared unusual, bar the toilet seat that was up and the open door of the bathroom. That's when I saw it. Directly behind and what would've been hidden had the door been closed was a poster, bordered with a black, glossy frame. ISAAC ENERSON it read, the poster of my first headlining gig at The Pink Elephant. Above my name was an illustration of the latter, drunkenly tilting his feet on the top of the letters bearing my name. He was guffawing in delirium, with pink bubbles floating around and to the side of his gaping mouth, all of them containing HA-HA's. Bubbles waiting to burst. I didn't even know she had that poster.

"Well? Do you like it?"

"I love it, Sandra. I'm really touched," I said.

But a strange feeling arises in me... I've seen that elephant before, but I can't place where. He wants to tell me something. Some secret he thinks that I think I'm desperate to know. I begin to feel queasy... unsure of myself... almost unattached. Sandra's fingernails run down the inner-thigh of my leg. I swing my head to face her, but the room, or more, the elephant, or elephants... I cannot tell, come with me, swaying sideways in an unfocused overlay, all behind, or somehow blended with the steam. They sweep between the space of me and Sandra, collapsing in a dust of pink, blanketing its debris over the foam. Now all the bubbles glimmer with its hue. Sandra's moved to her knees and both of her hands are under the water by her crotch. Her eyes appear to be rolling around the back of her head. But I'm not sure because of the steam enveloped over my own eyes. We're both... eyeless to each other. I'm not sure what to think, or whether I'm even capable of doing so. A narcotic drowsiness or drunken giddiness makes me giggle, but each guffaw carries nausea. There are rivulets of sweat running down my lungs. I can tell she's speaking, but the words are muffled as if we're under the water instead of above it. Her mouth hangs open, black except for a prismatic shimmer that expands in sync with her lips...

Out pops a bubble... shaded in a darker, more violent pink.

"Oh Isaac," says Sandra, gurgling a little. An iridescent pool sits inside of her mouth, tipping and streaming over the edge of her bottom lip and chin. Ever so slowly, she blows another inflated but now reddened dewdrop towards my nose. For a reason beyond me, I make no movement at all. It pops instantly on contact. The splash is sticky and metallic. Gooey. Sandra giggles whilst gargling the mixture of prismatic colours, but instead of spitting, she swallows it. "You haven't been hitting the sniff again, have you Isaac?" she asks. I wipe my nose at last with the tips of my fingers. It's thick like bile. Too thick to be blood, surely, oozing and stretching out into a stringy line as I pull my fingertips away.

"No," I say. My hand cross-fades to focus on Sandra. She's playing with herself underneath the soapsuds. More bubbles appear out of nowhere, all popping in what seems to be through their own will. My hand is nothing but red now. Where are they coming from? Sandra's head tilts to the side. "You make me so hard, Isaac," she says. The freckles on her shoulders have all turned into a deep glistening red. My head sways out of its own accord, looking away to the side again. That's where they came from. Three baby-sized, yet somehow adult bright pink elephants are floating in the air, sipping on martinis, giddily drunk and hiccupping bubbles out of their trunks in delicate streams. "I want you to fuck me with a knife against my throat again, Isaac," says Sandra, "nothing ever made me burst like that before."

"ha-eh-*oh!*" says the middle elephant, with the voice of some deranged, perverted entertainer. "Looks like we're in for some—*hiccup*—cutting-edge comedy tonight boys, ha-he-*oh!*"

"Oh yeah. Cut me up like you used to, Isaac. Oh, god. I'm so fucking hard. Do it for me Isaac, and I'll laugh when I come, I swear. I'll give you the biggest load of laughter you've ever had in your life. Make me snort."

"ha-*hiccup-oh!* That's Utterly Smutterly!"

I don't remember this happening. I must be having a bad trip... but I didn't take anything... why can't Sandra look at me?

"What do you say, funny man?" asks Sandra, rising from her knees. I don't know how she can move in this swamp... my legs aren't even here. I cannot feel them at all. I'm just a torso without a lower half, looking up at the bubble-coated Sandra. Her legs are apart. She looks down at me, lustful and loathing. Through the bubbles... from between her legs... I see something protruding—poking through! It's grey—no, black—no, grey and black! It's a fucking microphone! I can't tell if it's strapped on or coming out of her vagina, but she's got a microphone for a cock!

"HA-HE-*OH!*" the three elephants chant.
-HICCUP!-

"So you wanna see your name in the big bright lights, do you pretty boy?" Sandra says.

"ha-he-*oh*! You betcha' he does!" the elephants guffaw in a chorus line, delighted to be gagging and choking and suffocating on their own chuckles. "His only dedication is for his own admiration. He's a whore, of that we're sure, poke him, choke him, make him beg for more, more, more!"

"Suck it then you fame hungry slut," Sandra says, pointing at the tip of the mic. Her hands thunderbolt towards my ears and pull. The pain is so instant and piercing that my eyes wince and my jawbone snaps open. The microphone hits the back of my throat before I can even blink!

"Fuck the funny out of his mouth, girl! ha-he-*oh*! That's it. Harder. Yeah, make sure he gags! We wanna hear lots and lots of gags tonight! A whole lotta giddily-gag-gagging! Come along now, harder. We know he can gag better than that!"

I now see what the swamp is. It's not mud or sludge but thick, congealed blood... it's everywhere, slowly sucking me under... this can't be possible—

"He sure is choking tonight! I hope he becomes the butt of his own joke pretty soon! Did you ever notice... that—hiccup—you're being throat-fucked by a microphone right now?!"

"What's it gonna be, Isaac," says Sandra, "me or the mic?" She slaps me over the skull, then yanks my face forward by the ears, thrusting in and out of me... my eyes feel like their bleeding... but the shock outweighs the pain. This can't be real. This can't be real. This can't be—

"HA-HE-*OH*! It's real alright!" the elephants chuckle, whilst Sandra digs and scratches over my scalp. She grips a clump of my hair and twists it, forcing me to face her. "Look at me when I'm throat-fucking you funny man, your fifteen minutes is almost here!"

"Make him swallow his pride! Ha-ha-ha! Blow the fuse all over his face! He-he-he! Fuck him in the eye sockets! *Oh-oh-oh!* Yay, the eye sockets! Eye sockets make for perfect cock pockets! HA-HE-*OH!*"

The water is splashing but rising. Burps and bubbles and gurgles breathe over the surface. The elephants can't stop chirping, hiccupping, laughing—

-SLAP!-

Sandra's palm knocked the bathroom completely out of whack. The elephants now circle around her and behind my head. Their laughter sounds like harsh feedback from a sound system. Each hiccup causes a jagger in their movements, but it only makes them guffaw even harder, despite the pain it inflicts. "You chose the mic over me Isaac," says Sandra, her voice distorted, *demonic.* "You made your choice, now fucking swallow it!" I'm not even sure I'm breathing anymore. She grabs my paralysed chin and squeezes, making me look at her in her entirely blackened eyes. "This is the last time you'll see me squirt," she says, thrusting so far down my throat that my eyes feel like they're about to burst. The blood's boiling all around us, thrashing and tossing and spurting. "Argghhh... arggh..." moans Sandra. She clamps my nose shut! "*ARGGGHHHHHHH!!!*" She pulls away, only for a gush of blood to spurt out of her as she spasms inside a violent fit. The mic is too far down my throat, I cannot cough it up! The blood hits the elephants, instantly burning their skin—but they only enjoy the burn, find it funny and impossibly hilarious! Before

I can blink, Sandra has both hands over my mouth and nose, forcing me to swallow the mic... the lights above us begin to shutter. The elephants now begin to have hysterical seizures, their bodies see-through just like the bubbles! Sandra shoves my head under the bloodbath, her body thundering with electricity along with mine... this is it... I'm going to fucking die!

-SMACK!-

My body forces me to take a huge breath as if I really was under water. All I can see and smell is blood and vomit. My head is in the toilet. The seat rests above my skull. It was a dream. All just some sordid nightmare. My relief is so instantaneous that I throw up again immediately, but I'm laughing as I do! Ha-ha-ha! I'm alive! What kind of fucking nightmare was that?! My body folds under its own exhaustion and flops onto the floor. The bathroom rug is the most welcoming place of rest I've ever known. I'm crying, soaked in sweat, enveloped in fumes of blood-stained puke, but I'm so awash with the release of stress and euphoria... that it's minutes before I see the bathroom cabinet above my head.

The mirror. Cracked at the centre. Ha-Ha scrawled inside one of the shards, written in neon pink. Sandra's favourite shade of nail varnish. The most toxic smell imaginable. A blended chemical imbalance... like that of paint. Why does it feel like a memory I've forgotten?

My face appears disjointed, its identity fractured. Did the fragments fall and were they pieced back together again, or did they just sit there the whole time? What does this person in front of me want me to fucking see?! Is he in on some joke I can't comprehend?

The Ha-Ha shard falls free and lands inside the sink in a scattered circle. Face down its nothing but black. I look back up at my shattered, unrecognised reflection. The left eye is cracked like a broken television screen. The right one nothing but the hole left behind by the shard. Have I disappeared? Is the best part of me somewhere else... or did he ever exist?

Why do you always have to have the last laugh, Isaac?

The remaining shards tumble away from the frame, landing in what feels to me like a revelation, yet still, nothing comes to mind. I'm just hollow. Empty. But there's still some sort of awful, knowing dread stirring up inside of me. My head swings by instinct to the poster on the wall. It still hangs there, slightly askew like always. But wait. The bottom corner of the frame used to point towards the kitchen. Now it points across the corridor towards the living room. As if in a trance I begin to approach it, numb in body and mind, spiritless, detached from the potential disaster this bathroom seems to convey.

It looks the same on close inspection. There's no damage to it at all. In truth, I never cared much for the poster. The pink, almost albino elephant always freaked me out. Did I ever tell Sandra that? No, I didn't. I'm sure of it. Maybe subconsciously though, she knew. The poster looks clearer somehow. The glare cast by the bathroom light is less intense, almost not there at all... because the glass of the frame is missing...

The tissues. The trail which led me to the bathroom. That's all I can see by my feet. No glass. Nothing else.

But the path didn't end at the bathroom... that was just a detour. Now I see where it loops and takes you back towards where you started, only to derail by the bannister of the stairs before the straight, one-way stretch into the living room.

I gulp. A string of vomit slithers down my throat like the after drip that follows a line of cocaine. My legs shake so much I'm forced to use the walls of this closed-in corridor to keep me upright. It only occurs to me now, that I must've wet myself during the nightmare. The cold sweat I'm coated in kept me ignorant of it. Sandra was right. I am a lowlife, drunkard, piece of shit.

I'm at the door now. Or back at it, maybe I should say. The doorknob rattles inside my hand. I don't need to twist it, yet here I am doing it anyway. Part of me wants to close it, to shun what's inside, turn around and run. But I push instead of pull, and it shudders as if stricken by some terrible, undetectable force. All I can see is the clock, with the minute hand on the five, the hour hand edging over the eight. The clock must've stopped working, transferring its tick to the inside of whatever remains of me. Eight. The ceaselessly looping number; trapped ad infinitum.

More tissues are scattered over the carpet, but no longer in a path. This is where their intricate order is lost. Obliterated.

I blink.

Now I stand amongst the blood-soaked tissues, which look like flakes of fallen ash. My eyeline shifts ninety degrees like my head is being pulled by a rope. And there she is... arms stretched-out in a position of self-sacrifice. ISAAC on her right arm, ENERSON on her left, both carved with the severest, most jagged cuts imaginable, by the shards of glass which once protected the poster she'd gifted to me. The advert inside of the advert. The promise of what was to later pass. Inside the haphazardly wrapped, wrinkled duvet sits an upright martini glass, close to spilling its remaining liquid. The smeared blood across the hem of the otherwise milk-white quilt appears pink, in patches light, in others a violent crimson. Below the waist it twists away to the side, revealing her... and my favourite dress. The same long, black gown with the slits at the sides of the upper-thighs. The dress she wore when she sabotaged my chances of winning the competition. The dress I removed to see her naked for the first time. The dress she wore when I first saw her, during my debut as a stand-up comedian. The dress of her demise.

But it was the look on her face that did it, that transcended me and her into a different place. The thin smear of blood that had pinkened her already rosy-cheeked skin. The crimsoned freckles appearing like bubbles... the deep, blackening red layered across her entire eyes... the abyss that I've been sucked into... the crooked, self-righteous smile across her countenance, the satisfaction she derived from knowing I'd find her there, only for her to send me here. She'd died in a fit of hysteria, of the most palpable spasm of cruel, indignant laughter I had never before thought possible. Sandra had got the last laugh, but I never expected her to achieve it through me.

And so I screamed. A scream so loud my own eardrums popped and distorted, creating a ringing of interference that has since ceased to stop. I cannot tell you where I am because I do not know myself.

But what I can tell you is that Sandra is inside that ringing crackle somewhere. She no longer speaks to me... as she's too busy laughing. In the end, she got her wish. We are finally together as one. I'll tell you where I think I am. I'm on a stage somewhere with the brightest of lights bearing down on me. I've tried to look around, but the light is so blinding I can never make anything out, except for an audience that surrounds me from every impossible angle, inside of this awful, perfect cube. At first, I thought the guffawing was them. But I know better than that now. They sometimes applaud inside an inescapable echo, but their faces betray no emotion, as they have no distinctive features at all. I think they came here to see me, but I cannot be sure. I mean to ask them one day, but I'm scared that they'll leave me here... if I ever stop laughing.

ACKNOWLEDGEMENTS

I'd like to thank my partner Myriam for her endless patience and belief in my ability; especially when my own is lacking; my dog Benito for reminding that sometimes all you need to do is take a walk and have a shit, and my two cats, Leonardo and Tabitha Antigone; the former because of his independence and easy-going nature, the latter not so much as she was a kitten at the time I was finalising this work, thus delaying its release for a good number of weeks. And my parents and brother, whose names I shall not mention due to the contents of this piece.

To my ever-declining list of friends, whatever. You know who you are.

ABOUT THE AUTHOR

G.C. McKay was born and raised in Brighton, England. When he's not writing, he's probably drinking or speaking about himself in the third person. He currently resides in Almeria, Spain, with his aforementioned and ever-suffering partner and their three (for now) pets.

For book recommendations, writings tips and all the latest shits and giggles, head on over to gcmckay.com today and sign up to the newsletter for your chance to win some books and booze!

OTHER WORKS BY G.C. MCKAY

Fubar

a novel

Made in the USA
Monee, IL
04 January 2022

87916315R00173